PRA [illegible] SAVED *THE WORLD IN A WEEK*

'A fabulous page-turner'
Abi Elphinstone, author of *Sky Song*

'A compelling and timely survivalist journey'
Sita Brahmachari, author of *Where the River Runs Gold*

'A brave and powerful story'
Jasbinder Bilan, author of *Asha & the Spirit Bird*

'A fast paced heartfelt thriller that will
have you on the edge of your seat'
Gill Lewis, author of *Sky Hawk*

'Compelling, beautifully written and just
so much fun. Every kid needs this book'
Nikki Sheehan, author of *Swan Boy*

'A rollicking adventure with family
and friendship at its heart'
Joseph Coelho, author of *If All the World Were...*

'Tense and gripping with the most wonderful narrator'
Rashmi Sirdeshpande, author of *How to Be Extraordinary*

'A brilliant and unique story'
Nicola Penfold, author of *Where The World Turns Wild*

'I gulped this book down in two sittings!'
A. M. Howell, author of *The Garden of [illegible] Lost Secrets*

'Th [illegible] comes

ALSO BY POLLY HO-YEN

Boy in the Tower

Where Monsters Lie

Fly Me Home

How I Saved The WORLD in a Week

POLLY HO-YEN

Illustrations by George Ermos

SIMON & SCHUSTER

For Dan

First published in Great Britain in 2021 by Simon & Schuster UK Ltd

1 3 5 7 9 10 8 6 4 2

Simon & Schuster UK Ltd
1st Floor, 222 Gray's Inn Road London WC1X 8HB

www.simonandschuster.co.uk
www.simonandschuster.com.au
www.simonandschuster.co.in

Simon & Schuster Australia, Sydney
Simon & Schuster India, New Delhi

A CIP catalogue record for this book is available from the British Library.

PB ISBN 978-1-4711-9354-5
eBook ISBN 978-1-4711-9355-2
eAudio ISBN 978-1-4711-9996-7

Typeset in the UK by Sorrel Packham
Printed and bound by CPI Group (UK) Ltd, Croydon, CR0 4YY

RULES FOR SURVIVAL

1.	*Always be prepared*	–	*have everything you need ready and with you at all times*
2.	*Pay attention*	–	*keep constant observations of your surroundings*
3.	*Trust no one*	–	*you may only be able to rely on yourself*
4.	*Master your fears*	–	*through practice, planning and taking action*
5.	*Never stop trying*	–	*you must never give up!*

PROLOGUE

No one believed us at first.

They didn't think it could be true.

But now we're running for our lives . . .

PART 1

HOW TO MAKE A FIREBOW

It's the week before Christmas, the kind of pinprick cold where you can feel it needling into the tips of your fingers. I don't know what Sylvia told the school office but just before we are about to go out for break, Mrs Tombo the school receptionist comes in to say that my mum is here to collect me.

We're playing a game Miss Browning made up called 'Blankets'. One of the class has to go out of the room and then someone else hides under a blanket, completely covered, so you can't see any part of them. Then the person who went out comes back and has to guess who it is.

We're playing games because it's the last day of term. After break we're going to watch a film and then there's a party in the top hall this afternoon. There's going to be *every* kind of party food and I can't wait.

It's my turn to guess who is under the blanket so I'm looking at the lumpy mass in the middle of the room. All the other children's faces are staring at me with big bug-eyes which makes it harder to think, somehow.

I'm concentrating so hard on the game that I don't even notice the classroom door opening but then, in a quiet voice, I hear my name.

'Billy,' Mrs Tombo says. 'Um, your mum's here to collect you. Do you want to get your things together?'

There's a groan from someone in the classroom. I look round to see who it is, surprised that anyone would miss me. I've never felt like I settled at this school even though I've been here for about six months now, which is almost as long as I've been at any school in the last couple of years.

Dean has tugged the blanket off his head and looks over at me crossly.

'I was going to win then,' he splutters, red-faced and sweaty. 'Billy was never going to guess it was me!'

I try not to look at him, or at the exchanged glances between Miss Browning and Mrs Tombo, or at the eyes of everyone else which look wider and glassier all of a sudden. They think I can't hear them whispering to each other.

Why's he going again?

What is it with his weird mum?

I quickly go to get my bag and coat and follow Mrs Tombo. I try not to look surprised; Sylvia didn't mention picking me up early when she dropped me off this morning.

Sylvia's my mum. I always call her by her first name. She prefers it that way.

As we get closer to the school office, through the window I can see the dark shape of her, prowling like a shadow.

When I walk into the room, she doesn't give me an explanation of why she's here, simply reaches towards my hair as though she is going to touch it but then stops herself just before she does.

'Let's go,' she says and marches out of the glass doors.

I mumble to the receptionist as I leave, 'Happy Christmas, Mrs Tombo.'

'Happy Christmas, Billy,' her voice rings back. 'Hope you have a good holi—' She's cut off by the doors closing as I hurry out to catch up with Sylvia.

She marches ahead of me to the train station that's close by. I almost have to break into a run to keep up with her. I want to ask where we're going and did I really have to leave school early today of all days. This morning I'd told her about the fun things that we were going to do because it was the last day of term but I had known she hadn't been listening properly. I can feel the disappointment of missing out humming around my head but I keep it all on the inside. It's something I've learned is best to do.

The train doors have already starting bleeping when we get to the platform. Sylvia darts forward and rams her body in between them.

'Quick,' she says, pulling me into the carriage as the doors close behind us like a jaw.

Now, I feel so far away from school, from the other children, from Miss Browning and Mrs Tombo, from the station and the train, from anybody else in the world, in fact. We got off at the last stop and walked briskly to these woods, about half an hour's walk away. Now we are here, I recognize that it's somewhere we've been a few times before. Sylvia always seems to bring us here a different way, so it took me a little while to remember, but as we walk deeper into the woods I know where we are.

A breeze whistles through the trees above us. Their black branches, stark against the pearl of the sky, make me think of hands with long, beckoning fingers, or claws.

'Matches,' Sylvia says. She holds out a hand for them without even looking down.

She's not impatient, at least I don't think she is. Yet.

I pat my pockets (although I know they are empty) and then I rustle through the plastic bag she brought but they're not in there either. I even look in my school bag although I know it's pointless.

I check my coat again, feeling Sylvia's eyes hotly on me now, but my fingers only close around the tiny scraps of white fluff that line my pockets.

'Don't we have any?' Sylvia asks. She likes to be direct, she doesn't like what she calls 'waffle'.

'I don't think so,' I say and look away from her stare, holding my breath.

'What's the number one Rule, Billy?'

'Always be prepared,' I mumble quickly. Sylvia has been drilling the Rules into me for so long now that the words feel like they have almost lost their meaning.

I start to try to explain why I don't have the matches on me. 'I didn't know that today—'

'That's okay.' She cuts me off. I breathe again and for a tiny moment I want to crawl into her lap like I used to when I was little. It's silly, because it's not something I have done for years. I try to brush the feeling away but I can still feel it there, niggling me.

The last time we were in these woods, we forgot to bring the penknife with us and Sylvia got upset. She didn't shout or yell but her face seemed to crumple in on itself, like a piece of paper being screwed up into a ball. Then she had stalked off through the trees, leaving me alone for what felt like ages, although it was only twenty minutes when I checked my watch.

I'm glad she doesn't react like that today. But I'm on edge, worrying I might do something that will make her leave me here alone again.

There's another voice in my head that whispers to me too; it tells me that I'm supposed to be in school enjoying the last day of term with everyone else, that I wasn't meant to be remembering things for an adventure – not today. I feel myself blink, willing the voice away.

'It's best that we learn other methods, too,' Sylvia says. 'Our matches might be limited. Or we might not have any at all.'

She turns towards me and this time she does place her hand very lightly on my head, so she's only just touching the outer strands of my hair.

We have similar colour hair that sometimes looks brown,

other times blondish and in some lights, can look a little bit grey. Sylvia's is long, silky and straight. It snakes around her neck and down her back, but mine is tufty and wiry and sticks up in all the wrong places. Sylvia told me once that I get the tuftiness from Steve, my dad.

She doesn't talk about him very often – my dad – and when she does I've noticed that Sylvia seems to look over her shoulder as though she's worried she's being overheard. The details I've gathered about Steve feel dustlike: scattered and insubstantial. I can't seem to bind them together to make him feel like a real person. They split up when I was really small, and after that he used to come and see me, not that much but at least sometimes, but I haven't seen him for over two years now. I remember the last time because it was just before Sylvia stopped going to work. Steve came to where we were living at the time but Sylvia wouldn't let him inside, so he took me to the park instead. He asked if I wanted to go on the swings and when I didn't reply he said something about how fast I'd grown up and how much I loved them when I was very small and would shriek with laughter each time he pushed me.

I used to ask Sylvia when I would see him again, but whenever I did I could tell she didn't like it. When I mentioned Steve's name, her mouth went in a line, pinched and taut, and shadows gathered across her face.

So I stopped asking.

I've learned the things to say and not to say to keep things calm. Almost normal. And right now, I know to keep my mouth shut about Steve – even if I'm thinking about him.

'Right. What shall we do? Let's try . . .' Sylvia's eyes look a little misty as she mentally works through a list in her mind. 'Firebow!' she proclaims. 'Let's make a firebow!'

I nod, my neck almost jarring from the movement. I feel glad she's not thinking about the forgotten matches any more.

'What do we need?' Sylvia asks and hands me the slightly tattered book from her coat pocket. It's thin, with paper that has yellowed and dimpled like skin. The title on its cover reads *How to Survive.* It doesn't look like anything special. But to Sylvia it's everything.

The book has a musty odour, not horrible, but the sort of smell that you notice immediately. A previous owner has underlined words here and there. A few of the page corners have been bent over in neat triangles.

I like these traces of others but none more than the name written into the book's front in a curly, looping scrawl.

Sylvia Weywood.

My mum wrote her name here when she was my age, when she first owned this book, years and years before she was my mum. When she was just Sylvia, and I didn't even exist.

I look up 'firebow' in the index and then turn to the right page and read aloud what we need.

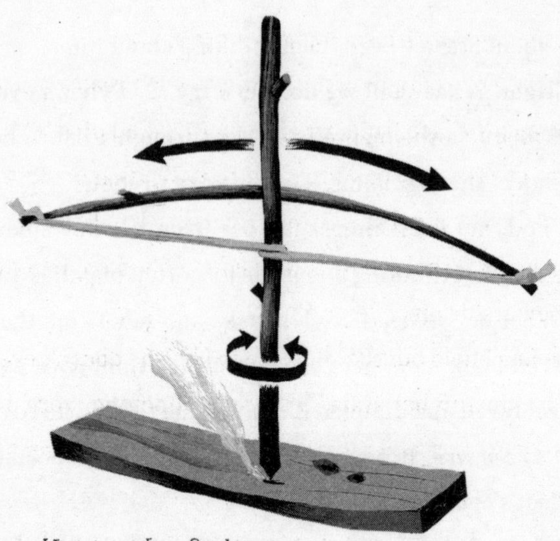

Fig. 1. – How to make a firebow

'Why don't you find a stick that will do for the bow?' Sylvia says, handing me her penknife.

It's heavy in my hand. I don't tell her that I'm a little afraid of its sharp blade, that I don't find it very easy to use. When I find a suitable branch, I snap out the saw blade from the penknife – it only takes four attempts this time – and cut away a piece. I take care to close the jagged teeth of the blade before I walk back to her.

'Perfect, Billy,' she says when she sees the wood. Quite suddenly she kisses me on the head and leans into me. 'Perfect,' she says again. I start to press into her half-hug, making the most of the unexpected closeness, but in the following moment she pulls away.

'We need some cord,' she murmurs. 'Your shoelace would

do,' she says, with a small, barking laugh.

I bend over immediately, without even really thinking, and untangle the lace from my trainer. I try and do it as quickly as I can, but when I look up, I see that Sylvia isn't hurrying me, instead she's staring out into the distance. She takes a deep breath and exhales slowly, as though she's enjoying the taste of the outside air.

When I hold out the shoelace to her, she doesn't even notice, she's so lost in her stare. It's been happening more and more, these moments when she seems to be in a different world to the one I am in. These moments when I feel that although she is right beside me, she is somehow slipping away, between a crack, to a completely different kind of place entirely.

I can't remember exactly when it started happening but I think it was around the time she left her job. She used to work as a scientist but she doesn't do that any more. Since then, sometimes, she just seems to turn inwards and disappear, even though she is standing right there in front of me. They build, these moments, as Sylvia drifts away. It's like darkness at twilight, creeping in so gradually at first that you don't realize it's turning dark but then when you look outside again, you see that night has dropped all around you.

'Sylvia,' I whisper and then, as if something inside her snaps, she breaks off from staring and looks over to me and the shoelace dangling in the air. I try to ignore the look that flashes across her face; the one which for just a fraction of a second does not seem to recognize me, the one that's unsure of what we're doing. She gives her head a shake and then the moment is over – she's reaching for the shoelace and tying it to one end of the branch that I found.

She works quickly, placing a stick here, looping the shoelace there, and then she leans back with a satisfied sigh, finished.

I look at the arrangement of sticks and can't understand how we are going to make fire from this.

'Get ready with that tinder when it starts to catch,' she tells me, pointing to some dried-out moss we collected earlier. She takes a leaf and places it carefully at the bottom of the arrangement. 'This will catch the embers,' she explains.

Then she begins, moving the bow from side to side as though she is sawing a piece of wood, making the pointed stick spin from the movement.

Her breath is heavy. I look for a flame but I see none, only a thin trail of smoke.

'There,' she says, through a half-breath. There's a small pile of black, smoking powder on the leaf. She takes a bundle of the dry moss and places the tinder on top of it.

'Come here, Billy,' she says. 'You need to learn how to do this. Blow very gently.'

I do as she says and blow on the moss in little puffs of gentle breath.

It smokes.

It smokes a little more.

It looks like it's breathing.

I blow a little harder and then smoke builds and builds until

I see it.

A flicker.

Something as slight as a flutter of eyelids.

It's that small.

But then the flame licks around the moss hungrily – the handful of moss is consumed by it and I can't stop myself from squealing in delight. We feed it dry pieces of bark and very small twigs. The fire devours them all and grows bigger still.

'We did it,' Sylvia says. She leans into me once again and we are both quiet for those few seconds, watching the flames grow, dance and flicker.

Just then, there's a ripple in the sky overhead. The clouds hang grey and low.

There's a flash.

Lightning.

It seems to come from nowhere.

Sylvia looks up to the sky as the first raindrops fall. I see them land on her forehead, making wet circles that trickle down her pale face. But in the next moment she turns suddenly as though she's spotted something I haven't and then she's up, grabbing our things, filling her arms. I look all around us, thinking of our second Rule: *Pay attention – keep constant observations of your surroundings.* Sylvia tells me that's the one I particularly need to practise because I'm always missing the things she sees. But as my eyes travel over the trees, trying to see what Sylvia has spotted, she says: 'We've got to go. Help me pack everything up – quick!'

It's a scrabble to get everything together.

Though she's carrying the bags, Sylvia still has a hand free to hold mine and I'm glad of it as she pulls me away. It feels warm and dry and strong in mine.

'It's not safe here,' she says and we start to run. It's difficult to keep up with her: my trainer doesn't have its lace any more and with every step I feel like it might come off completely. But she seems so worried that I don't want to have to tell her that I don't think I can run, so instead I keep it all inside and try and make my foot hold the trainer in place.

'Don't stop, don't look back,' Sylvia says and her pace quickens.

But as soon as she tells me not to, it's all I want to do. I can't help myself.

The fire we made has been transformed into a smouldering pile now, dampened by the rain, its heat extinguished. The hungry flames may as well never have existed.

And there is someone there; standing, where our fire had once been burning.

HOW (NOT) TO MAKE A FRIEND

I've always known my mum is a bit different to other people's mums.

Sometimes other people's mums seem so alike it's hard to tell them apart.

They dress in normal clothes like jeans and a T-shirt, and the T-shirt might have writing on it or something sparkly and a picture of something or other. They wear different colours; coats that are the bright red of a cherry, jumpers with black, bold stripes.

Sylvia wears old-looking clothes that are all the same shade of grey-green. And she wears the same pair of trousers and boots every day. She has this funny green thing that's a bit like a jacket, only it has no arms, and it's got loads and loads of little pockets on the front. I've never seen anyone, let alone a mum, or a dad, wear anything like her jacket.

Other people's mums speak in the same way. In fact they speak a lot, with so many words that they run into each other and sometimes I can't hear much more than a whirring drone.

Sylvia is silence. There have been days where she hasn't spoken to me at all. Sometimes that means that I might not speak to anyone if it's the school holidays. I don't mind, but I know it's not how other mums behave. It's not even how Sylvia used to behave.

When we first moved here, one of the boys from school, Emmanuel, invited me round to his house one night, before he knew what being my friend would mean.

We haven't been here long. We move around a lot. Sylvia says it's not good to stay in one place for too long or to get to know too many people.

The last placed we lived was on a houseboat while the owners were away and before then, we had a room in a house with other people who came and went and we never got to know properly. Sylvia says it's best not to trust other people. It's Survival Rule number three: *Trust no one – you may only be able to rely on yourself.* The places before then have blurred in my head and I get mixed up because there have been so many. I like the South London flat that we're in now – it's just the two of us living here and it's got way more space than the boat.

I don't like having to start at new schools, although you would think that I would be used to it by now. It's funny how sometimes the more times you do something, the harder it becomes. It's kind of the opposite to what Sylvia has been teaching me; that practice makes perfect, that each time you repeat something, you get a little bit better at doing it. That's another one of the Rules: *Master your fears – through practice, planning and taking action.*

The teacher sat me next to Emmanuel on my first day and we got on okay. He asked me round to his a week later. I didn't really want to say yes, but there was another bit of me that couldn't help but say yes. I'd not been round to someone else's house for so long, I wanted to see whether I was exaggerating how different Sylvia had become to other people. Maybe it was all in my head and she was like other mums after all.

Emmanuel's mum was called Patrice. She told me that I could call her that, and she asked me questions even if she didn't always listen to what my answers were because Emmanuel had a little brother called David who was still a baby and kept crying.

'Oh, David, David, David,' she said, rocking him back and forth. 'Can't you see that I'm trying to get to know Billy?'

We ate pizza which Patrice ordered from a takeaway place because she said she was too tired from looking after David to cook and it was nice to have a treat sometimes. I didn't tell them it was the only time in my life that I'd ever had takeaway pizza.

'Just help yourself, Billy,' Patrice said, yawning loudly. 'Eat what you want.'

I kept going back to the large flat box again and again to have another thick, greasy triangle. I couldn't stop myself; it tasted so delicious. I could feel it settling in my tummy, a lovely weight that made me feel whole and complete.

And I knew then that I was right about Sylvia being different.

So I didn't ask Emmanuel to come over to our flat for dinner. I didn't even ask Sylvia if I could; I just didn't want it to happen.

I knew that we'd eat something like kidney beans with wild rocket that we'd pick from the verge on the side of the road on our way home from school. Or maybe Sylvia would insist that we try to cook outside on a fire. She does that sometimes. It takes ages for the fire to get hot enough to heat anything and even then the food might still only be lukewarm.

It would never be something that Emmanuel would want to keep going back for, like me and the pizza. I knew dinner would be embarrassing and odd but, more than anything, I just couldn't imagine it ever happening. I couldn't picture him in our little flat with just Sylvia and me; I couldn't imagine how it would be. It was easier not to have to think about that at all.

Emmanuel doesn't even talk to me any more. I think that he might have forgotten that he ever tried to be my friend.

I'm absent from school so much that I often feel like my classmates have forgotten who I am. They learned pretty quickly that there was no point in getting to know me because I would most probably not be in the next day, or the day after that.

And I don't know when Sylvia will move us away completely. I've had the feeling recently that she might pack everything up and we'll be gone. There's an energy that she gives off when she's thinking of starting over. A new home, a new school. All new people, again.

I mean, what's the point in trying to get to know someone when you might disappear at any moment?

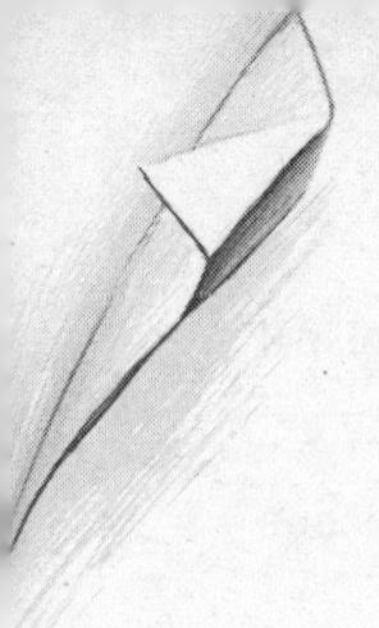

HOW TO USE A HELIOGRAPH: PART I

On Christmas morning, I wake early.

It's completely dark outside and the flat is still and quiet in a way that I know means Sylvia is not yet awake.

I reach around the end of my bed and find a few small packages have been placed there while I was asleep. Taking care not to make too much noise, I shift myself gently out of bed, but I'm not quiet enough. A moment later, I hear the creak of Sylvia moving in her room.

When I get dressed and go into the living room, she's standing straight-backed in front of the window, sipping from a mug. She told me she chose this flat because of the trees that surround our block. Their branches are almost level with our window, as though we live in a treehouse. It makes it harder to see in, she says.

I notice there's a few cardboard boxes stacked up in the corner that weren't there yesterday. I wonder if that does mean Sylvia is thinking about moving again. I don't want to ask her. I don't want the answer to be yes.

'Happy Christmas,' I say, but she doesn't turn around.

'Sylvia,' I try again. 'Happy Christmas.'

This time, she turns her head towards me.

'Happy Christmas, Billy.'

I go to stand next to her and look out at the skeleton branches of the trees in the dark light of the morning. The wind makes the branches wave and tremor and for a moment I imagine them as the limbs of some kind of giant creature coming to life.

'What do you see?' Sylvia asks me, breaking my daydream.

I blink, chiding myself for not paying attention to my surroundings like I'm supposed to. Sylvia's right, I do need to work on that Rule more.

'Trees,' I answer quickly.

'Just trees?'

'Trees and . . .' I peer out of the window. 'Squirrels!' I spot them, two of them, racing across one of the branches.

'Anything else?'

I look at the ends of the branches, at a dancing leaf, one of the last to fall. And then at the thick trunk which leads down to a car park below. That's when I spot him, a man sitting in a car. I can't see what he's doing but I think I see him staring up towards the windows of our block of flats.

'There's a man in a car.'

'Good,' Sylvia says, turning away.

'What's he doing?' I ask. 'Why is he just sitting there like that?'

'Who's to know. Maybe he's waiting for someone. Maybe he's a taxi driver. It could be completely innocent.' Sylvia slips her hand in mine and leads me gently away from the window. 'Or maybe he's watching us, maybe he's come for us and we have to make sure that he doesn't see us—'

'But why would—' I start to say, but Sylvia interrupts me.

'Remember Survival Rule number two, Billy.'

'*Pay attention – keep constant observations of your surroundings,*' I say immediately.

'Good. You have to take notice of what's around you, Billy. Then if things change, if something happens, you are the first to notice and you can get a head start. Remember that, okay? That's another reason why Rule three is so important, too.' She looks at me expectantly.

'*Trust no one – you may only be able to rely on yourself,*' I say without hesitation, eager to please, but the words fall like stones, dull and heavy. It makes me feel alone, somehow, just saying them out loud.

'That's right,' Sylvia says. 'You must keep all the Rules at the forefront of your mind. Don't let yourself forget them, even if it's Christmas Day.'

I nod although I don't understand what she's saying really. 'Can I open my presents now?' I ask.

Sylvia gives a little snorting laugh. 'Ah, so you noticed *those*, did you?' she says. 'Go and get them, then.'

It takes me just a few seconds to pull off the pages of the old magazine that Sylvia has used as wrapping paper.

There's a new pair of gloves (my old ones have holes in them) and a small tin cup that's red with a black rim and something else that's covered in bubble wrap and is the size of a credit card.

I rip it open to find what looks like two small mirrors.

'They are heliographs,' Sylvia tells me. 'You can use them to direct a ray of sunlight in a certain direction. When it gets properly light, I'll show you how to use them, okay?'

Throughout the morning, Sylvia keeps looking out of the window to check the man in the car has gone until finally deciding it's fine for us to go out on the balcony. The sun is now shining brightly, but there's a sharp coldness in the air and I'm grateful for my new gloves.

Sylvia shows me how to hold the credit card-shaped mirror between my thumb and finger and make my beam of sunlight dart from place to place using only the smallest of movements. I watch as the sunlight dances on the tree trunks. Two spots of light, one of them directed by me, the other by Sylvia, jump from tree to tree.

'That's it,' Sylvia says. 'That's perfect.'

I feel a glow inside at this small amount of praise.

'You can use a heliograph if you're trying to signal to get someone's attention. Like if you need rescuing and are trying to alert someone to where you are,' Sylvia says.

She points to the small hole that's right in the centre of the mirror. 'This hole is here to help you aim the beam directly towards a moving target – like a plane or a boat – because that can be tricky, but you can use it to direct the light towards any specific target. Like, if I wanted to get a person's attention, I might try to aim the light right into their eyes so they would notice it straightaway. Understand?'

I nod, but to make sure, Sylvia asks me to repeat back everything she just told me. She gets me to say the part about directing it into someone's eyes twice over.

Then she takes out *How to Survive* and shows me the page about heliographs.

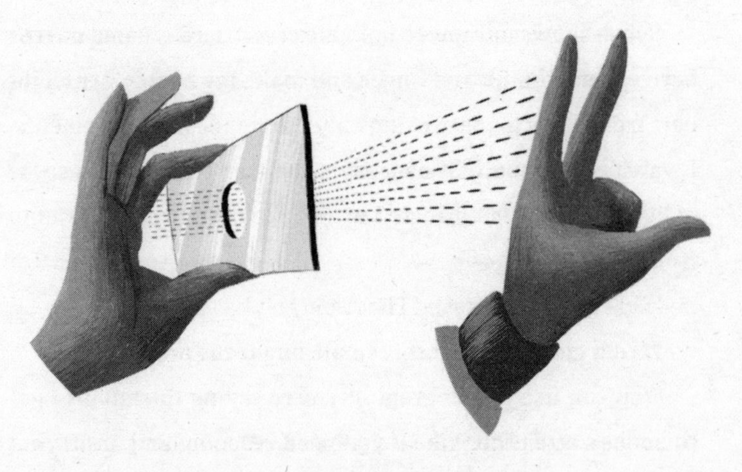

Fig. 2. – How to use a heliograph (Part 1)

She shows me how to look through the hole and extend one of my arms out straight in front of me, making a V-shape with my fingers.

'That should help with directing it. The book says using a pencil on a string and holding it out straight helps too. That way might be better than your arm, but it's good to know both ways because you don't know what equipment you'll have to use. We can try the pencil and string another day.'

I nod but I continue to practise directing the heliograph to line up exactly with an imaginary person's eyeline. I feel Sylvia watching me.

'You're getting good,' she says and I feel her warmth beside me. I think that she is about to move away but instead she pulls me closer into a hug. She kisses me on the top of my head.

'I love being your mum, do you know that, Billy? You mustn't ever forget that. Whatever happens. Remember that – I love being your mum.'

I pull away, embarrassed, not sure what to do or where to put the words that she is telling me.

'It's okay,' she says. She dusts herself down and points her heliograph to the sky and I immediately miss her warmth and wish I'd leaned into her to keep the hug going for longer.

I wondered whether we might go on an adventure today but Sylvia says that there are too many people about, going on Christmas Day walks.

I can't stop thinking about the kind of Christmases other

people will be having. I've heard my classmates talk about them, seen them in the films they show at school sometimes, even vaguely remember what they were like when I was really small. Tables heaving with food, stacks of presents beneath a glittering tree, long walks together as a family where you say 'Happy Christmas' to everyone you meet. I remember a 'Christmas Day' I spent with Steve a few years ago. It wasn't on the actual day, I'd been with Sylvia, but it was just a few days afterwards. He'd made a big fuss over it; there was a proper dinner with crackers and we'd decorated a tree with gaudy baubles the night before and put so many lights on it that it lit up the whole room. I try to think of something else because I can feel a lump growing in my throat as I remember it. The lump gets bigger and bigger and it feels hard to swallow but at the same time, I feel empty, like I haven't eaten for ages.

I always get that feeling when I start thinking about Steve and what it used to be like, which is why I try not to do it. It's hard today though, I can't seem to bat away the thoughts like I usually can.

We stay in the flat and Sylvia spends most of the day packing up the boxes in the living room. Her face is set in concentration as she examines papers and sorts tins and packs them tightly together as though they are a jigsaw puzzle. I watch her for a while and as I do, I start to think of Steve again. I'm not sure if it's a real memory or something I've made up myself, but I have a hazy image of Steve packing his things into a bag when he left us. I try to shake the memory as the feeling of emptiness builds up inside me. I wish Sylvia would stop but I can tell from the way that her shoulders are hunched together, how her fingers flick through things deftly, that her mind is completely focused on the task and she has no thought of stopping.

'Are we moving?' I ask, in the end.

'Not yet,' she says quietly. 'I just need to put some of this stuff in a safe place.'

'A safe place?' I repeat, but I don't get an answer. Sylvia continues to pack.

That night, after eating dinner – we have toast and baked beans with melted cheese on top, as a Christmas treat – she kisses me on the head and tells me that she is going out. She says that I am not to worry, that she'll be back in the morning.

Sylvia leaves me with a couple of instructions: 'Stay away from the window and don't open the door to anyone while I'm gone. I'll do the knock when I get back so you know that it's me that's opening the door.'

A few weeks ago, Sylvia insisted that we knock in a certain pattern when we come in so the other person knows for sure that it's not a stranger. You knock once, leave a pause and then knock quickly twice – that's our code.

Then, without looking back, without me having time to ask anything, without me having a moment to protest that it's Christmas and does she really have to go, she leaves, carrying two of the boxes that she packed up. The front door clicks closed and then the silence feels deafening as I'm left alone.

I decide to go to bed, but I can't relax, my ears straining at every moment to listen out for her coming back. I'm sure that I won't sleep, but I must doze off because suddenly I'm awoken by the code – one knock, pause, then two in rapid succession – and, finally, the sound of the front door opening. Moments later, I hear Sylvia's soft tread outside my door. I check my clock, it's 4 a.m. She's been gone for hours.

The same thing happens the next night, and the next, and the night after that.

But she won't tell me where she is going.

She won't tell me what she's doing.

HOW TO HAVE AN ADVENTURE

We used to call them adventures. I can't remember when Sylvia stopped calling them that but I still call them adventures in my head.

Whenever Sylvia said we were going on one, I always got excited because I knew that it meant special time, just Sylvia and I. We'd spend weekends together, somewhere I'd never been. Not like to the cinema or the library or a café like other people. It would always be somewhere outside, usually someplace where there wasn't anyone else around.

Sylvia would bring something for us to eat when we got there. A square of dark chocolate, perhaps, or a tangy, squashy clementine; a handful of walnuts or the corner of a Kendal Mint Cake. That's how I knew we had arrived: because she'd hand me a snack to eat.

Then she'd pull out *How to Survive* and let me pick what I wanted to do. I'd flick through the pages and it didn't seem to matter which activity I suggested, somehow Sylvia would have everything that we needed to do it in her rucksack, all ready to go.

Sometimes whatever we were trying wouldn't work particularly well. But she never seemed to mind. She had more patience then and she wasn't as good at the survival stuff either. We were learning together almost.

Those days felt fun. Special. And I felt lucky to have a mum who wanted to spend time with me like this, rather than one who didn't really care where I was or who I was with, who just ignored me while she chatted on the phone to friends.

But somewhere along the way, our adventures changed.

We started to go on more of them. And then it stopped being just at the weekends.

The first day that I missed school Sylvia took me out of class in the middle of the morning saying that there was something more important that we needed to do. My teacher had looked a bit shocked but didn't say anything. It was a one-off so it was okay.

A week later, Sylvia just decided out of nowhere as she was walking me to school that we should go on an adventure instead.

And it kept on happening.

Each time I tried to tell myself they were just our fun adventures like always, but I knew really that they were different now. It was almost like Sylvia *needed* us to go and practise, to keep calm. Like it stopped something spilling out from her.

Then Sylvia left her job in the laboratory and things got worse.

It was just a few weeks after the time with Steve in the park, and he was supposed to be coming down on Saturday to see me again. On the Friday I saw Sylvia standing by the school playground. The window of my classroom looked out to the patch of the playground where the parents would wait for their kids at home time and I could see her standing at the gate, waiting to get in. There wasn't anything particularly unusual by then about Sylvia picking me up from school much too early and I thought she might be collecting me for another adventure, but she didn't actually come in to get me. There was a class that were having their P.E. lesson in the playground and Sylvia just stood there outside the gates the whole time, not really watching them; her gaze seemed to stare past them. She looked almost like a statue; she didn't seem to move the whole time. I could make out the sun picking out the silvery grey of her hair.

When school finally finished, I ran down to her as quickly as I could. She wrapped me up in the tightest hug and she didn't let go. It went on for just a bit too long. This felt like more than a greeting, it was like a prison. I wiggled a little but she only clung on tighter. Her arms felt rigid around me.

'Sylvia,' I said. 'It's hurting.'

She let go of me then but immediately kneeled down, so her face was just centimetres away from mine. She studied me as though she was looking for something. Then she locked eyes with me and I saw, just for a moment, a flood of emotions that seemed to dart from the hazel of her irises right into me, like a beam of light: pain and hurt, worry and tenderness, fear and love.

'I thought that you had come to pick me up for an adventure,' I said. 'I saw you come early.'

Sylvia whipped her head quickly from side to side, as though she were trying to shake something off.

'I just had to think,' she murmured. 'I just needed some time . . .' She trailed off.

'Is everything all right?' I asked.

She didn't answer.

'Let's go,' she said, standing up. She gripped my hand tightly and set off at a pace that was just a little too fast.

That was the night she wrote up the Five Survival Rules. She made me copy them down on to the inside of the back cover of *How to Survive*.

Early the next day, before it was even properly light, Sylvia took me on an adventure. I asked about Steve, and the fact I was supposed to be seeing him, but she just told me he wasn't coming after all. She didn't say why, even though I asked her. It had never happened before. I couldn't quite understand how I felt when I first heard Steve wasn't coming. I was disappointed, but then we were out for nearly the whole weekend and stayed overnight in the woods in an emergency shelter that we made, so I was distracted from thinking about it.

Sylvia didn't mention anything about her job to me until Monday morning. She said that I didn't need to go to school. That we were going out again.

'But don't you need to go to work?' I'd asked.

'Not any more,' she replied with a firm, brisk shake of her head.

'Why not?'

'You're my job now,' was all she said.

We moved house for the first time that very week. And I haven't seen Steve since.

HOW TO HAVE AN ARGUMENT

Sylvia has gone out every night since Christmas Day, and on New Year's Eve I decide I have to say something.

She's holding another box of stuff and is heading towards the front door when I confront her. As though my legs are not my own, I feel myself run over and stand between her and the door.

'Thanks, Billy,' she says, misunderstanding me. 'I don't think I can manage the door with this one.' Her fingers grip on tightly to the large box she's struggling to keep hold of. It's stuffed full of papers, old work documents that I didn't know she still had. She has spent the day sifting through them and packing them away.

'Sylvia.' My voice comes out much quieter than I think it will, more like a whisper.

She shifts the box in her arms, heaving it upwards before it begins to slip again.

When I don't open it, she says, 'Hurry up, will you, Billy. I can't hold on to this for ever.'

Part of me wants to move out of her way and pull the door

open for her, but the other part keeps my feet rooted to the floor, my arms rigid at my sides.

'You have to tell me where you keep going each night,' I say, in a burst. 'You have to tell me what's happening.'

Sylvia heaves the box up one more time and then, quite suddenly, she drops it. It falls with a huge thud and I leap backwards. The lid flies open from the impact and some of the papers scatter on the floor around us.

I catch sight of reports with CONFIDENTIAL stamped across them, in red. There's a notebook filled with Sylvia's handwriting that lies open at an angle.

I don't dare look at Sylvia's face. I am sure she is upset. But then her hand is on my cheek. I can feel the ridge of the calluses on her fingers, smell the scent of the soap she uses, feel the warmth of her palm on my face.

'Billy,' Sylvia says gently. 'You have to trust me. You know everything that I do is for you. To keep you safe.'

I nod.

'Do you trust me?' she asks.

I hesitate in replying for just a second too long.

I see Sylvia's mouth twitch.

Words spring from my lips. 'I do trust you, I do. But I don't understand what you're keeping me safe from. Where are you going to each night? Are we moving? Please tell me if we are leaving again.'

Only as the question is spilling from my mouth do I realize how much I fear that we are going to start again someplace new. It isn't that I love my current school or have any friends or anything like that, there is just a grey tiredness inside me that tells me I can't move yet again.

Sylvia sighs but it sounds more like a hiss.

'I told you already that we're not moving.' She speaks through clenched teeth.

I hear myself exhale, I hadn't realized I'd been holding my breath. I'm glad to hear that we're not moving again.

'I just have to take these things to somewhere safe. We need to get ready.'

'Get ready for what?' I say. I hear my voice rising. It doesn't sound like my own. 'What are we getting ready for?'

'I have to keep you safe. I have to keep you safe.'

'Safe from what?' I question her again. 'What's happening?'

Sylvia just shakes her head.

'Is this about Steve?' I suddenly blurt out. I've stopped myself from mentioning him so many times but now his name just bubbles up; it's out of my lips before I know it.

Sylvia's face jolts and for a second I see it flash across her face. Naked worry. It *is* about Steve.

'He's my dad – doesn't he want me to be safe too?'

'He doesn't understand.' Sylvia's voice comes out like a growl. 'He doesn't want to understand.'

'Why don't I see him any more?' Suddenly all the things that I've been bottling up are fizzing up, out of my control. 'Why doesn't he come?'

Sylvia clamps her hands over her ears and shuts her eyes.

'Tell me,' I continue. 'You need to tell me.' I feel desperate with a longing that I didn't know until that moment was living inside me always. Where was my father and why didn't he want to see me any more?

All of a sudden, Sylvia roars: 'Your father doesn't want to know, okay? He'd much rather believe in something convenient. I've tried to talk to him, I have . . . I did try. I tried to explain. But he doesn't believe me, okay? His mind is closed. That's why you don't see him any more. Because he just doesn't understand how important this is. And I can't risk it, I can't risk you not being ready. This is serious, Billy.'

I try to absorb what it is that she's telling me. I realize that there's always been a voice telling me that I'm the reason that Steve doesn't come to see me. I'd done something wrong, something that made him not want to see me any more. That was why I felt so empty whenever I thought about him. But now Sylvia is saying it was something else, something he wouldn't believe. That it's not my fault, it's his.

'What is it? What doesn't he want to know about?' I ask urgently.

'I'll tell you soon, I promise. And I will show you – where it is that I am going to.' She says it again: 'I promise.'

'When?'

'In the next couple of weeks,' she says. 'I've got more that I need to get ready before then.'

Instead of answering I step out of the way of the door and swing it open. I feel exhausted, like I've been running non-stop for hours on end. My mind flashes again with the hazy memory of Steve packing things into a bag when he left. This time, though, I remember more. I see myself stepping towards him and reaching out. His fingers closed over my hands as I see tears streaming down his face.

Sylvia stuffs the papers back into the box. I go to help her but she grabs the papers from my hands as I do. I read a snippet of a sentence from her notebook before she jams it into the box. It's just a fragment and it doesn't make much sense at all: *has to be a better way.* I try to read more but Sylvia closes the notebook with a thump and shoves it on top of the papers.

She hauls up the box into her arms.

She doesn't say goodbye. She doesn't look back.

HOW TO LEARN (THE HARD WAY)

I don't go back to school when the new term starts up.

The days before I'm due to go back I'm on high alert, looking for any sign from Sylvia that she might know it's approaching.

Perhaps she'd start thinking aloud about what to buy for my packed lunches. Maybe she'd dig through my school bag to uncover the reading project I'd forgotten to do. But deep down, I knew none of these things were going to happen.

On the first day of term, I lie in bed past the time I know I should be up and the funny thing is that although I don't really want to go to school, I feel sort of twitchy and hot because I know I'm doing something wrong. Eventually, I put on my school uniform, picking it up from the floor where it has sat since we got home from making the firebow in the woods. There is still dirt from the wood clinging to the trousers that I try to brush off as best I can. But when Sylvia sees me, she tells me to 'get dressed properly', that I need clothes to keep warm because we'll be out all day. We spend the whole day navigating using a compass and Sylvia teaches me how to use the sun to measure time as it sets, when you can see the horizon.

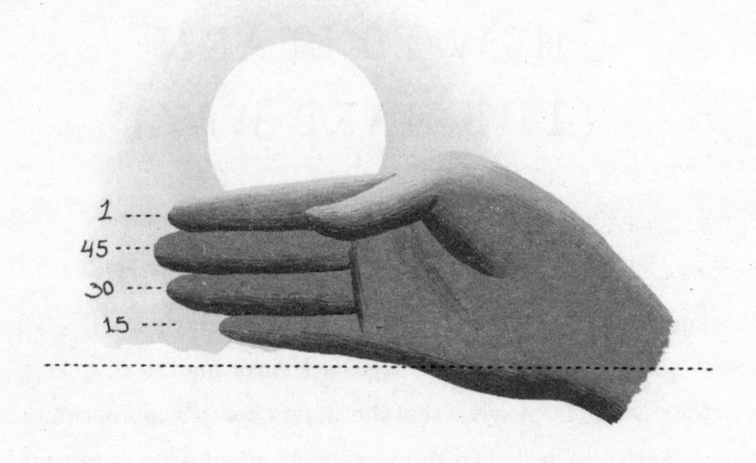

Fig. 3. – How to measure the time using the sun

The next day, Sylvia wakes me early, and we are out before it's even light. That whole first week of term is the same, each day like a repeat of the one before; we spend most of the day on an adventure and then Sylvia leaves in the evening to go to the 'safe place', wherever that is.

Now it's Monday morning, and all I can think about is how I should be going into assembly at just this moment. But then, Miss Browning is probably telling everyone off for being too noisy in the corridor; what does it really matter if I'm missing out on that?

I try to ignore the little part of me that wants to be just going into school, like any other day, like any other person.

I can't help but think about the assembly we had at the end of term. The head teacher presented a brand-new bike to the junior who had the highest attendance in the whole school. There were lots of people who thought that they might have a chance of winning and just before they announced who'd won, excitement filled the hall. I felt as if I could almost see it: an oversized, quivering jelly, balancing in the air.

I knew that there was no way that I was in the running, partly because I hadn't been at the school that long and partly because, in the time I had been there, I was absent so often. But even I hoped for a second that it might be my name that they read out.

I knew that Sylvia got in trouble for keeping me off school. I'd seen the letters that she received. But she didn't seem to care and at first neither did I. I loved our adventures. And the less I was in school, the less lonely I felt. I didn't have friends and so being with Sylvia, learning all the survival stuff, was much more fun than being in school.

But somewhere along the way it turned into something different.

It changed from fun to me being worried about what might happen if I wasn't there with her.

It had transformed into me lying here in bed very still when I knew that I should be somewhere else and having a very different sort of day.

*

I hear the floorboards softly squeak in the room next to mine and I get up and get dressed. I go downstairs and have a poke about in the kitchen cupboards but can't find anything that will make a breakfast.

When Sylvia appears, her silver hair is scraped up in a ponytail, making her face look thinner than usual. She starts to pack her rucksack with matches, a ball of string, her penknife. She seems like she's in a hurry.

'Let's get out as soon as we can,' she says in place of 'good morning'.

I nod but I can't stop myself from saying the words: 'Do you think I should go into school today?'

Sylvia doesn't stop packing, and I think that she can't have heard me. But then, as she fills up one of the water bottles from the tap, with her back to me, she answers.

'I can teach you more about what you need to know than you will ever learn going to that place.'

I don't know how to answer.

I don't know how to explain to her that I don't want to go on adventures any more. That I'm all mixed up inside because I'm scared to leave her alone but I just want to do what everyone else is doing. That I'm full of complicated feelings, knowing a distance is growing and growing between me and other kids my age and not being able to do a thing about it.

HOW TO CONSTRUCT AN EMERGENCY SHELTER: PART I

Sylvia found a tree she said was dying.

It would be good to practise on, she said, and so that afternoon, we made our way over to the park. We'd spent the morning studying pictures of the lopped-tree bivouac, a type of emergency shelter, in *How to Survive* and reminded ourselves how to make one.

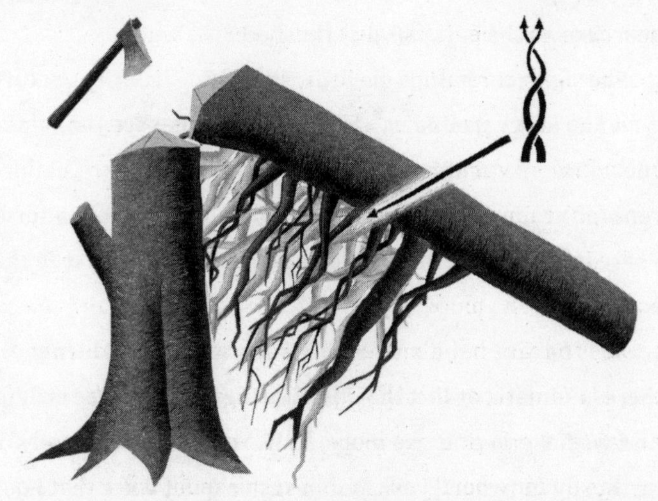

Fig. 4. – How to construct an emergency shelter (Part I)

Before we left the flat, Sylvia looked out of all the windows and insisted on checking the corridor too.

'All clear,' she told me.

We go on a complicated route to the park, with sharp turns down alleyways, and sometimes we break into a run. Sylvia keeps looking over her shoulder as though she thinks there is someone following us.

'There's no one there,' I tell her but it's like she can't hear me. She keeps turning back to look.

'Are you sure it's okay for us to cut it down?' I ask as we finally walk towards the tree.

'This tree's dying, they'll probably thank us for doing them a favour. If we do it, they won't have to.'

'Really?' I ask, eyeing the families all around us. The school next door to the park has just finished.

She sighs; it reminds me of air streaming from a punctured tyre. She looks around us and I think she must see the same as I do: mothers standing in groups by their pushchairs, children running around screaming, still in their grey school uniforms. There is no one else like us. No one else who has an axe in their bag.

'It'll be fine,' she snaps. She rubs her eye suddenly, like there is something in it that is irritating her. 'The tree is dying. And we have to practise more, Billy. You have to be ready.'

'Ready for what?' I ask, but in such a quiet voice that I don't think she hears me.

She swings the axe up high and when it hits the tree it's like everyone around us feels the cut, the way that they startle and look over. Sylvia's axe swings make dull, rhythmic thuds as she hits the tree again and again, her cheeks flushed from the effort. In no time, a crowd has started to grow around us.

'Umm, I don't think you can do that,' someone says.

Sylvia gives a small laugh.

'I can do that,' she says. 'Because I am.' She swings the axe again, hard, and it sinks deeply into the trunk.

I pull at Sylvia's sleeve. I want to go.

A man steps forward then. 'I really think you should stop,' he says, his hands on his hips.

Sylvia doesn't look at him but swings the axe again into the trunk. As she lifts it, the blade glints in the afternoon sunshine.

'Can't you see that this tree is dead?' Sylvia mutters. 'Idiots.' She lifts the axe once more and strikes the tree with all her strength. The axe bites deep, it's the final blow needed for the top of the tree to be pulled down, for us to start to thatch the inside branches to make the shelter.

'I'm going to call the police if you don't leave,' a mother says.

'Sylvia,' I say. 'Maybe we should go.'

Despite my worries that we shouldn't be using the tree, I had actually almost been looking forward to making the shelter. If we did it right, it would resemble a sort of wigwam by the end and I thought it would be fun to have our own den of sorts. But now I just want to leave.

'Oi!' shouts a man who is walking a sausage dog. He is

running towards us; his dog's stubby legs can barely keep up with him. 'You can't cut that tree down! Is it even legal to have an axe like that in the park? There are children here.'

'Sylvia, let's go,' I say.

I can feel people watching us. With every person that arrives I can feel another pair of eyes boring into our skin as though they are fierce rays from the sun, as though they can burn us.

'Fine,' Sylvia says. But I know it's not.

She leans the edge of the axe handle against her shoulder, so its dull, sharp blade rears into the air, and stalks through the middle of the crowd that has built up around us.

They part as we approach.

I see the first woman who had spoken to us grab hold of her daughter as we pass by, as though she is worried that Sylvia might swing the axe towards them.

Don't be worried, I want to tell them. *We are just practising*, I want to explain. *She wouldn't ever hurt anyone*, I want to say.

But then we hear the sound of sirens in the distance and Sylvia tells me to run.

HOW TO STAY SILENT

There's a growing list of things I want to ask Sylvia about.

I want to know if I am ever going back to school. It's been almost a month now since the new term began and I've not been in once.

I want to know where it is that she still goes to almost every night and what it is she is doing.

I want to know what we are getting ready for.

But Sylvia stays silent.

And so I do too.

HOW TO CONSTRUCT AN EMERGENCY SHELTER: PART II

You find a fallen tree.

If you can't find one, a largish rock will do.

You clear away any old leaves or branches on one side of it (where you want to make your bed) and light a roaring fire on this spot.

This will dry out and heat the ground. After the fire has been burning for about half an hour, you push the embers a couple of metres away from the log, where you want your main fire for the night to be.

You cover the ground where the fire once was (taking care there are no embers left) with a deep layer of leafy branches, then fern leaves, then moss or grass. This will be your bed.

You know that if you lie on this bed of plant material as close to the log as possible, you will be sheltered. You know that with the heat of the fire nearby, you will keep warm.

If there is the possibility of rain, you support branches against the log on the side that you are not sleeping. You cover them with leafy branches to make a roof of sorts.

Fig. 5. – How to construct an emergency shelter (Part II)

'That's exactly right,' Sylvia says.

She's driving us somewhere in a white, battered van and asking me questions to stop me from falling asleep.

'How do you make a fire using a magnifying glass?'

'How do you navigate using a shadow-stick?'

'How do you build an emergency shelter?'

'Tell me the Rules for Survival.' Over and over.

I yawn. My eyes blink closed, even though I am excited that I'm finally going to find out where she has been going each night.

'Why do we have to go at night?' I ask her, trying to sit up straight in an attempt to stay awake.

'Too many eyes in the daytime,' she replies. 'Strictly

speaking, we are not supposed to be going to this place and so it's best to go when there aren't many people about.'

As she explains this, I feel worries knot through me.

What if we get into trouble?

What if we are found?

'Don't worry,' she tells me. 'It's a safe place. It's our safe place.'

The van jolts to a stop and this is what wakes me.

It's dark outside. I can't see any light coming from anywhere. Not from a neighbouring house, not from a streetlamp. We must be in the middle of nowhere.

Sylvia doesn't speak. She clutches at the steering wheel and pulls herself forward so she is closer to the windscreen. She is looking up at the night sky – looking for something. For stars, perhaps, but when I look up the sky is overcast.

'Ready?' she says. She climbs out of the car and closes the door softly behind her. I copy her but when I stand, I feel the weight of tiredness pulling me down. I feel disconnected from every footstep I take. I follow her in a slow shuffle, unable to see where we are going or to work out what has brought us here.

'Where are we going?' I ask, but Sylvia does not answer me. She ducks in and out of shadows and I have to hurry to keep up with her. I can smell salt in the air – it lines my nostrils and stiffens in my hair. 'Are we by the sea?' I ask Sylvia's disappearing back.

I don't notice the building at first. I'm concentrating so hard on following Sylvia that I don't see the squat, grey tower in front of us. It looks like a huge, oversized chimney that is growing up from the ground.

'It's called a Martello tower.' Sylvia's voice rings out clearly. 'Defensive forts that were built in the nineteenth century. Some of them are just ruins now. Or they've gone the other way and have been turned into holiday homes. This one's somewhere in between. It's not in bad nick but there's no one using it. It's good for us.'

'Good for us, for what?' I say, although I can feel the answer lingering just ahead of me. I know Sylvia well enough to understand why she would have more than a passing interest in an unused defensive fort.

'It's the perfect place for an emergency shelter,' Sylvia says. 'And I've been making it even more suitable, every chance I get.'

This is where Sylvia has been coming each night, this is what she has been working on.

We walk around the tower to a small, narrow door. It almost looks like it's just a shadow in the wall. Sylvia bends down and pulls out a pick and a wrench from her pocket and begins to fiddle with the lock. I hear the lock turn and Sylvia opens the door for me and hands me a torch.

'You go first,' she says. 'I want you to see it. I want you to see everything that I have done.'

I click the torch on and direct the thin beam into the tower. For a moment, I do not want to go any further. I do not want to follow the light of the torch. I do not want to see Sylvia's preparations. I wish I was somewhere, anywhere else.

'Go on,' Sylvia urges me, cutting through my thoughts. She gestures towards the door. 'See what I've done.' Her voice sounds high and taut, like a kite that's being pulled by a strong wind.

I let the torch beam travel across the sides of the entrance. I can't see anything in there – there's nothing pinned to the walls, nothing blocking the pathway.

'Hurry up, Billy.'

I take a step in, and then another.

'Take the door on the right,' Sylvia says.

I turn and push the door open. It's stiff; I have to give it a hard shove to move it. My eyes struggle to adjust to the new darkness in this room but then I see it.

There are tins and tins and tins piled up so they make a wall. There's other food too – longlife cartons of milk, bags of rice, of oats.

Lining every wall space, there are articles tacked up which have been circled and highlighted. In the darkness I can only really make out a few words and odd phrases. I recognize some of the pages as reports on climate change and the melting ice caps that used to be plastered to the walls in our flat. Sylvia had taken them down when we were being visited by someone from social services. I thought she'd thrown them away but clearly she had just found them a new home.

There are other diagrams too. Images of the human body that are pinned up and have scribbled notes all around them.

They've been shaded in with pencil or something so you can't see their skin, only a grey sheen where the colour should be.

'What are these?' I ask, but Sylvia steps in front of the diagrams.

'Don't worry about those. Come on, I'll show you where everything is,' she says.

She walks me round every part of the Martello tower, showing me exactly how she has organized it and where to find everything. There's a room that already has two sleeping bags laid out, side by side – one for me and one for her. It's a dark, dank room and smells like old mushrooms. I can't imagine sleeping in it.

'Are we moving here?' I ask Sylvia when I see it, worry in my voice.

'Well, that's the thing, Billy,' Sylvia says. 'We may have to move here. I'd hoped that we wouldn't but we need to be ready in any case. Remember the number one Rule . . .'

'Always be prepared.' I speak the words without thinking, they are so etched into my mind.

'There's a strong possibility that we will have to stay here. I wish it weren't the case but wishing doesn't make things go away.'

I swallow hard. I don't understand why we would ever have to live here.

'It's not for now,' Sylvia says, and I feel a tightness in my chest release. 'But you need to know how to find it, just in case we get separated and have to make our own way here.'

She pulls a map from one of the shelves and spreads it out on the floor.

'But how will I know if it's the right time to come if we're not together?'

'You'll know,' Sylvia says, without meeting my eye. 'You'll know.'

HOW TO START A FIRE USING A SPLIT MATCH

The wood of the match is spindly, almost impossibly thin.

Sylvia holds it with a shaking hand.

She places one of her fingers on the head of the match and presses it against the striker.

'Your finger will be burnt,' I call out to her. 'Don't light it!'

She looks over to me. She sees me.

She sees me.

This morning there have been longer periods where she hasn't seen me. I've spoken and my words have fallen around her like dead leaves. I've reached out to her and she has shaken me away, shrugged out of my grasp.

But now she sees me.

'It won't burn me,' she tells me. 'I'll lift my finger as soon as the head flares. I'll show you again.'

She's taught me how to split matches before. She put the knifepoint just behind the match head, the sharp part of it angled towards its tip and drove the blade down so it would split into two.

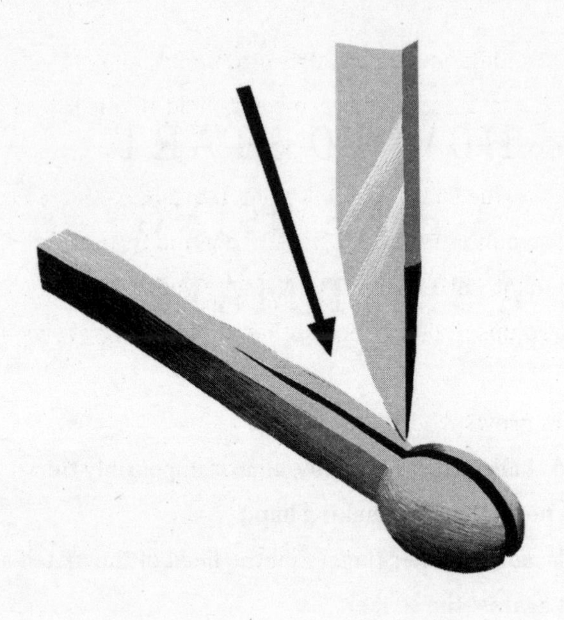

Fig. 6. – How to start a fire using a split match

'If we split matches,' she had told me, 'we can double our supply.'

But the problem came when lighting them. They would break easily now they were half as thin. You had to press the head on to the striker with your finger and take it away at the very last moment.

'Don't do it,' I plead with her now. 'Let's not start a fire. We don't need one.'

'It's easy,' she says. 'It's easy to do.'

Her hand shakes only a little, her finger is still pressing the head of the match against the striker.

She draws the match along, holding it firmly within her

thumb and middle finger. It sparks into flame.

'See?' Sylvia says. 'You just have to hold it carefully so it doesn't break.'

She lights the little pile of tinder that she collected and flames lap around the twisted newspaper and the candle ends.

She feeds it with the papers that arrived in the post and made her so upset, one after another, and the fire grows and grows.

The fire grows where she made it.

In the middle of our living-room floor.

HOW TO FALL

The flat fills with smoke. Not just like the smoke when rice burns on the stove or something like that; these are heavy, dense clouds of smoke that seem as impenetrable as walls.

The fire grows across the carpet and spreads towards the sofa. She'd used something to make it catch, a spray, a liquid that fed the fire with a roar.

Her eyes are wide with alarm and fear. I know that she did not mean for it to be so big.

I know, too, why she was so upset about the letter that made her decide to burn our post. I read it when she crushed it into a ball and threw it down on to the floor. It was something legal about who was going to have custody of me. Steve wanted me to live with him and the letter said there was going to be a hearing.

Steve. I felt the old familiar hole opening up inside of me as I read the letter, the emptiness that grew in my stomach any time that I thought about him. It had been so long since I'd seen him now that he felt like just a name to me. I couldn't quite admit to myself that I couldn't even properly remember his face or the sound of his voice. But he *did* want to see me again, the letter proved that.

What would it be like if I didn't live with Sylvia? However difficult it could be, I knew with a heavy, sure certainty that I couldn't be separated from her. I just couldn't.

I'd scrunched the letter back into a ball and left it on the kitchen floor so that Sylvia didn't know I'd read it too.

For ages she had paced the flat, walking from wall to wall to wall, an energy raging inside her. Then she had the idea that she wanted to burn it . . .

Now the smoke from the fire grows thicker and thicker.

I think of ringing 999. I think about the very small fire extinguisher that we have in the kitchen; it seems far too tiny to be able to put out a fire like this. I think of wrapping wet tea towels around our faces. But in the time these short thoughts have darted through my mind, the fire has grown even bigger. Too big.

Then I feel Sylvia's hand in mine. She is coughing violently from the smoke and I can feel it too, a burning in my chest. It feels like I will never be without it, that pain.

She pulls me towards the fire but I'm paralysed with fear. I don't want to move.

'Come on, Billy, you must,' she says.

I shake my head violently.

'You can do this,' she says. 'I know you can do this.'

I find that I am on my feet, that I am following her past the raging fire.

Sylvia drags me towards the window and wrenches it open. She lifts me and suddenly I am spiralling out of the window, tumbling in the air, waiting for the moment that I land, my eyes tightly shut.

I think I can't possibly survive a fall this big, I think: I am going to die.

HOW TO SAY GOODBYE

I cough and I cough.

I can't cough hard enough.

I feel like I need to cough something up before I will ever be able to breathe again, like a black twisted piece of tar or a jagged stone that has sharp, cutting edges. There are tears welling in my eyes although I'm not crying, not really, although I can still feel the weight of heavy teardrops forming. And the funny thing is that I want to cry. I want to curl up and sob. I am suddenly very aware that there's a hole inside of me: a pit, a black and bottomless pit, and I could fall down into it at any moment, I know this. But for now, I must just—

'Breathe, breathe,' a voice commands.

They try to fasten a mask over my mouth. At first I try to push them away but there are hands, strong hands, that hold me down and keep me still. And then the mask is on me and I can feel it helping.

I can breathe without coughing.

I can breathe even though it still feels that something inside me is torn.

I can hear voices talking all around me and my ears strain to hear the sound of the only voice I want to hear.

Sylvia.

Where is she?

I struggle to get up and try to pull the mask from my face but someone, a paramedic I think, leans over me and says, 'No, no, keep it on, mister.' She presses the mask back over my face. 'That's it,' she says.

But then I hear her radio scramble. A voice rings out, tinny and faraway. I hear scraps of the words it is saying: 'Urgent assistance required – code 119 – all available units respond.' She turns her back to answer it, I wrench the mask off in one movement and struggle away from the bed and the blankets that feel like ropes tying me down.

There are people gathered outside our building. Our neighbours mostly, but also people that I do not recognize. I look for Sylvia's face amongst them but I only see strangers.

I want to shout out her name but my lungs are too painful; if I try to shout I will only make a strangled-sounding wheeze. I know that my voice has shrivelled, like a plant that hasn't been given enough water and its leaves have turned into crispy spirals.

Flashing lights from police cars bathe everything in a pulsing blue beam.

I look up to our flat, to the window that Sylvia had thrown me through. It's dripping with water; the glass is blackened, cracked. How did I survive falling from such a height? But as I look at the ground beneath the window, I instantly know the answer. There are large shrubs growing which must have acted like a cushion; Sylvia had known they would break my fall, made sure that was where I'd land. But even though I'm here, alive with just bruises and cuts, I still can't believe the height, the fall.

The fire crew are milling around the entrance to our building. I wait for the right moment, when they have walked just far enough away, and then I make a run for the door. Sylvia must still be upstairs, I decide. I have to find her, I have to know she's okay.

But I am not as fast as I want to be, my legs move sluggishly beneath me as I try to run, and they easily spot me.

'Hey, stop there!' someone shouts as someone else comes stomping towards me.

I only just manage to slide past them and run up the stairs to our flat.

Everything has been blackened and singed by the fire and the smell of smoke hangs in the air.

'Sylvia!' I call out in a cracked whisper. I run from room to room.

She is not there.

I hear the pounding of the fire crew's footsteps down the corridor.

I am suddenly sure that I will not be here again. I know that I will be taken away. It will be just like in the letter that Sylvia received this morning.

I reach out for something, anything that I can take with me. A piece of us that can come with me.

My fingers grip around Sylvia's old penknife that lies on the floor. It's tarnished from the fire but it feels just the same in my hand.

And then there are arms around me, there's blankets and more flashing lights. They smother me, they carry me away.

I still can't find Sylvia. And no one will tell me where she is.

HOW (NOT) TO SAY HELLO

The blanket feels scratchy around my neck. I keep shrugging it away but each time I do someone comes along and pulls it back around me again. The seat of the ambulance bed feels hard beneath me.

My voice feels hoarse from asking about Sylvia, although the paramedic says that's just because of the smoke I inhaled.

They took me downstairs from our flat back to the ambulance and I don't know how long I wait there but in the end the ambulance pulls away and drives to a hospital I've never been to before. A woman called Talia is there to meet me. She has short, tufty blonde hair and wears large, dusty boots that look like they are a size too big for her.

When I ask her about Sylvia, she looks at me straight in the eye and tells me that she is being seen by doctors, but not at this hospital. I think someone had told Talia about me running back into the flat because she stays close to me all the time we are in the waiting room, even staying close to the doors of the toilets when I need to go.

After I see a doctor, Talia takes me into a little room that has a stack of magazines with curling covers and games for children much younger than me.

'Not much for us to do in here, is there, Billy?' Talia says, looking around. 'Fancy something to eat?'

I nod, although I'm not really hungry. I have the oddest sensation that I will never feel hungry again; I just feel completely blank.

'I think I spotted a vending machine back there. Let's go and choose something,' Talia says.

I follow her down the corridor in silence.

'What do you reckon?' she asks as we stand in front of the glass machine. When I don't say anything, she fills the quiet. 'There's apples and cereal bars or a little box of dried fruit. Does anything take your fancy, or shall I just get a few things?'

Back in the room, Talia digs through her rucksack and starts placing things out on the low table. She finds a bottle of water and a half-eaten bar of dark chocolate, a notepad and a couple of pens.

She looks up at me brightly.

'Hangman, Billy,' she says. 'We've got to pass the time somehow, don't we?'

'Does it have a "d" in it, Billy?' Talia asks me.

But I'm not listening. Instead I'm looking up through the narrow window in the door where a man's face has appeared. There's a tiny inkling of recognition, but mostly I'm just wondering who it is that's looking in. It's something I will have to keep inside of me, something that I will have to carry, but feels too prickly to hold properly. It's like a spiny horse chestnut, with needle-green thorny spikes – the fact that I didn't know who he was at first.

Then the man pushes the door open and rushes towards me. Before he gets to me, though, he stops. It takes me a moment to realize that it is me who has made him stop so suddenly in his tracks. It's because I am looking at him like he's a stranger, like I don't know who he is.

It's Steve.

Talia leaps up when she sees Steve and introduces herself noisily, almost as though she knows that I can't face him right there and then.

I squirm on the chair, wishing that there is somewhere I could hide in this blank, almost empty room as they try and have a hushed conversation in the corner.

But I make out snatches of sentences:

'Looks like he's been through a lot.' (Steve)

'No permanent damage.' (Talia)

'Been a while since we've seen each other.' (Steve)

'His mum's been seen by a psychiatric team.' (Talia)

I jerk my head up at that and see Steve nodding away. He exhales noisily. 'It's been escalating, I think,' he says, but then he spots that I'm listening and turns his attention to me.

'Hey, buddy,' he says. 'It's so good to see you.'

He moves towards me and leans in to try and hug me. But I stay frozen where I am, so he crashes into me with his weight and I almost fall off the chair. He catches hold of my arm so I don't fall, but as I feel his hand grasping me, I begin to struggle. I don't know why I do it. It's like I'm not in control of myself and I've been cornered into a tiny space that I cannot escape from.

'Easy, Billy,' Talia says.

'I was just trying to stop him from falling,' Steve says to her.

'Maybe it's best,' Talia says, 'if you wait outside for a moment.'

HOW TO (BE FORCED TO) MOVE HOUSE

'How do you feel about going home with your dad today?' Talia asks me. 'He would really like you to go and live with him in Bristol.'

I wait for her to say something more. Something like 'until your mum's better' or 'for just a little bit', but she leaves the words as they are, with no promise of anything else.

'He lives in Bristol?' I didn't know that he had moved out of London. 'What about Sylv— my mum? Why can't I live with her?'

'Your mum needs to concentrate on getting well. So I'm afraid you can't live with her while she's getting the help she needs.'

She leaves the unspoken question hanging – *Don't I want Sylvia to get the help that she needs?*

'Okay,' I say, almost in a whisper but not quite.

'That's great, Billy,' Talia says and then she pauses. 'I know that it's a huge amount to take in . . . but I'm glad that you've decided to go with your dad today.'

There's more that's unspoken in the air but I know exactly what she's getting at.

If I don't go home with Steve, who else would want me?

HOW TO SURVIVE

I lie unmoving on the bed, my eyes wide open and glassy. I'm not sleeping– in fact I find it hard to go to sleep – it's more like I have been switched off, like some kind of toy with dead batteries.

This morning is just like all the others before it. Steve brings me breakfast clattering on a tray and talks to me as though there is nothing unusual about the fact that I'm not getting up and that I haven't lived with him since I was six years old and that we don't really know each other even though he is my dad and I am his son.

He pulls open the curtains and though the winter light is feeble and dim, he says, 'I think it's going to be a nice day today, Billy.' He lingers for a few moments more, straightening the corner of my duvet cover unnecessarily, picking up Sylvia's penknife that lies in the middle of one of the empty bookshelves and putting it down again. Then he says, 'Well, see you later, then,' and though I haven't said anything in reply, he says as if he is answering me: 'I'll just be downstairs if you need me.'

'My room' is a powder-blue room that doesn't have enough things in it. When I arrived, Steve told me he moved to this house for his job about two years ago, but it looks to me like he hasn't really done any decorating since he arrived. I think about the timing and realize that he must have come to Bristol around the same time he stopped coming to see me. I've been wondering if that was the real reason why he stopped our visits. Sylvia had told me it was because he didn't believe her about something but maybe it wasn't that at all. Maybe his life had just got too busy to have me in it. Maybe I was right when I thought it was because he didn't want to see me any more. It makes me feel like I am so small, as though I am shrinking down to nothing. But then there was the letter asking for custody. Had he changed his mind? And remembering that letter makes me feel so torn up inside when I think back to how it was what made Sylvia start the fire. It's the reason why I am here and she is far away, it's why I have not seen her since that day. My mind feels like it's in a constant swirl of questions and unknowing.

I wasn't allowed to get anything from our flat, so there's nothing of me in this room. Just some clothes that Steve bought me quickly so I had some things when I arrived. He'd put some of his old books on the shelves for me too, and I placed Sylvia's penknife right in the middle of one of the empty bookshelves.

As soon as Steve leaves the room, I take a deep breath in and out. I can smell the porridge on the breakfast tray but I can't bring myself to eat it although I know it'll be worse if it's cold. It will turn jelly-like and slimy and I'll never be able to stomach it.

It's just as I'm bringing the first spoonful to my mouth, that I hear the sharp rapping on the front door.

Someone's knocking furiously and hard but as quickly as it starts, it stops.

The floorboards creak as Steve stomps towards the front door in large strides. He opens it but there is a missing moment when he should have spoken to the person who was there. Instead he just shuts it again and there's the stamp of each of his footsteps back to the living room.

All goes back to being quiet again.

Then, there's another sharp tap. This time it's different to someone knocking on the door. It pings against glass. Something is hitting my window, a stone, most probably. First there's one. Then two in quick succession.

It's the knock. The one that she would do when she got home so I would know it was her.

I drop my porridge spoon. It's Sylvia; she has come to get me. It has to have been her at the door, and Steve wouldn't let her in.

Quickly I turn to the window and peer down in front of the house. There's no sign of Sylvia, but that must be because she's hiding. My eyes scan over every detail of the front garden and the street. I try to absorb everything. Rule number two: *Pay attention – keep constant observations of your surroundings.*

That's when I spot it.

It's just the corner poking out from beneath the black bin, but even from that I know immediately what it is. The edge of a book I know so well that I can quote whole passages from it by heart, that I could pick it out in the darkness by its scent alone.

I pull on my shoes and come clattering down the stairs so loudly that Steve looks up in astonishment.

'Billy – you're up!' he says, a huge smile lighting up his whole face. But I turn away from him and run to the front door and out to the wheelie bin.

I pull the book from under it. I can't believe she's left *How to Survive* for me. That I have her treasured book in my hands. The cover is a tiny bit crumpled, like it's been stuffed into a bag or something. and it feels ever so slightly damp, but it's definitely Sylvia's book.

'Sylvia?' I call out. 'Sylvia?' I look down the street one way and then the other but there is no one there.

Then Steve is behind me. 'What's going on, Billy? Are you all right?'

I quickly hide the book behind me and tuck it away into the top of my pyjama bottoms. I can feel its pages dig into the small of my back.

'Are you all right?' Steve asks me again.

'I'm fine,' I lie. 'I just wanted some fresh air, all of a sudden.'

'That's great!' Steve beams. 'Why don't we go for a little walk? We could go to the park? Go and get dressed and we'll get going.'

I nod and hope my face isn't giving anything away.

When I get back up to my bedroom, I hide the book under my bed, behind a box, but not before I check it all over, looking for a note or anything at all.

There's nothing in it – no message to me, no hidden letter – but on the first page, in curly handwriting, written a long time ago, there's a name: *Sylvia Weywood*. And on the inside of the back cover, in my handwriting, are the Rules for Survival staring back at me.

I don't see Sylvia that day. She doesn't come back to the house. I look for her as I walk around the park with Steve, pretending that everything is normal, but there is no sign of her.

We loop around the park a couple of times. We stop to look out over the city and Steve points out to me different buildings that we can see in the distance. The tower on a hill. A church spire.

'When will I see Sylvia again?' I blurt out, in a rush.

'Oh, Billy,' Steve says. His face falls into a frown and his eyes look down and won't meet mine. 'I can't say for sure. We'll try to visit her in hospital when she's ready, we will. But, Billy, your mum's not well. She's not been well for a while. All of that – ' he waves his hands around as if there is something in front of him although there isn't – 'all of that . . . survival stuff she'd been doing. It's got really . . . out of hand.' Steve's voice keeps tripping up over the words.

'But she'd want to see me, wouldn't she?' I ask.

'Of course she does. We just need to make sure it's when

she's a bit more . . . steady. Then it will be better for both of you.'

I swallow hard. I try to imagine Sylvia in hospital and find that I can't.

'And are they not letting her do the . . .' I try to remember how Steve put it, 'is she not allowed to do the survival stuff any more at all?'

'Well, it's a . . . symptom. Of her illness. None of it's real, Billy, and it's better that she doesn't do any of that stuff any more.'

I speak in a whisper: 'The skills we learned *were* real.'

But Steve shakes his head furiously. 'No, Billy, it was all in your mum's head. It was the illness making her believe things. Wrong things,' he says. 'But she's getting help now. It'll get better – I promise. And then we'll go and see her.'

I can feel something binding and coiling around my heart. Sylvia's urgency to prepare and teach me how to survive had started to scare me and felt out of control, but could it really be true that none of it was real? That she was wrong about us needing to be prepared? It was everything to Sylvia, and so it had been everything to me.

'But it can't be,' I hear myself say. Sylvia's face flashes through my mind. I can almost feel her steady hazel eyes holding me in her gaze as I'd try to learn whatever skill it was that we were practising. 'Everything she taught me, she said that we were getting ready for something, that it was all so that she could keep me safe.'

Steve doesn't answer, he looks away from me, to the ground, embarrassed.

I feel a surge of anger rise up in me. He doesn't believe me, he doesn't believe Sylvia, just like she said. But what does he know?

'You don't get it,' I spit out. 'You weren't even there. You can't just say all this stuff about Sylvia if you weren't even there.'

'Billy, I—'

But I'm shouting now. I can't stop the anger coursing through me, red, hot and liquid. All of the weariness that had sunk into my bones since the fire, the dead feeling of heaviness of being separated from Sylvia, was gone. 'She said you wouldn't understand, that you didn't want to know. She was right.'

'I . . . I . . .' Steve splutters.

'You haven't seen me for over two years!' I scream. 'You don't know Sylvia. And you don't know me!'

'Calm down, Billy. I know this is a huge amount to take in. And you're right – we haven't seen each other for a long time. Although that was not how I wanted it, believe me. Your mum kept moving you around, she didn't want me to see you.'

'That was only because she knew that you'd act like this. And she was right, she was right to keep me away from you. To keep me safe.'

Steve flinches, as though he's been slapped. Then he takes a deep breath and swallows hard. 'I'm sorry you think that, but the reason you're here, living with me, is because I'm not the only one who believes that your mum needs help. There are professionals, doctors, who understand that your mum needs to recover before she can look after you again. There's nothing either of us can do to change that. When she gets better, I hope we can find a way where we can both take care of you. But I don't want it to go back to me not seeing you like before, I never wanted that. It doesn't have to be just your mum, or just me. But she needs to get better before we can think about any of that. And, I'm sorry, Billy, but I don't believe that she was keeping you safe because well . . . Billy, you had to be thrown out of the window of a burning flat because of a fire she started. That wasn't keeping you safe, was it?'

I don't answer. The anger I was feeling has drained from me and I feel depleted and raw.

I can't argue with the fire. I still dream about the smoke filling the living room, almost engulfing us. Sometimes I'm sure that I can still feel it in my lungs, in my next breath.

But he was wrong. I wouldn't, couldn't, believe that everything Sylvia had taught me was all for nothing.

When I had found the book, part of me knew that I wouldn't find a message from her. The book itself was the message. It said, don't give up, don't stop learning, keep yourself prepared. Don't forget to follow the Rules.

And now, to be prepared I had to make sure I hid the book from Steve. He couldn't ever find it.

I couldn't let him know that I was thinking about any of 'that survival stuff'. He'd think that I was ill too if he thought I believed in it.

And I didn't want to find out what he would do then.

HOW TO GET IN TROUBLE (ON YOUR FIRST DAY OF SCHOOL)

'Hey, you want to see something awesome?'

I don't look up at first. The boy can't possibly be talking to me because I've just been staring at the ground for the whole break time.

I've learned from moving schools so often that the best way to get through it is to keep myself to myself. I keep my head down; stay out of trouble, do as I'm told. But I also mean I will actually keep my head down; I won't look up, I won't meet anyone's gaze. I've spent the last five minutes just studying the many greys of the playground tarmac.

But then he says: 'You'll want to see this, seriously!'

I look around, but there's no one but the two of us. 'What, me?' I ask. When you're the new kid you get used to no one talking to you at break. In class, it can be different because the teacher makes us talk to each other for paired work or table talk but when we're all set loose in the playground it's a different story. I'm used to being ignored and mostly I prefer it that way. Well, at least that's what I tell myself.

'Yeah,' he says and passes me an empty drinks can. 'Just hold this for a second, will you?' He has very dark curly hair and his bottom lip sticks right out. He holds what looks like a piece of plastic piping.

'What's that for?' I ask.

'You'll see,' he says. He rubs the plastic pipe with a cloth he takes from his pocket and then he says, 'Okay, put the can on the ground.'

He moves the pipe towards the can and it immediately starts to roll away. Then he moves the pipe to the other side of the can and this time it rolls back the way it came.

'How are you doing that?' I ask, and he answers me with a grin. He moves the can back and forth – never touching it – controlling it with the pipe this way and that until a gust of wind takes the can clattering off. He bounds off after it and I think that he won't come back but he returns beside me moments later.

'Cool, huh? Want to have a go?' He hands me the pipe and cloth. 'You're Billy, right? I'm Anwar. We're in the same class,' he says as I make the can roll.

I worry for a moment that he's going to ask me about why I had started school so late in the year or where had I moved from – questions I don't want to answer. But he doesn't ask me anything. Instead we just play with the can, shifting it back and forth, until it keeps getting carried off by a breeze.

'It doesn't work when it's too windy,' Anwar says.

'Well – thanks,' I say, a little awkwardly, handing him the

pipe. I walk back towards the wall. But as I do, Anwar walks with me.

'What shall we do now?' he says, although it's not so much a question to me, but to himself. His eyes glance upwards as though he's examining the options in his brain.

'Bob,' he says finally.

'Bob?'

'Have you met Bob yet?'

Bob has twitching whiskers, ink-drop eyes and a tiny wrinkled nose.

He has such soft fur that it tickles me as he walks along the line of my underarm.

Bob is golden brown and has a fleck of pink for a tail.

He is, of course, a hamster, which I didn't know until Anwar ran over to his cage, shouting 'Bob!' and plucked Bob from his food bowl and let him run from one hand to the other.

We've snuck into the Year 3 classroom where Bob lives. He's only supposed to be for the Year 3s, Anwar tells me, and we're not allowed to be in here really, but Anwar has been coming back to visit Bob over the years.

'When I was in this class,' Anwar says, 'I used to make him things to do – like the longest tunnel out of about fifty old toilet rolls – or once I made him a kind of seesaw. And a tightrope – but he didn't really like that. I don't think the Year Threes do anything for him like that, they just want to pet him and cuddle him, but Bob needs some excitement.'

I can't help but smile. Anwar reminds me of how Sylvia used to be. How she'd always be on the lookout for exciting things for us to do. How she'd get carried away showing me how to make something and so time would just disappear. For a moment I imagine that she's there with me, I can almost smell her. I feel a hollow pit in my stomach, and my eyes burn, so I quickly shake off the memories.

'Well . . . should we do something fun for him now?' I suggest.

'Yes, Billy!' Anwar says and I smile. We look around the classroom for inspiration – it's not long until we both settle on the large water tank in the corner of the room.

We make a boat out of an old food container – we looked at quite a few different options from things lying around the classroom before deciding this was the best one: it would take Bob's weight easily and it had high enough sides and so hopefully he wouldn't fall over the edge into the water.

'If he does go over,' Anwar says, 'we'll just fish him out straightaway. A little bit of water won't hurt you, will it, Bob?'

We fill the tank and then set Bob on the water in his little plastic boat.

At first, he doesn't move – I think he's getting used to the motion of the boat as it swings gently from side to side – but then he starts sniffing around the plastic container as it drifts around the tank.

'You're a pirate now, Bob,' Anwar says.

That's the moment we're caught.

'What are you two doing in here?' says a deep-barrelled

voice. 'Outside, now!' the teacher roars.

Anwar and I look at each other, both unsure of what to do. If we step away from the tank to face the teacher then he will be able to see Bob in the boat.

'Outside!' From the way he speaks I can tell the teacher isn't used to people not doing what he tells them to do right away.

He marches over to us and peers over at the tank.

'What on earth . . .'

'Sorry, Mr Belvedere,' Anwar says solemnly. He points towards Bob who, whiskers twitching, explores the hull of his plastic ship, oblivious to it all. 'No animals were harmed in the making of this boat.'

Mr Belvedere has a funny little moustache and at first, it starts to bristle and tremor and then it wobbles violently before he begins really shouting at us.

He tells us that we are a disgrace, he tells us that we don't even know how much trouble we are in, he tells us that he can't believe how stupid we are. Once he starts shouting, it's as though he cannot stop himself. He's a tornado of shouting.

'You're both going to the head immediately,' he says finally. 'I don't expect anything less from you, Anwar, but you . . . you—' For the first time he realizes that he doesn't even know who I am. 'Who are you? What's your name? What class are you in?'

I mumble a reply.

'You're new here, aren't you?' he asks me.

I nod.

'And this is how you choose to spend your first day at this

school? It's not a good start, is it? I'd think very carefully about who your friends are and how you want to spend the rest of this year.'

I look down at my feet.

'Now, follow me this instant. Both of you.'

'But, Mr Belvedere,' Anwar says.

'Silence! I said follow me – nothing else.'

'But shouldn't I put Bob back in his cage?' Anwar asks and looks over to the golden hamster still bobbing in the water tank.

'I'll do it,' the teacher says. 'I think that you've done enough.'

He reaches roughly into the water tank and makes a grab for Bob. Then he shrieks loudly.

'He bit me! He just bit me!'

I really want to laugh, I can feel it tingling inside my belly. All I would need to do is open my mouth and I know that it would come ringing out. I clamp a hand over my lips to stop myself.

'I'll put him back,' Anwar says and Mr Belvedere doesn't speak as Anwar scoops Bob up gently and returns him to his cage.

We follow Mr Belvedere to the head's office but she's in a meeting and so we have to wait outside.

'I'll be back in ten minutes when you'll need to explain yourselves to Mrs Oglivie and we'll decide what to do with the pair of you. Neither of you are to move or speak.'

He stamps off, huffing with every step.

As soon as he's turned the corner, Anwar looks over to me.

'I'm sorry. I didn't mean to get you in trouble on your first day.'

'Don't worry,' I whisper back. 'It was worth it.'

'I think Bob enjoyed it.'

'He definitely did. He really didn't want to leave that boat.'

Anwar snorts with laughter which makes the school secretary glare over at us.

'I wouldn't be laughing if I were you,' she says to us.

But I don't care that we're in trouble, I don't care that everyone's cross with us because there's one thing that I'm suddenly sure of that makes everything seem all right: I have a friend.

HOW TO SHARE

Anwar lives in a flat not far from Steve's house and so we've got into the habit of walking home together each day in the last month. It sometimes takes us much longer than it should because Anwar often spots things that he wants to investigate as we walk along.

Today it's a petrol-coloured beetle in the bush of someone's front garden.

'Look at the size of it!' he exclaims as it scampers over his fingers. It looks like a jewel, in a colour in between green and purple, shiny and iridescent. It opens its wings and flies off with a buzz back on to the open flower of a pink rose with petals that are starting to shed and fall away.

'Have you ever seen a beetle like that?' he asks me.

I shake my head.

'Want to come up?' he asks casually when we get to his block.

'Better not,' I say. 'Steve's still being a bit funny about the Bob thing.' Steve had wanted to have a 'serious chat' when the school contacted him to tell him what had happened on my first day.

'I think you'd better stay clear of this Anwar character,' he'd told me.

'He's not a character,' I said hotly. 'He's . . . he's my friend.'

'You don't need friends that get you into trouble,' Steve said.

But that hadn't stopped us. At school, Anwar and I spent as much time together as we could and we would walk home on the days that Anwar didn't stay behind late for Science Club.

'Oh, he'll get over that,' Anwar replies. 'Parents forget. Or I've found you can usually wear them down over time. You just have to be persistent. Or a pest. One of the two.'

I grin.

'Well, see you Monday, then,' I say.

'Not Monday!' Anwar groans. 'Let's do something over the weekend. Are you doing anything?'

I think of the next two days stretching ahead of me with nothing to fill them. No adventures. No Sylvia. Only Steve and I, not being able to talk to each other. I've been thinking about ways to keep practising things from *How to Survive*, but I don't know how to without Steve finding out. I'm starting to worry that I'm beginning to forget the things that Sylvia had taught me. But I know I must find a way. I've been thinking about Rule number five for some time now: *Never stop trying – you must never give up!*

'No, actually. I don't have any plans,' I say.

'Well, let's meet up. I've got some experiments I want to try out that need two pairs of hands. Or at least someone else to witness them. Tell Steve it's educational or something. Parents love that.'

'Okay,' I say with a smile. 'You're on.' And then I have a thought.

'Spit it out!' Anwar says, seeing the look on my face.

'What?' I ask.

'Whatever it is that you're thinking of saying . . . I know you, Billy Weywood, you've had a thought.'

'Well . . . it's just silly. I just wondered if maybe, as well as doing your experiments, whether we could do some other kind of experiments too . . . Like survival skill things? Making fire, shelters . . . things like that . . .' I tail off. What if Anwar thinks I'm mad, just like Steve thinks Sylvia is?

But Anwar's eyes widen. 'Do you know how to do things like that?'

'A bit,' I say. 'Sylvi— I mean, my mum taught me a lot.'

'Amazing. Yes! Teach me.'

Relief rushes through me. I should have known Anwar would understand. He's nothing like Steve or the other grown-ups judging Sylvia.

'She knew so much,' I tell him. 'She had this book. It's this old kind of book really – she found it in a second-hand book-shop when she was about our age and it's got loads of great techniques for how to do things. Sylvia said it's the best survival guide out there. I've got it now, she left it with me. We can use that to learn how to do stuff.'

Anwar nods so enthusiastically it looks like his head might fall off his body.

'Bring it along, I can't wait to see it. I just wanted to make parachutes but your book sounds more interesting.'

'It's my mum's book really. I'm just borrowing it.'

I pause for a moment but before I think any more, I hear the words flowing from me. Suddenly I want to tell Anwar everything. Maybe because he never asks me questions about Sylvia or my life before I came here, it makes it easier to talk to him about her.

'I used to live with my mum before I moved here. But there was an accident and so we got separated. That's why I live with Steve and started at school so late in the year. I haven't seen her for about a month now and . . . and . . . I don't know when I'm going to see her again. But she managed to get the book to me. She found out where Steve was living and threw stones at my window and so I knew it was her. And then I found *How to Survive* left under the bin for me.'

It feels good to be able to tell someone. It's as if it makes it real and not just a story that I have made up and am telling myself over and over.

'Did you get to see her when she left the book?'

'No – she was hiding. She had to keep hidden from Steve because he won't let her see me. Not yet anyway – because of the . . . the accident. But it had to be her.'

Anwar nods. I know that he believes me.

'Well, definitely bring your mum's book this weekend,' he says.

As I walk the final bit of the way back to Steve's house, I realize that I feel lighter than I have in a long time. I don't just have a friend, I have a best friend.

HOW (NOT) TO MEET YOUR DAD'S GIRLFRIEND

'Billy! Billy? Are you ready? They'll be here soon!' Steve yells up the stairs.

Even though the walls of our house are so thin that he has no need to yell, he shouts. He can't seem to do anything quietly.

Steve will crash through a room.

His footsteps fall heavily on the stairs.

His breath whistles.

He can't stop himself from sighing loudly in *humphs* and gasps.

I can hear him right now, humming along to the radio downstairs; he thinks he is doing it to himself but I can hear every off-key note.

Sylvia could move around a room without a sound.

I think of her as a cat – a silent prowler, padded paws in place of feet. Often she'd surprise me by appearing behind me as if out of nowhere. She'd ruffle my hair and I'd startle, thinking I was alone.

But now that we're not together, when it's all quiet and still,

I'll feel my neck straining round to look for her. Waiting for her to appear. But now the shock comes because she's not there, because she won't surprise me.

'They'll be here soon,' Steve bellows again.

My bedroom door quivers.

'Billy? Did you hear me?'

I can hear Steve, of course, but I stay where I am.

Steve first mentioned to me that he had a girlfriend last night. It came as a surprise because although I'd been living with him for a couple of months now, Steve hadn't mentioned her at all and had never been to see her that I'd known of. I'd been about to go to bed. I thought he was just going to say goodnight but instead he blurted out: 'There's a couple of people I'd really like you to meet tomorrow' and held my gaze with large, worried eyes.

When I didn't say anything, he muttered, 'my girlfriend' and then looked away to the floor.

'You have a girlfriend?'

'Julie,' Steve said. 'She's very nice. She can't wait to meet you. I didn't want to spring this all on you, too soon – after . . . everything.'

'I said that I'd meet Anwar . . .'

'You see him every day at school.' Steve pursed his lips and then blurted out: 'I want you here to meet them. You're not spending the whole weekend with Anwar.'

'But—' I'd tried to protest.

'That's final, Billy,' Steve said.

'Who's the other person?' I suddenly thought to ask.

'She has a daughter, your age. Angharad.'

'Oh,' I'd said because there didn't seem to be anything else to say.

'Billy? Are you okay?'

'Yes,' I'd answered, but I spent the whole night thinking about it.

I can't really describe how I feel about it now other than I know that I don't really want them to come round. I don't want to get to know them and have to talk to them and pretend that everything is normal.

So instead I lie across my bed at an angle, my arms and head hanging off one side of it.

From where I am, I can see out of the window, its glass flecked with diagonal dashes of rain. It feels like it's *always* raining here. There are rows and rows of little houses all squashed up, going up the hill. They lean into each other as though they are holding one another up, huddling together for protection against the weather.

A man is walking, trudging, up the hill. His face is grey with effort; it's so without colour that it almost looks like he could be wearing a Halloween mask. One that's made of rubber, making his cheeks sag and look like half-deflated balloons.

The wind and the rain surge all around him like a whip that flails and lashes and could land just about anywhere; just one nudge here, and another there and it could throw him off balance. The weather feels on edge, as though the rain and the wind could tip over at any moment into a full-blown storm.

I reach down to turn another page of *How to Survive*, that's lying open on the floor in front of me. Reading the book seems to calm me somehow, it makes me feel closer to Sylvia.

'*Billy?* What are you doing up there?'

Steve again.

I turn another page of the book and stare hard at the words but they blur in front of me, turning into just shapes and shadows. I'm not really reading any more.

There's a little voice inside of me that's asking quietly whether maybe I should go downstairs. Try and be 'normal'. Make Steve happy.

I hear Steve stomp across the kitchen and open the oven door. Then there's the shuffle and a clang that means he's checking on what's cooking in there. *Slam!* The oven door closes.

I turn back to the yellowed pages of *How to Survive* and read:

Modern living may be convenient, but it does not help us to prepare for a variety of survival situations.

But then Steve is thundering up the stairs.

Thud, thud. Thud, thud. Thud, thud. Thud, thud.

I imagine each stair bending a little under his weight.

I flip the book shut, slide it under my bed in a single movement and then he's there, knocking on my door. Saying my name again and again, like it's a question.

'Billy? Billy?'

'Come in.'

'Hey,' he says, peeping around the door. 'What are you doing up here?' He looks at me, his head held to one side, his eyes large and trusting. Sometimes I think that Steve looks like the Labrador that belongs to the woman down the road: eager, expectant, and a little bit worried all at the same time.

I try to think of an answer that won't sound like I'm lying but before I do, he carries on talking.

'They'll be here any minute now. Lunch is almost ready. Why don't you wait downstairs? They'll be here soon.' He's speaking fast. Little droplets of spit fly from his mouth. He runs a hand through his hair and seems almost surprised to find that there's not more of it.

Then the doorbell rings sharply and Steve's eyes widen in panic.

'Do I look okay?' he asks. 'Maybe I should change my shirt? Maybe you should change your shirt? Do you have any that are more . . . more clean?' He glances over at the teetering pile of washing in the corner.

He asks me something while he turns his head to look down towards the front door and so I don't hear him.

'What?'

'I asked if you were ready.'

I don't answer him.

I'll never feel ready.

'Billy likes reading. Don't you, Bill?'

Steve does not usually call me Bill.

We are sitting at the table in front of our empty plates, the remnants of lunch smeared across them, with Julie and her daughter Angharad.

Angharad has long caramel-coloured braids with neon-coloured beads at the ends that cascade down her back. They jangle each time she turns her head.

She looks at me with a scowl that she makes no effort to hide, as though I am something disgusting she has stepped on. When Steve introduced us, she just said to her mum in a loud voice, 'When can we go home?'

Julie laughed, embarrassed and pink. 'Angharad!' she hissed, but didn't really tell her off.

We never usually sit at the table, Steve and I, and there aren't enough chairs for all of us: I'm perched on a stool from the sitting room and Steve's on the office chair from his study.

'Angharad's always got her nose in a book, haven't you, love?' Julie looks over at her daughter encouragingly, her eyebrows raised.

'Muu-uum,' Angharad complains. She makes the word sound like it has two syllables and shakes her head so the beads rattle and clink.

Julie ignores her: 'What was it you were reading last week that you liked so much? Why don't you tell Billy about it?'

'Don't go on about it, Mum,' Angharad says with an exaggerated sigh, raising her eyes up to the ceiling and scowling. 'It's no big deal.'

But Steve has already pounced upon it. 'Yes! Billy's got quite the collection now. Maybe he's read it already. What was the name of that book, Bill, the one you couldn't put down?'

I don't answer but stare hard at my fork on my plate. The sauce from the baked beans has started to congeal around it.

It's been like this all lunch: Steve and Julie batting questions at us across the table that we bounce away unanswered.

It doesn't seem to matter what Angharad or I say (or in my case, don't say) because the conversation continues without us. 'It's practically a *library* up there,' Steve goes on. 'Billy has a knack for finding books. He's always bringing them home. He found a big box that was dumped on the street the other day.'

I let myself glance at Steve; I can't quite tell if he likes this fact about me or not, whether he thinks it's a gift or a curse. There's a suggestion of a frown on his forehead even though he sounds enthusiastic.

Ever since I found Sylvia's old book, I see them everywhere: tucked under bushes on top of a wall, discarded in piles with the rubbish, even crammed down the side of a bus seat. I can't walk past them without having a rummage and picking up at least one to take home.

Julie is smiling over at me; she pushes the sleeves of her jumper up over her elbows and leans towards me over the table. 'What was the last book you found that you really liked, Billy?' she asks.

The yellow-paged *How to Survive* book flashes into my mind but I don't want to share that with them. I end up mumbling: 'I can't really remember the title.'

'Tell me about it!' Julie says and she laughs with her head

tipped back, mouth wide-open. I can see bits of the spinach we had at lunch sitting darkly in her teeth. 'I can't remember half of the things that I've read either. Sometimes I start something new and don't realize until I'm halfway through that I've read it already!'

Steve begins to laugh too and then they lock eyes and it's as though they can read each other's minds for just a moment, because at exactly the same time they say:

'Billy, why don't you take Angharad upstairs and show her your books?' (Steve)

'I'm sure Angharad would like to see your books, Billy.' (Julie)

Their words blend into each other's as though they are one voice.

Suddenly it's clear: why Steve mentioned I liked reading, why they've been talking in circles. It was just so that they could get rid of us and make me and Angharad go upstairs. He and Julie probably planned this before they came over.

'You'd like to see them, wouldn't you, love?' Julie says.

They are both speaking in the same tone: it sounds pleasant, but it has an edge of something hard to it. Somehow I know they won't take no for an answer.

Angharad looks at her mum through narrowed eyes but then stands up so suddenly the table rattles.

'Come on then, Billy,' she says. 'Let's get this over and done with.'

She stomps up the stairs – she's almost as loud as Steve – and all I can do is follow.

HOW (NOT) TO SPEND TIME WITH YOUR DAD'S GIRLFRIEND'S DAUGHTER

Angharad goes straight over to my books and pulls one off the shelf before I've even made it to the top of the stairs.

'I like that one,' I say, but perhaps I spoke too quietly because she's already stuffing it back into the gap in the shelf and pulling out another.

I have the familiar feeling of being far away from the person in front of me, of not saying the right thing, of not saying it in the right way.

I'm not sure what to do; to go next to her or just to leave the room entirely. I settle for sitting on the edge of the bed and looking out of the window.

Outside, a child screams out as their scarf is carried off down the street by a gust of wind. It's a waving flapping rainbow of wool and everyone lunges to catch it.

Then I see the man I saw earlier when we were waiting for Julie and Angharad to arrive. The one who was climbing the hill, whose every step was a stagger and who looked grey with effort.

Suddenly, in a flick of a moment, the man falls. He drops to the pavement as though he is not a person at all, but a sack, or a stone, or a ball that rolls down the hill a little.

There's a still moment before anyone does anything. I can see everyone's faces panicked and white as they watch the man fall, not knowing what to do, then there's a bustle as people rush towards him. A car driving past stops suddenly and its driver gets out, shouting instructions.

I see people pull out their phones – they're calling for an ambulance, I think – and the driver of the car, a man wearing the sort of blue raincoat that people wear when they are walking in the mountains, rushes over to the man. I can't see him now, the person who fell, he is so surrounded by others.

I look back over to Angharad. She hasn't even noticed that anything has happened outside, she's still looking at my shelves and has pulled a thin grey hardback out. It's one of my favourites, titled *Ounce Dice Trice*. Its cover has almost come away completely and there are tea stains on every page but it lists funny words with black-and-white illustrations that always make me laugh. I found it abandoned in a pile outside someone's house, left out as rubbish.

'That one's *really* good,' I say.

Angharad glances up at me and the beads in her hair jingle from the movement. Without taking her eyes off me she opens it up to one of the centre pages. The way she moves makes me think it's a threat. She reads. Then turns another page, and another.

'It is good,' she concedes. 'I like the illustrations.'

Carefully, she replaces *Ounce Dice Trice* on the shelf.

I turn away to the window again. More people have stopped around the person who fell. I can see them explaining what has happened to others. Their mouths open wide as they recount the drama. They look like fish gulping for air.

'What are you staring at?' Angharad says and she flings herself on the bed next to me, so she can look out of the window, too.

'Someone fell outside. Look, an ambulance is coming now.'

'Are they all right?' Angharad asks.

'I'm not sure. One minute this man was walking and the next he just fell over and rolled down the pavement. It was like he'd suddenly gone rigid or something.'

'Maybe he is epileptic?' Angharad thinks aloud. 'Or had a heart attack.'

We both stare out of the window but when after a while the ambulance is still there and we can't see anything more, Angharad sits back and looks around my bedroom.

I try to imagine what it might look like to her. I still don't have much stuff. Nothing on the walls, although Steve said I could put up anything I liked. It's not even that messy; it almost looks like no one really lives in here. In the end her eyes settle on my bulging bookshelves.

'You *do* have a lot of books,' she says and she smiles over at me. 'Even more than me. They're everywhere!' she exclaims.

I see her point to the floor beside her foot. There, just

peeping out, is the corner of *How to Survive*, where I shoved it earlier on.

As though in slow motion, I watch her lean forward. She reaches towards it, the tips of her fingers just millimetres away from it, about to touch the dull sheen of its cover . . .

'Get out!' I shout. 'GET OUT!'

I am louder than loud.

I am louder than Steve.

I am louder than Mr Belvedere from school.

I am louder than I can believe that I can be.

'Get out! Get out of my room!'

Angharad jumps. She is unbelieving, but I keep on roaring, as I let my mouth spill out a rage that until that very moment I did not know I had inside me. It's everything I've been feeling, all screwed up together into a tight ball; it's that I don't know how Sylvia is, it's that Steve left us, it's that I don't know what's true any more, it's that I have to hide all the survival stuff, it's that I don't know how I feel about my family. All the confusion and worry and anger that I have been carrying is finally coming out.

'Get out!' I scream again.

Angharad stands up, tall, filling the room.

'Don't you shout at me!' she screams. 'Who do you think you are?'

I hear Steve's voice from downstairs, streaked through with concern. 'What's going on up there?'

Angharad looks at me, her nostrils flaring and wide as though she is a dragon who has just breathed a fireball. Then she turns away and clatters down the stairs with such heavy footsteps it sounds like she is falling down them.

Then I hear Julie's voice, comforting and murmuring, and then Angharad again, as clear as though she is beside me: 'He just started to shout at me to get out of his room, for no reason. Can we go now, Mum? Can we just leave?'

I know that in a moment Steve will be in my room. He will be upset. He will be bewildered. But he will also be angry.

I quickly take the book from under my bed and tuck it out of sight, into the waistband of my trousers, behind my back.

I can't let Steve find it.

I can't let him see it.

HOW TO ESCAPE

The hailstones distract them.

They begin lightly.

It's just as Steve is shouting at me to 'get down here this minute' while Angharad is continuing to steam that she never wanted to come here anyway and Julie is talking softly to her in low, soothing tones.

Thunder drowns them all out. The sky sounds like it's being ripped in two; a deep barrelling growl that lasts far longer than it should. Then I hear the soft patter as hailstones begin to hit the ground.

'Where's this come from?' Steve says and then he answers himself: 'It's come from nowhere.'

'They're hailstones,' says Julie.

'They're huge,' I hear Angharad exclaim. 'They're bigger than . . . than peas!'

I walk quietly down the stairs and see that they have all turned towards the window, almost entranced, to watch the hailstones fall.

Angharad's fists are still clenched into balls. She was shouting only seconds ago but for now her mind is elsewhere, on the ice-white peas thrown down from the sky.

The patter has turned drumlike now. The hailstones hit the ground with a crack. They grow bigger and bigger and louder and louder. We are surrounded by them, hemmed in; the room feels suddenly smaller and darker than it was before.

'Sounds like they're going to break the roof down,' Angharad says.

'It'll all be over soon,' Julie says.

But I see her hand reach down to Steve's and they clasp each other's fingers fiercely. The drumming grows louder, the hailstones beat at the window as if they want to get in. Their grip only lessens as the hailstones begin to fall a little more lightly.

This is my chance. While everyone's gaze is fixed out of the window, I turn away from them all. I run out of the door and into the storm.

The hailstones sting as they hit me. I feel the chill of them as they bury into my hair, burrow down my neckline, but I don't stop running. I don't stop until I get to Anwar's. I am breathless and cold though and so I can't speak properly through the intercom when I dial the number of his flat.

I can hear Anwar in the background say, 'It's Billy, it's for me, it's Billy,' although I don't know how he can recognize me from my mumbling.

The door buzzes. I open it and run through. It slams behind me.

Finally I feel I can take a breath.

'Hey man,' Anwar says. 'Perfect timing.' He shakes a tube of Mentos at me, in explanation.

I don't reply.

'Are you okay?' he asks, his head cocked slightly to one side.

'Yeah,' I say and then a moment later, I feel like I actually want to tell him the truth. I can feel the edges of *How to Survive* rubbing into my back. It doesn't hurt as such, in fact I feel comforted that I'm keeping it close. I think again of how Steve might react if he found out that I have it and I make myself stand a little straighter. It digs into my back a little more. 'Not really. But we can talk about it later. What are you doing?'

'Come in, come in. Let me explain it all.'

Anwar's mother and two sisters are perched on a sofa by the window in their living room. They wave hello to me and mumble a greeting as we pass them, but they stay by the window, watching the end of the storm. The ground is covered with white now – almost like there's been a snowfall.

'This way,' Anwar says.

I follow him into the bathroom where he's placed a large bottle of Diet Coke in the bath.

'Apparently, these,' he says, pointing at the Mentos, 'will make a kind of fountain when you put them in Diet Coke.'

'Really?' I look from the Mentos to the Diet Coke bottle

again, then to Anwar, and the memory of Angharad's shaken, shocked face dims just a little.

'Dad'll be back soon,' Anwar tells me. 'We'd better do it before then. He's said I'm not allowed to do experiments inside any more.'

I unscrew the cap and Anwar gets out a handful of Mentos.

'Apparently you're meant to put them all in at the same time,' Anwar says, 'so we'll use this.' He places a funnel on top of the bottle. 'Do you want to do it?'

'You do it,' I say.

'Okay, get ready to run, just in case.'

He drops the Mentos down the funnel.

Almost immediately the Coke explodes up out of the bottle in a spurting light-brown foamy fountain. It sails high into the air, hitting the ceiling of the bathroom and spraying us completely before we're able to escape.

As we sprint out of the room we collide into Anwar's dad.

'What's going on?' he asks crossly. 'What are you doing in there?' I'm a little afraid of Anwar's dad. He's as stern as Anwar is fun. He drove Anwar and me out to the countryside one weekend when Anwar wanted to test boats he'd made out of different materials in a stream. But he spent almost the whole time telling Anwar that he needed to stop this nonsense, so it wasn't really that enjoyable.

'Nothing, Dad,' Anwar says quickly. 'Nothing, nothing.'

But it doesn't stop his dad from opening the bathroom door. Everything drips with Diet Coke.

It is undoubtedly one of Anwar's more successful experiments.

'Let's go to the park,' Anwar says as we get downstairs. It hadn't taken too long to clear up the bathroom but Anwar's dad had not stopped glaring at us and so we decided to go out.

'But the hailstones,' I protest, but as we walk outside the sun is out and shining and has already melted most of them away. It roasts the pavement and so a hazy steam rises from it. The sky's a sunny blue and it's as if the hailstorm never happened.

I can't help but feel unsettled by the weather changing so rapidly. Sylvia always looked to the skies for markers. Her moods would be especially charged if there were any sudden changes in the weather.

By the time we get to the park, it's already full of families basking in the sunshine. We find a quiet spot a little away from everyone else, where we can see the city in the distance.

Bristol looks so different to London, the only place I have lived before. It's nowhere near the same size for starters: the buildings aren't as tall and there aren't as many people living here either. Though I thought I would never get used to it, there are some things, like meeting Anwar, that make living here not so bad.

'So what's going on?' Anwar asks me. 'Why were you being weird when you first came round?'

'Just – Steve . . .' I'm not sure where to begin. 'He told me yesterday that he had a girlfriend and today she came round with her daughter, Angharad. And I sort of ended up shouting at her.'

'Steve's girlfriend?'

'No. Angharad. Steve and Julie – that's his girlfriend – made us hang out and then Angharad picked up my mum's old book. I sort of overreacted because I'm trying to keep it hidden. I told her to get out.' I correct myself. 'Well, I *shouted* at her to get out.'

Anwar just nods his head gently and I know he understands why I behaved like I did.

'What's she like?'

'Kind of . . . fierce. She got really cross with me when I yelled at her. I don't think we're going to be friends anytime soon.'

'It'll be okay, you know. You could just say that you're sorry and you're, you know, missing your mum . . .' he says quietly.

I hear myself sigh or take a breath or something in between the two. I feel like a fire that's been doused, like I'm just the ashes, crumbling to nothing. Thinking about Sylvia makes me feel like I'm slowly falling apart, spilling away. I pull the book out from my waistband and press the cover down a bit from where it got crumpled when I had to hide it. I open the cover and trace my fingers over Sylvia's loopy handwriting where she wrote her name.

'So this is it?' Anwar asks.

'Yes.' I pause for just a tiny moment but then I pass it over for him to look at. Anwar handles it carefully as though he understands without me having to say a word how precious it is to me.

‘“It might be difficult to overcome certain hazards,”’ he reads aloud from the back cover, ‘“but if you have read this book then your chances are much greater.”’

‘Teach me something,’ he says. ‘From the book.’

‘Here?’ I’ve been hiding my survival skills training for so long, I can’t shake the feeling that I need to keep it secret.

Anwar nods. ‘Why not?’

I look around me. ‘We need something shiny and reflective – like a mirror. A pen or a pencil and a bit of string.’

Anwar digs around in his yellow backpack and pulls out a half-eaten pack of Fruit Pastilles, a leaking pen, a shrivelled conker, an empty box of matches and lastly a small compact of face powder which he hands to me.

‘Why have you got this?’

‘I was using the powder to look at fingerprints,’ Anwar says as if that makes perfect sense.

‘Okay, well this will work.’ I open the compact to inspect the mirror inside.

‘We could use a shoelace for the string,’ I say, remembering the time that Sylvia used my lace for the firebow. I turn to the page which shows you how to use it with the heliograph.

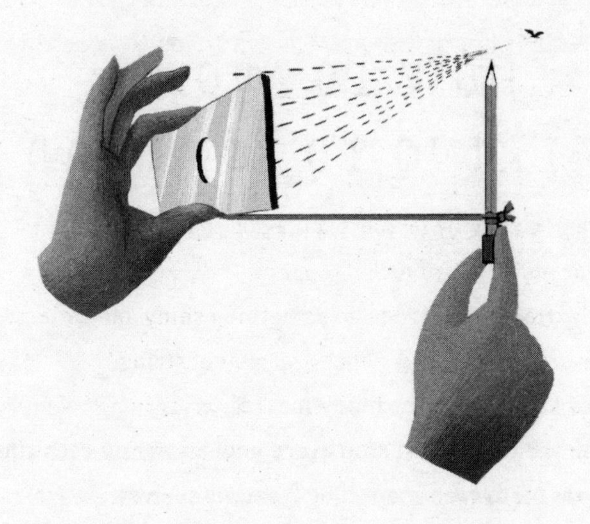

Fig. 7. – How to use a heliograph (Part II)

I had forgotten how much fun practising could be, but Anwar and I spend ages trying out the pencil-and-string technique until we've got it perfected. It's not the same as being with Sylvia, but it's something.

When at last we part and I walk slowly back home, I see his mirror flashing at me from all the way across the park.

I can't help but smile as I see it. Somehow it makes going home and facing Steve seem a little easier.

HOW TO AVOID TALKING TO YOUR DAD

(WHEN YOU KNOW HE WANTS TO TELL YOU OFF)

Steve and I trail down the ready-meal aisle.

I push the trolley and stop every now and again each time Steve leaps off to grab something from the shelves.

He wants to talk about yesterday. I know that from the way he keeps looking at me, like he wants to say something but is stopping himself. We haven't spoken about me shouting at Angharad at all. When I got back from the park, Julie and Angharad had gone and Steve told me that I'd better go up to my room and think it all over.

We'd eaten dinner in near silence and when we finished, without Steve having to tell me, I went back upstairs. I'd sat in my steadily darkening room, staring out of the window.

There weren't many people about, just a couple strolling hand in hand and someone walking their dog. Then, behind the dog walker, a few spaces away, I spotted a figure I recognized. It was because of the stagger. The same as before, throwing their whole body into each step. It was the man who'd fallen and was taken away in the ambulance. Only I realized then, that I hadn't actually seen him being driven away, I'd just seen the ambulance arrive and that was when Angharad had spotted my mum's book.

I stood up by the window to look closer and the more I studied him, the surer I was it was the same person. His face, though shaded beneath a cap, had the same greyish tinge.

He was just about to catch up with the dog walker when the dog, a white and brown terrier, darted round to face him. Even from my window and in the fading light, I could see the dog baring its teeth and then I heard it start yapping and barking so forcefully it was almost impossible to believe that the sound was coming from such a small dog.

The owner started to pull the dog away and shouted at him to be quiet, but nothing would stop it; its eyes remained fixed upon the grey man and it continued to bark as loudly as ever. The dog had to be dragged away. Its short legs danced backwards as its yelps continued to pierce the quiet of the evening even after they had turned the corner.

Just then I heard Steve climbing the stairs with heavy thuds and, thinking that he was coming to speak to me about the day, I quickly flung myself under my duvet and pretended to be asleep. It was too early to go to bed really, but I'd learned that Steve never wakes me when I'm sleeping. Sure enough, he opened my bedroom door with a creak and for a few moments, I could hear him breathing at the doorway. Then he walked across to the window, drew the curtains closed and walked out. When I heard his steps going down the stairs, I sat upright and looked out of the window again. But there was no trace of the man; he was nowhere to be seen.

I couldn't stop thinking about him this morning. I wondered what had happened and if he was okay after falling so badly and why he was not in hospital. There was no one to talk to about it though because it was just Steve and me. And if we started talking, he would want to speak about what went wrong with Julie and Angharad, so I kept quiet.

He's wanted to say something to me since breakfast but I've just managed to duck away each time. Now we are in the supermarket and he looks like he might burst if he doesn't say something soon. His fingers drum and fidget on the side of the trolley and he keeps looking over at me. But eventually he just says: 'Do you want burgers for dinner?'

'Yes please,' I reply.

We are being very polite with each other; it makes everything we say sound stiff and hollow.

Steve looks at the burgers on the shelf. There's a two-pack but there's also a family pack that has four burgers in it. He hesitates for a moment and then reaches for the two-pack.

'Billy,' he says as he places the burgers into the trolley. I can tell from the tone of his voice that the moment has come – he is finally going to tell me off and ask what I was thinking: what happened, why did I shout at Angharad like that? I can already hear the words before he has spoken them. Worry twists and writhes inside me.

'We need to talk about what—'

'I'll get the burger buns!' I say quickly, cutting him off and running away down the aisle.

I tuck away around the maze of the supermarket. There's a crowd of people by the newspaper stand and I have to go around them because they're blocking my path. I turn down another aisle and then another. I look behind me: although I know that Steve is not following me, I want to make sure. I want to be alone.

For a few moments, hiding among the long loaves of French sticks and boxes of plasticky-looking cakes, I have to remind myself to breathe slowly: *In and out, in and out.*

My chest feels tight, like someone is squeezing my heart. I've had the feeling before and the only thing I can do is breathe and wait for it to pass.

I had the feeling when I was parted from Sylvia.

I had the feeling when Steve told me that all the 'survival stuff' was in her head.

I know I have to think of another reason why I would have shouted at Angharad, so I can keep Sylvia's book secret and safe, but I just don't know what it is yet. All I know is that I can't let Steve know the truth.

When I feel the tightness begin to uncoil, I start to make my way back to Steve. I still haven't worked out what I will say but then I remember what Anwar said to say – I will say I'm sorry and that I'm missing Sylvia. Neither of those things is untrue.

I squeeze past the people by the newspapers again. There's an old woman who sees me coming and steps to the side, gesturing to the papers. 'What's the world coming to, eh?'

I glance over at the papers and I see him straightaway.

Amongst the screaming headlines about presidents and extreme weather, there's a blurry photo on one of the local newspapers.

It's the man I saw fall. Only this time, he's running away.

There isn't much to the piece because no one knew that many details and it also seemed like no one could really believe it actually happened. The article's headed:

Back from the Dead
Search for local man continues

Some parts of the story I know because I'd seen it happen – the man falling in the street and the ambulance coming – but there are other bits that I don't know. Like the fact the man was dead when the ambulance arrived, even though no one knew what had caused it.

An eyewitness they spoke to backed up just what I saw: 'One minute he was walking down the street, he was sort of shuffling along, but the next he just fell over in a heap.'

It didn't make sense that this was headline news, until I read on:

Paramedics who were called to the scene reported that they pronounced the man dead on arrival, but just moments later the man jumped back up and fled the scene.

'He sprang back to life,' an onlooker confirmed. 'Someone tried to follow him but he was too fast, too strong, to be stopped.'

Police and medical services are asking for anyone with any information on the man in question to come forward, so they can check on his wellbeing.

Alongside the article was a picture that someone must have taken on their phone camera as the man ran off. But it wasn't very clear and he just looked like a greyish blur.

I take a copy of the paper as I go back over to Steve who is looking around a little impatiently by the tills.

He looks at me and the paper in my hand quizzically.

'Where's the burger buns?' he asks.

'Sorry – I got distracted. I'll go get them now.'

'Hang on a sec, Billy. I've been thinking about yesterday . . . I don't know why you shouted at Angharad. Frankly, I'm not interested in why, because it wasn't okay for you to treat her like that whatever the reason. You need to say sorry to her. I've asked Julie if they will come round for dinner tonight and so you can apologize to her face to face. Okay?'

I look in the trolley and see that Steve has replaced the packet with two burgers for one with four.

Though I do want to say sorry to Angharad and I'm glad

that Steve's not trying to make me tell him why I yelled, I also feel small and hot when I hear they are coming over again. But I manage to nod and I go back towards the bakery aisle.

'Get enough for four of us!' Steve calls out from behind me.

HOW TO SAY SORRY

As Julie and Angharad arrive, Steve's emptying frozen chips on to an oven tray. They clatter as they fall, glinting cuboids that don't even look like food.

'You answer the door, Billy,' he tells me. 'Go on.'

When Angharad sees me she glowers but Julie greets me with a smile as though nothing has happened.

'Hello, Billy,' she says brightly. 'Us again!'

'Oh . . . yes,' I stutter and step back to let them in. 'Steve's in the kitchen cooking dinner.'

'I'll go through, shall I?' Julie says. 'Give you two a chance to talk.' She urges Angharad and me towards the living room as she heads to the kitchen. Angharad starts to pace around the living room, like she's looking for a way to escape.

I take a deep breath.

'Sorry I shouted at you,' I say quickly, all in a rush.

Angharad ignores me and moves the empty packet of crisps on the seat of the sofa to the coffee table and then slouches down on to the sofa.

'I . . . umm . . .' I know I can't really explain why I acted the way I did. She might tell her mum who might tell Steve. And so I just say I'm sorry again without looking her in the eyes.

'It's easy to say sorry,' she mutters.

'Well, I mean it,' I say.

She doesn't reply but I see her looking at something just past me on the ground. It's the newspapers that Steve had shoved in a pile to be recycled when he was clearing up. Somehow he must have mixed up the old and new ones because the local paper I bought in the supermarket today is on the top – the headline about the grey man shouts out from its front page.

I pick up the paper and hold it up, trying to change the subject. 'Remember that man from yesterday? The one who fell over and the ambulance came for? This is about him. It says that the paramedics thought he was dead but then he jumped up again and ran away.'

'What?' Angharad says. Despite yesterday, despite her not wanting to be here, she can't hide her interest. 'Really?' She points to the greying blurry face in the photo.

I nod.

'He came back to life?'

'Apparently. And no one can find him. They don't know where or who he is, but the thing is that I'm sure I saw him again last night. Walking up the hill.'

'Are you sure it was him?'

'I think so – he doesn't look like most people and he walks in this weird way.'

Angharad looks up at me and for a moment I can see that she's confused. One minute, we're not talking and she thinks she might hate me and the next, we're just having a normal conversation like we're friends or something. 'Don't shout at me again, okay?' she says in the end.

'I won't,' I say.

'I mean it,' she says. I think if she were able to growl then she would.

'I promise,' I say.

'Well, let's just see how much you mean your promises. Because if you shout at me again, I just won't speak to you again. Simple as that. So whatever is going on with you and your mum and dad or whatever, remember if you treat me like that again, I just won't speak to you. And I keep my word. Okay?'

'Okay,' I say.

'Okay,' she says. She looks vaguely amused that I'm agreeing with her. 'I mean it. No second chances.'

'No second chances,' I repeat.

'All right then. As long as we're in agreement.'

We nod at each other.

'Why did you?' she asks me.

'Why did I shout?'

She nods.

'Because . . . because . . .' I pause, not sure if I can trust her. 'Well because you were about to pick something up that I'm trying to hide from Steve and I wanted to stop you.'

She rolls her eyes. 'Oh. Well, you could have just said that.

I've got lots of stuff that I keep hidden from my mum.'

'Yes – that might have been a better idea,' I say.

'Billy,' she says, looking at me like I'm possibly the most stupid person she's ever met, 'that *definitely* would have been a better idea.'

Dinner's not quite as bad as lunch was yesterday. Julie and Steve still do most of the talking but after we've eaten, I start to clear away the plates and Angharad offers to help me. Julie raises her eyebrows at Steve but doesn't comment on it. They say that they are going to look in the garden because Julie's going to help us plant some things.

Angharad scrapes the food we didn't eat into the compost bin and I load the dishwasher.

'I've been thinking about that fallen man,' she says as she closes the lid of the bin with a thump. 'If you saw him again last night, he can't have gone very far away, can he? He's probably still close by. You should tell the police that you saw him or . . . or . . .'

'Or what?'

'Or we could try and find him,' she suggests. She tucks a braid behind her ear and I see curiosity in her eyes, like a small flame. 'The police probably won't believe you – or they'll have more important things to do. But the man must be close by, right?'

'I don't know. And, even if he is, if no one else can find him, why would we?'

'Well, you know what he looks like for one thing. And you've seen him more than once. You've got insider knowledge. Both times were out of your bedroom window, right?'

'Yes, always on the same bit of the hill.'

'Well, we could keep watch. He might come back again and this time we could follow him.'

'Follow him?' I'm surprised at how much she's clearly thought about this over dinner.

'Yes,' Angharad says. She pulls at a braid that's threaded through with purple and loops it round and round her finger until it becomes coiled, like a length of rope. 'If we can see where he goes, we can call the police or ambulance or something when we know where he lives. Don't you want to know what happened to him? How he supposedly came back to life?'

'Well, yes – I guess—'

'We could work it out!'

'But what if . . . I don't know . . . he's dangerous or something?'

'It'll be fine,' Angharad says, swiping her hand to the side, dismissing any dangers that lay before us. 'We won't get too close. We'll just see where he goes if you spot him again.'

'All right,' I agree. I get the feeling that whatever I say, Angharad is not going to let it go. '*If* I spot him again.'

HOW TO MAKE A SNARE

I'm teaching Anwar to make a snare trap. We can only do it on a mini scale in the playground but it's sort of working.

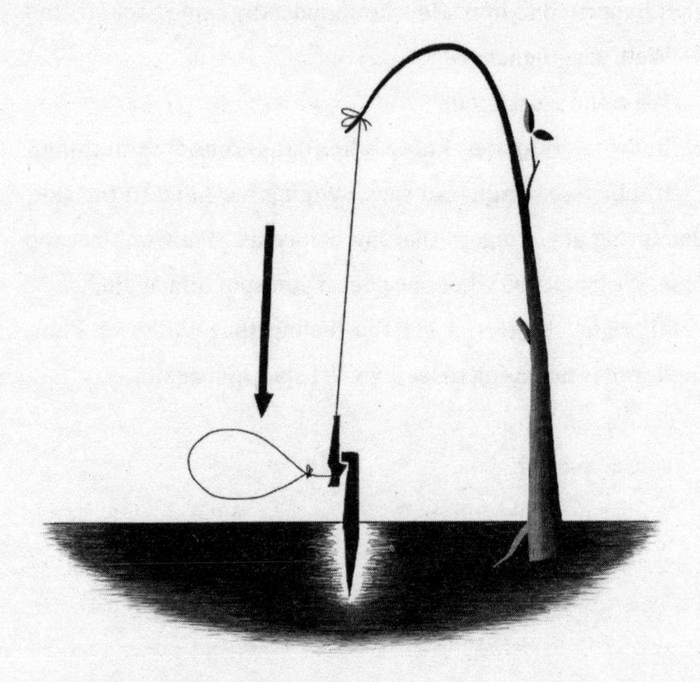

Fig. 8. – How to make a snare trap

'So how did it go when you got home?' he asks.

'Well, they came round last night, Julie and Angharad.'

'Again?'

'Yeah, for dinner. Steve wanted me to apologize.' I pause for a moment, remembering. 'Actually she was all right about it, Angharad I mean.'

Anwar looks up from our snare construction.

'I thought that you didn't like her.'

'I don't know, I don't know her really. But she was okay. When I told her a little bit about why I shouted and she kind of understood. Said that she hides stuff from her mum too. She was more interested in the fallen man though.'

'What's a fallen man?'

'I saw this guy fall over really badly on the street outside my bedroom window. Lots of people went to help him and an ambulance came and everything. And then the next day I read an article about him in a local newspaper. It said that he was dead but somehow sprang back up again and ran away.'

'That's mad! Did they find out what happened?'

'No, he just disappeared. But I'm pretty sure I saw him again later that same night.'

'What? Really?'

'Yeah. And I told Angharad about it because she was at my house the day he fell. But now she's fixated on trying to find him because she says that she loves a mystery. She's going to get her mum to bring her round next weekend so we can try and look for him.'

'I thought that we were going to build a snare in the park next weekend,' Anwar says in a rush with a funny look on his face.

'We are,' I say quickly, worrying that I've hurt his feelings. 'They'll probably come round on Saturday, so we can hang out on Sunday. Is that okay?'

'Okay,' says Anwar, sounding relieved. 'You know, I could see if I could find anything online about him, the fallen man guy?' He pauses. 'I suppose it's good, isn't it? That you're getting on a bit better with Angharad.'

I think about that for a moment, and then I say: 'Yeah, I guess it is,' and realize that I mean it.

HOW TO FIND THE FALLEN MAN

'Is that him?' Angharad asks for about the billionth time.

She's lying across my bed, her eyes glued to everyone who passes on the hill and making notes in a little spiral-bound notebook she's brought with her. When I asked her why she was doing it, she sniffed ever so slightly and said, 'Observations. Just observations.'

I glance over at the dog walker, a man with a sandy-coloured greyhound which walks with long, loping strides.

'No, I told you – when he walks, he looks like he's falling over.'

'How can you even walk if you're falling over?' Angharad says with a huff.

'I don't know but he was. Anwar said—'

'Anwar?'

'Yes. He's my friend from school.'

'You told him?'

'Course,' I say.

'And he believed you?' Angharad asks, narrowing her dark eyes.

'Yeah. He knows how to do lots of stuff online and said he'd help with research. He's good at that kind of thing.'

'Oh, right.' Angharad turns away to look out of the window, the beads in her braids clattering together as she does. I get that same feeling of having said the wrong thing, but I don't know what.

'Anyway,' I add, pointing to the man with the dog as he walks away. 'Dogs don't like the fallen man, so he wouldn't be walking one.'

'I don't remember you saying that.'

'When I saw him the last time, there was a dog that wouldn't stop barking at him. But what does it matter?'

'Because there's a dog that won't stop barking,' Angharad says, getting up and slinging her notepad shut. 'Can't you hear it?'

Now she points it out, I can hear a dog barking away in the distance.

'That could be anything, Angharad,' I argue. 'It could be barking at a cat or maybe its owners have left it alone too long.'

'Or, Billy,' she says back to me in the same tone. 'It could be something to do with the fallen man. Let's go and find out!'

Steve and Julie are in the garden digging out a flowerbed. They are both pink-cheeked and keep looking down at the muddy patch of ground they've dug in a pleased sort of way. When we tell them we're going to the corner shop and will be back soon, they beam at us so much that I almost feel bad about lying to them.

As we go back inside I hear Julie say to Steve, 'They're getting on really well now, aren't they?'

I have to run to keep up with Angharad as she sprints down the pavement, stopping now and again to look one way and then the other.

'I think it's coming from that direction. What do you think? It's hard to tell because it could also be coming from over there.'

'Let's go this way,' I say, picking one of the directions she's pointed out at random.

It seems I chose correctly, as the dog barks build in intensity and volume as we walk along. We're not too far from Steve's but have gone down an alleyway and rounded a corner to some old rundown garages.

The dog is in the back garden of someone's house. We can't see it. But we can just about make out the voices of its owners arguing about what to do.

'Ted, we've got to put Bailey inside. He must be driving the neighbours up the wall . . . He's driving *me* up the wall,' a woman's voice calls out from the house.

'I've tried,' comes the reply. 'But he keeps running off when I get close to him and he won't come for his treats. Here, Bailey, here, boy! Come on!'

'What is it he's barking at anyway?' the woman says.

'I don't know what it is. I can't see anything. We'll have to corner him. Bailey! Bailey!'

Angharad's eyes light up as we overhear them.

'This has got to be the right place!' she says, punching my arm.

'Ow!' I say.

'Oh, come on,' she says, 'that couldn't have really hurt. I could do one that does though.'

She lunges towards me and I dart away quickly.

'Oi! Stop it!' I say.

'Your face,' Angharad says, doubled up with laughter. 'Don't worry, I promise I won't hurt you.' She laughs so hard that she can't quite catch her breath.

'Are you okay?' I ask her, when I hear her wheezing.

She stands up tall but when she sees my face, she collapses again, laughter shaking her spine. 'Your face.' She keeps wheezing with laughter and then after a moment or two, she scrabbles in her pocket and pulls out an inhaler that she puffs on. 'Look what you made me do,' she says. Her breath starts to calm. 'My asthma's bad at the moment. Wooo. Okay. Where were we?'

We peer round to the garden where we heard the dog. The couple must have finally got it inside because now its bark is slightly muffled.

'Let's have a look around to see what the dog was barking at,' suggests Angharad. 'Maybe the fallen man is here?'

We loop round the garages a couple of times but there's no sign of anyone. The ground is cracked tarmac that's coming away in places. The garages look unloved and unused; the paint of the doors is peeling away in curls and long grasses are growing out in angles around them, but they are all securely locked.

'Let's go,' I say. 'There's nobody here.'

'Hold on,' Angharad says. 'There's a bit around the back, I think. Look! There's a path in between the gardens and the back of the garages.'

I can see the overgrown path that she's pointing to; it's almost disappeared because of the weeds blocking the narrow passageway.

'Down there?' I say dubiously, when I hear a voice behind us.

'Are you two all right? Are you looking for something?'

It's the same man who was trying to get his dog inside. I recognize his voice. What did the woman call him? Ted.

He looks a bit like a teddy bear with a roundish belly and small circular glasses that make his eyes look a little beady. He has short gingery hair that looks like fur that's started to wear away.

Angharad steps in front of me before I can think of an excuse and says, 'We're looking for our cat. He's black and white – have you seen one like that?' She's so convincing that for a moment I imagine it's true; that we have a cat, that he's mostly white with black splodges and hasn't been home since last night.

'No, sorry,' Ted says, scratching his gingery beard. 'But he could be back there. Our dog's just been barking at something and he doesn't like ca—'

Ted suddenly spots something in the passageway behind us that makes his voice falter.

He adjusts his glasses on his nose and looks again, peering round us.

'Did you see something?' Angharad asks. We both turn but there's nothing there, just the entrance to the narrow path.

Ted blinks a few times. 'I thought I saw . . . Never mind . . . Maybe you should head home. Where should I go if I spot your cat?' He takes his glasses off and begins to clean them on the yellow fabric of his T-shirt.

I tell him the road that Steve's house is on, but give a different house number.

'Okay, I'll keep my eye out.'

'We might have a quick look down that path,' Angharad says. 'While we're here.'

She tugs at my arm and is about to turn when Ted calls out suddenly.

'Wait! Stop!'

'What?' Angharad says.

'There's something there,' Ted says, but then he corrects himself. 'I think there's some*one* there. But I'm not sure. If there is someone, they don't look very well.'

Angharad clutches my arm. 'It must be him,' she hisses.

Ted steps forward to the entrance of the passageway. 'Hello?' he calls. 'Anyone there?'

There's no answer.

'Hello?' Ted calls again.

'Can you see anyone?' Angharad asks, peering behind Ted.

'No. Maybe it was a shadow.' But he takes another step into the passageway and calls out in a softer voice, 'Do you need any help? We can get you help if you need it.'

Then I hear it.

A rustle.

A definite rustle in the passageway.

I move past Angharad so I can look round to see.

There's the sound of someone moving, the sound of someone in the overgrowth.

Everything that happens next rolls into one.

There's another rustle and then a crash and I hear someone gasp: Angharad, I think. Then I see him – the fallen man. Before I know what's happening, my hand is in Angharad's and I'm dragging her, yanking her away, and she has no choice but to follow. My legs almost stumble beneath me but I run with her away from the dark-green mouth of the passageway. I know we were looking for the fallen man, but now all I'm sure of is that we have to get away from here.

'What is it? Why did you drag me away?' Angharad asks, pulling my hand to make me stop running when we're back on the main road. When she speaks, she's breathless.

'Didn't you see?' I say. 'It was the fallen man, but he didn't look like . . . like a person any more. He's . . . something's happened to him.'

'I couldn't see anything.'

I can still hear snatches of Ted speaking from the alleyway behind us. He's talking in a strangled sort of way, trying to sound like he's in control.

'Oh, mate. It's all right. It's going to be all right. I can get you help. I'll call an ambulance.'

I can hear it all swirled up in his voice: panic, fear and concern all bleeding into each other.

'Stay here, Angharad,' I say. 'I'll be right back.'

'I'm okay,' Angharad says, but her breath is coming in a wheeze again.

'Sit down,' I tell her. 'Use your inhaler. I need to go back and see if that Ted man is okay. Just wait here.'

I can see she doesn't want to be left behind, but her breath is ragged and she reluctantly slumps to the ground and brings out her inhaler once more.

I run back down towards the garages.

The fallen man is standing just behind Ted.

'I'll get some help,' Ted is saying and when he notices me he shouts: 'Get back!' in alarm. There's panic written all over his face. I know it's because of what the fallen man looks like.

His clothes are hanging off him in tatters and now that I'm closer I can see that it isn't really a greyish tinge to his face; instead his skin is the colour of dull metal. There's no sign of normal skin colour at all and his face is mottled, like the grey is fluid somehow, almost moving like it's alive.

He doesn't look human, and yet he is.

He doesn't look real, and yet he's standing there.

He opens his mouth to speak, but it's not words that come out; it's a strangled, desperate, piercing cry that I feel as something physical, stabbing me right through the chest.

Ted holds his hands up as the fallen man makes a move towards him. His stagger is gone and instead his movements are agile and flowing, almost as though his legs aren't legs at all but rolling wheels or waves curving over the sea.

He starts to lift one of his gnarled grey hands towards Ted. It is distended, grown larger than any hand I have ever seen, and looks not unlike a claw, hooked and sharp. The movement is slow, as though there is some invisible force that is holding the man's arm in place and stopping him from reaching out.

But then, in a single, sudden movement, his clawed hand hooks around Ted and all at once, they are locked together. I can't describe the embrace exactly, it's like nothing that I've ever seen. It's as though he's all around Ted, on top of him and beneath him at the same time. And then Ted is released; they are no longer bound together.

Ted starts to shudder.

It begins in his head, in his shoulders – a convulsion that travels in a wave through his body. He jolts and trembles and twists.

His pinkish skin changes colour so it resembles something closer to metal than flesh. His tufts of ginger hair begin to melt away to silver strands. His blue eyes dull and darken until they are a cold, iron grey that seems to dapple and breathe of its own accord. But it's when he opens his mouth that I know it's too late.

It's that same piercing shriek of the fallen man.

It makes me feel hollow inside. Settling as a dead weight on my back, pulling me down.

The fallen man screams back at what was once Ted.

As though they have understood each other, they both slowly turn their heads towards me.

I turn to sprint and I run as fast as I can. When I get to Angharad I skid to a stop.

'We've got to get out of here,' I tell her. 'Something's happened, come on.'

'What is it?'

I flounder, trying to put into words what I've just seen, but I can't.

'There's no time,' I tell her.

I clamp my hand to hers and pull her away.

HOW TO REMEMBER NOT TO MENTION YOUR MUM

I'm faster than Angharad.

Although her long legs extend out effortlessly, I can see she is still struggling to catch her breath but I pull her along with me anyway. We have to get away.

Only when we finally reach Steve's house, do I let us slow and stop.

'What happened?' Angharad asks.

I try again to describe the fallen man, the way that he transformed Ted.

I remember all that Sylvia taught me about soaking up your surroundings, being aware of all the details, and so when I picture it again, I feel like I'm reliving it all over again as though it is playing out in front of me. I can't stop the questions flooding through my mind. What's happened to them? Why have they been changed? And can they be changed back? I can't get the sight of their grey, shadowy skin from my mind, it fills my head and makes everything else around me seem too garish and shocking in its colour.

It seems unbelievable, made up, when I put it into words, but Angharad doesn't question me on any of it. She listens. She believes me; I feel sure of it.

'We've got to get help,' Angharad whispers fiercely. She looks both terrified and determined at the same time. 'We've got to call the police.'

I nod and reach into my pocket for my key but my hands are shaking. They feel detached from my body, jellylike and cold.

'Rule number four: Master your fears.' I hear Sylvia's voice ring out from somewhere inside me. I take a deep breath, reminding myself to keep calm.

My hand closes around the cold metal of the key and I shove it into the door and we rush inside and to the back garden where Julie and Steve are still digging, laughing together.

'Something's happened,' Angharad announces. 'We've got to call the police.'

They look up with astonished faces.

'Just tell us one more time,' Julie is saying. She and Steve are sitting on the sofa calmly although Angharad and I can't stop pacing the square of the living room.

'We've told you already and there's no other way of saying it,' Angharad rants. 'We need to call the police.'

I see Julie and Steve exchange a look.

'You both saw it?' Steve asks.

Angharad and I look at each other for a tiny moment.

'I was right there,' Angharad starts to say.

'But I saw it,' I finish for her.

'Did you see any of it, Angharad?' Steve asks her. His eyes crinkle and I see doubt flash across them.

'Well, no, but that was because Billy pulled me away. For my safety. I was having a bit of an asthma attack. But that Ted guy was there.'

'You had an asthma attack?' Julie's voice rises sharply.

'It was nothing serious.' Angharad shrugs.

'So let me get this straight,' Steve says. 'You didn't see this man at all, and you didn't see anyone . . . transform.' He cringes as he says it.

Defeated, Angharad shakes her head.

'But I did. I saw it. It happened, I swear.'

'It's just that it's . . . it's hard to believe,' Julie says. 'There's a man who's come back from the dead? And he can turn people grey?'

'It's not like he turns them grey,' I say. 'It's like they catch something from him, the same thing that turned *him* grey.'

Suddenly a memory flashes back to me. The diagrams that Sylvia had pinned to the wall in the Martello tower. They look so clear in my mind, it's as though I am back in that dark room, standing in front of them.

'What is it, Billy?' Angharad asks, seeing the look on my face.

'I think I've seen something about this before. I saw some diagrams where people were coloured in grey.'

'Where did you see diagrams like that?' Steve asks.

I hesitate. But I have to say it, maybe it's an important clue to help us save Ted and the fallen man. 'Sylvia,' I tell him. 'Sylvia had them.'

Steve and Julie don't say anything but they look at each other, in shock and something else that I can't quite pinpoint; fear, worry, alarm?

'You see! Maybe we weren't the first to see this happen. Maybe it will happen to more people,' Angharad says. 'If we don't do anything about it.'

'You didn't actually see anything, sweetheart,' Julie says gently. 'It was just Billy.'

Angharad opens her mouth as if to protest and then realizes that she can't. Julie looks at Steve again, another silent conversation happening between them.

I can feel my heart thumping in my chest. It feels as though it might burst out. Every part of me is tensed with a mixture of anger and hurt at not being believed. Sylvia would believe me in a heartbeat, she would never think I was lying.

'Umm . . .' Steve rubs his chin. His face looks strained and a little white. 'Look, I need to speak to Julie for a moment alone.' Again I feel a bolt of rage and sadness flash through me. I didn't know until then that not being believed could feel like a pain. It hangs over my shoulders and drags down my spine, a kind of shame that eats away at me. And it's all mixed up with a hot, lashing anger. I feel like I am shaking, trying to contain it all inside me. But Angharad doesn't hold back.

'What do you need to talk about?' says Angharad in a shot.

'I can't believe that you don't believe us. Why would we make it up?'

'Angharad!' Julie exclaims. 'Don't answer back like that. Stay in here, Steve and I will speak in the kitchen.'

Angharad waits until they've left and then she goes straight up to the door and presses her ear against it.

'I can't really hear them,' she whispers. 'Hold on.'

I walk over and strain my ears too to catch any part of their conversation, but they are keeping their voices low and quiet.

'I think they said something about humouring . . . I'm not sure. They're coming back!' Angharad hisses.

We dart away from the door and slump on the sofa as we were before.

'Right,' Steve says. 'Julie and I think that we should all go back to the garages and see if we can find these people. I'll take my phone and if we find them we'll call the police straightaway.'

'Let's go,' Angharad says, standing. 'We need to find them quickly, but just make sure you don't get too close to them or the same thing might happen to us that did to Ted.'

'Ted? How do you know his name?' Steve asks.

'Because we heard him talking to his wife about the dog,' I say. 'Remember? The dog was barking, that's how we found them.'

'Oh, yes,' Julie says, unconvincingly.

We set off for the garages, Angharad leading the way. The sun has come out now and all we can hear is the sound of children playing in gardens, the diluted chimes of an ice-cream van from a far-off street.

There's no dog barking. There are no strange shrieks.

When we get to the garages, there's a white car with its engine exposed at the entrance of one of the garages, and a young man wearing a black cap and whistling while he works.

No fallen man.

No grey skin.

No shrieks.

The man gives us a nod when he notices us.

'Excuse me,' Angharad says, walking over to him despite Julie hissing at her to come back. 'Have you seen anyone else just here? Someone with grey skin? There might be two of them?'

The man scratches his beard. 'Grey skin? Like they were wearing make-up? I haven't seen anyone since I got here about ten minutes ago. Apart from you lot, of course. It's a bit early for Halloween, isn't it?'

He laughs, but Angharad stays put. 'If you do see someone like that, call the police,' she says. 'Call them straightaway.'

'Are they going to get me?' the man says, a teasing tone lining his voice.

Angharad stalks away then, back towards us.

'I know you don't believe us,' she says to Steve and Julie, looking them straight in the eye, standing taller than I ever could. 'But Billy and I know what happened here. I still think we should call the police. We could knock on the door of Ted's house too; his wife will be able to tell us that he's gone missing. It was that house, wasn't it, Billy?'

Despite Julie and Steve not believing me, the way that Angharad is acting, like there's no chance I'm wrong, even though she didn't actually see it, makes me feel stronger.

'Yes, that house there,' I answer. I catch Steve's eye. Only a second passes before he looks away.

'We're not bothering anyone else,' Julie says sternly. 'That's quite enough now. You,' she says to Angharad, 'always get swept up in telling these stories. I think that we'd better go home.'

'Fine by me,' Angharad says. 'It's not safe here.'

'Is that what all this is really about?' Julie says. 'I thought you were getting along, but all the while you were just plotting this ridiculous story so you wouldn't have to spend time with each other?'

'It's not like that,' Angharad says, hotly. 'Billy. Tell them.'

'Sylvia always said she was getting me ready for something bad that was going to happen. Maybe this is it.' As soon as I speak the words I wish I could take them back.

Steve's face turns stormy.

'That's enough,' he says. He speaks in a hard tone I've not heard before. It's both quiet and loud at the same time. It feels like something physical, like a punch.

Julie looks embarrassed and unsure of which way to look. Even Angharad looks like she feels sorry for me now.

But before I can say any more, Julie and Steve separate us.

HOW TO FEEL LOST

The clock ticks.

It ticks too loudly. It gets louder with every tick, I am sure of it.

We are waiting in a room with a vase of fake, plastic pink carnations and a pile of tatty magazines. The seats are hard, plastic-moulded and uncomfortable against my body. There's a television on the wall, with the sound off, which plays news stories with subtitles on, in a never-ending loop.

Steve sits opposite me, his hands placed on his knees, looking straight ahead. He's nervous. He's been nervous all morning. From the moment he woke me; passing me a plate of half-burnt toast at 7 a.m. and telling me that we were going, we were really going to see Sylvia. We left the house so quickly that I forgot my phone and only when we were squashed on to the second train did I remember that I was meant to be seeing Anwar today and had no way of telling him that I couldn't come any more. We had to travel across London and then take another train, then a taxi which finally led us here.

This is where Sylvia lives now. It's meant to be somewhere she can 'get the help that she needs'. At least, that's what I overheard the doctor say to Steve outside this little waiting room we're sitting in.

I wish that I had brought something for her. We talked about it briefly but in the rush of leaving and being late, the moment slipped past. I looked at the bunches of sad-looking flowers in a bucket at the train station but I knew she wouldn't really like them and then Steve was calling me to go.

'Are you okay?' Steve asks me.

I give him a nod although I feel tired and disbelieving that we are here. We've been travelling for most of the day and my body feels stiff and cramped from sitting on trains. 'Are you okay?' I ask back.

Steve doesn't answer but smiles at me, just a little.

'Why now?' I ask in a small voice. 'Why have we come to see Sylvia now?'

'Umm . . . I've been thinking about it for a while, and after yesterday, Julie thought, well *we* thought that it was time. If you see your mum, you might understand everything that's happened a bit more.' He sighs loudly and rubs his hands together nervously.

'You don't believe what I saw at all, do you?'

'I believe you think you saw something,' Steve says. He has a pained look on his face. 'But it might not have been what you think it was. Being with your mum might have given you . . . a different idea of reality,' he finishes awkwardly.

'What do you mean?'

'Just that. I haven't been making it up, Billy, your mum's still not well. She's still recovering. And maybe living with her on your own for so long has made you see things that possibly aren't really there.'

'So you do think I made it up?'

'I don't think you meant to,' he tells me. 'Just like your mum didn't mean to do some of the things that she did.' He looks at me, weighing up what to say next. 'But, no, I don't think that you really saw a grey man turning someone else into a monster.'

I stay silent. I know it sounds mad when it's put like that, but I also know what I saw. And I know that Sylvia was teaching me to look after myself because she thought that I needed to be ready. Maybe she didn't know exactly what was coming, but that doesn't mean she was wrong.

'Billy, the important thing for you to know is that this is a good place. That everyone here is helping your mum and I want you to see that for yourself. Your mum has spent time in here before and it has helped her to get better.'

He falls into silence and looks at his feet.

I can't look at him either, so I stare from the tattered, dusty carnations to the magazines to the television screen where a woman with short, straight blonde hair stares out, a serious look on her face. I glance at the subtitles.

The cause of this mystery illness has yet to be established – there have been two fatalities so far but medical staff at the BRI in Bristol have confirmed the surviving patients remain in a 'severely critical state'. Police are trying to identify what links this group of people and ask if anyone has any more information that they come forward immediately. Our local correspondent Nita Chowdni is in Bristol now.

The image switches to another woman standing outside a hospital. She's going into more detail about how quickly the illness struck and then the screen fills with photographs of different faces. The subtitle reads: *Victims of the mystery but fatal virus which has yet to be identified by medical authorities.*

My mind races and I look again at the screen full of faces. Among the group are two young paramedics. I know that's who they are because in the photo they are standing by an ambulance in their uniforms. They are smiling, looking like they might have just been about to start laughing about something.

There is a photograph of a man standing outside somewhere, the sun hitting his face so he has to squint slightly. The landscape behind him looks rugged and wild.

I almost have to stop myself from leaping up from the hard plastic chair as I realize that I recognize him. It's the man who was driving the car and jumped out to help the fallen man. I remember he was wearing a blue jacket that made me think he did a lot of walking.

Suddenly, I'm sure. These are all the people who helped the fallen man. For whatever reason, they didn't get changed by him like Ted did, they just got really sick.

'They got infected by him, too.' I think aloud without meaning to. 'But in a different way. It's all connected.'

'What did you say?' Steve says.

Just then the door opens and a nurse wearing a lilac-coloured uniform comes in.

'Hi, Steve, hi, Billy, I'm Jo. I'm going to take you to see Sylvia today. I know that she's been really looking forward to seeing you both, especially you, Billy.'

I try to push away my spiralling thoughts about the fallen man, and concentrate on why I'm here. Sylvia. I'm finally going to see Sylvia. And just like that, everything else melts away.

Jo has a calming sort of voice. I feel that she could lull you to sleep if you listened to her for long enough.

'Now, it's been a few months since you saw your mum, is that right?'

I nod.

'Okay, well, it's important to remember that your mum is working hard on getting better, and while she's doing that some things might seem different about her. She might not be the same as you remember her right now because she is having to put a lot of her energy into her recovery rather than just being herself. Does that make sense?' Jo asks me.

I nod my head again, although I don't really understand what she is saying.

'Can I see her now?' I ask instead.

'Of course – follow me.'

We go down a corridor – the floor is mint green and smells fiercely antiseptic.

I can't help but look into other rooms that we pass.

Sometimes the doors are just swinging closed and I catch a glimpse of the inside. I don't see any faces, only the backs of people or sometimes just a pale green sheet covering them, still in bed. We go through some swinging double doors and then some more. I look back the way that we came and wonder if I'd be able to find my way again if I came here alone.

Each door that swings closed behind us makes my heart contract. I can feel a sort of heat or wriggling sensation climbing from my stomach up over my shoulders. It makes me feel quite sick, makes my footsteps smaller, slower.

'Are you all right, Billy?' I hear Steve asking me. I've come to a standstill and when I look down at my hands, I can see that they are trembling. I'm nervous, I realize, to be finally seeing Sylvia. Then out of nowhere I hear a voice in my head. *Master your fears, Rule number four.* I make myself take a deep breath. I straighten my back, look forward and force my feet to work.

'I'm okay,' I say.

We carry on walking, down another corridor and then another.

'Here she is,' announces Jo, pushing open the door of one of the small rooms. We arrive next to a bed that looks like all the others that we have passed. It has a body within it that is looking away, that is sheltering under its covers.

'Sylvia,' Jo says softly, 'you have visitors, love.' And then, quieter still: 'Billy's here.'

The body in the bed does not move. The body in the bed does not respond. I cannot see how the body in the bed can be

Sylvia. The woman who has taken me on so many adventures, who usually has so much energy that it's like she can't sit still at all.

'Sylvia?' Steve says gently. 'We're here.'

He reaches out a hand to touch the green-clothed figure in the bed in front of us but still she does not move.

'Billy, why don't you speak to her?' Jo suggests. 'Just talk to her like you normally would, if you can. She might not wake up, but I know she'll want to hear your voice.'

But I am wordless. I feel choked up with what to say and what not to say. I feel like I'm watching everything play out from a distance – me, Steve and Jo standing around the hospital bed – as though I am quite separate from it happening, as if I am watching it happen to someone else.

Jo pulls back the covers a little so we can see the face of the person in the bed. She is asleep, her eyelids are firmly shut. But the body looks like Sylvia. It's got the same colour hair, although it's a bit longer than I remember and it's fuzzy from not being brushed and lank from not being washed. The nose is the right shape and the mouth, though a little pale and dry, looks like Sylvia's mouth.

But it's not Sylvia. Not really. This still, silent body seems so far from the Sylvia that I know. Her light is gone. The light that drove her to take me on adventures and make sure we were prepared. The light that made her lean into me quite suddenly and sweep me up in a close, tight hug that would take my breath away – that light is gone. So much so, that part of me doubts that this is Sylvia at all.

There's a commotion suddenly from one of the other rooms. An alarm rings out.

Jo hurries out of the room. I hear her call something to another nurse who runs towards her down the corridor. Then a doctor comes, and another nurse, and then another.

'We'd better go back to the waiting room until they've dealt with this,' Steve says to me. He puts a steering hand on my shoulder.

Everyone is so distracted by the other patient that I don't think anyone sees but me:

Sylvia has sat up. She's awake.

And, just like that, I know that she is herself again.

She's looking right at me. I can see in her eyes that there's so much that she wants to tell me. I can almost see it spilling out of her.

But her eyes flicker to Steve and then back to me and it's as though she is swallowing everything down.

Instead she clenches one of her hands into a tight fist and then brings it down on to her open palm – first in one thud and then two in quick succession. Tapping our code. Letting me know it really is her.

But then Steve is dragging me away. He turns to look back at Sylvia. And, as quickly as she sat up, Sylvia has fallen back on to her bed. Lying still and empty, just like she was before.

Steve has gone to see if he can find us some food. I said I wanted to wait in the corridor close to Sylvia, in case they say it's fine to go back in.

Jo comes down the corridor, with a smile.

'Okay, Billy? Sorry about all the kerfuffle. When your dad comes back, maybe you can go and see your mum again, if you'd like that?'

I nod and she nods back at me, her lips pursed together as though there is something else that she wants to tell me, but then she turns and I watch her walk away towards the nurse's station down the corridor.

Other nurses go past, they all acknowledge me with a kind smile or a nod.

For a few moments, though no one is paying any attention to me, I don't make a move. But then, very slowly, I walk towards the door where Sylvia's room is.

Just as I put my hand on the door to push it open, I see one of the other nurses step out a little from the station, her back towards me. If she doesn't turn, she won't see me.

'Who's that wee chap waiting by himself?'

I hear Jo reply: 'It's Sylvia Weywood's son. He and his dad are here . . . for their first visit since she was admitted.'

'That's Billy?' another voice says. 'She's been asking for him since she got here. That time she escaped, I was sure she was going to him.'

'Well, she'd been gone long enough to make it to Bristol and back, that's for sure. I didn't know if we were going to see her again.'

'She wants to get better. She told me that when she came back. Amongst other things. She wants to get her son back and knows this is the only way.'

I hold my breath as I listen to them talking about us. Sylvia ran away?

Without looking back, I push through the door into the corridor and make my way to Sylvia's room.

She's lying still again.

Like she's not really there.

When I get closer, I can see that she's sleeping again.

'Sylvia?' I say, and when she doesn't respond: 'It's me – it's Billy. I'm here.'

I remember what Jo said and try to talk like normal even if she doesn't reply.

'I miss you,' I say.

She doesn't respond, her breath coming in soft waves.

'It's been kind of weird at the moment,' I tell her. 'I've made some friends in Bristol now. Anwar, from school, and Angharad, sort of, I guess. Angharad isn't from school though, she's Julie's daughter, Julie is . . . well, anyway, they are the only other people that know what's been happening. I saw this man. He had kind of grey skin and walked in a funny way. Now I think he made some people really sick and I saw this other man change when he got too close to him.'

I've been staring at a tiny patch on the hospital bed cover as I've been talking, so when Sylvia's eyes fly open, I don't notice at first.

'Billy!' Her voice comes out like a wheeze.

'You're awake!' I can't help but cry.

'Was I asleep? They've put me on medication and sometimes I feel like I can't tell the difference between being awake and asleep. But, Billy! My Billy, you're really here. I thought I might be dreaming before.'

She reaches for my hand and I feel her vice-like grip around my wrist. Her eyes lock with mine, wide and urgent.

'Are you okay, Billy? Are you safe?' It feels like she is able to look right into me. 'Has something happened?'

I tell her again about the fallen man and the way that Ted was changed, the people that got sick.

'Have you told Steve?'

'Yes,' I say.

'Does he believe you?'

I give the smallest shake of my head.

'Do you believe me?' I ask in a quiet voice.

'Of course! You wouldn't lie, Billy. And this is too important.'

'Do you think,' I begin to say, although I know it's a silly thought, 'that if you spoke to him about it then he would believe me?'

Sylvia shakes her head fiercely. 'He wouldn't believe me either and I think it's best if I don't speak to your dad. It will only end in an argument. If he comes back, I'm going to pretend that I'm sleeping, okay? Like before.'

'But maybe if we both told hi—' I start, but Sylvia cuts me off.

'Billy,' she says. Her voice is hoarse, unused to speaking, but she talks rapidly. 'You know what you've got to do. You've got to rely on yourself: Rule number three. You remember where I took you that time – our safe place?' she whispers.

'The tower?'

'It's not very far from this hospital. Do you remember the map I showed you?'

I nod.

'The name of the place is Sandgate. Repeat it back to me.'

'Sandgate.'

'If something happens, if things get worse and you need protection – you know everything you need to look after yourself. You found *How to Survive*?'

'Yes.'

'Remember everything I taught you, Billy. Keep practising and never give up, okay? It's important. I know what they are saying to you about me – that I'm sick. But our adventures, what I taught you, it's all important. And you know where I'll be if you need me. I'll be at the tower at Sandgate. I'll find a way to get there so we can be together.' There's urgency in her eyes.

'Okay,' I whisper.

'There's something else – remember the heliographs?'

'Yes.'

But then I see something change. The light is gone again and Sylvia suddenly falls silent. She lies back on the bed and closes her eyes.

'There you are,' I hear Steve say from behind me. 'How is she?'

'She's asleep,' I say. 'She's just sleeping.'

HOW TO FALL OUT WITH YOUR DAD

We're on the train on the way back from seeing Sylvia. I feel glad that it's so crowded that Steve and I can't sit next to each other. I'm wedged into a window seat with a woman who looks like she is about to fall asleep as she reads things on her phone while Steve is a few seats away at a table sitting opposite two businessmen and a woman who has a tiny sausage dog puppy on her lap.

I look out of the window at the countryside that blurs past. I stare at it so hard that it stops seeming like trees and fields and instead I just see threads of colours – greens and browns and yellows – that can't be identified as one thing or another. I feel a little bit like that. That I don't really feel like myself, that I'm just lines and blocks of colours merging into one another.

I can't work out what I think about seeing Sylvia. Whether I'm glad that I've seen her, or that it's made things worse somehow. Unlike Steve, she believed me instantly about the fallen man, but seeing her in hospital made me wonder how ill she really is. She said it was medication making her drowsy but I can't stop thinking back to the shock of seeing her lying in the hospital bed, as still as a sack.

The train announcer tells us that we are about to reach another station and the woman next to me starts to rouse herself and reaches down for her bag. She's getting off.

Before she's even left her seat, Steve is inching his way past the woman with the dog and is heading towards me.

'Just so I can sit with my son,' he tells the woman when she sees him there waiting for her to leave.

'Oh, sorry, you should have said,' she mutters as she reaches for an umbrella and a coat that she stuffed into the shelf over our heads. Steve goes to help her but only seems to get in the way as she tries to move past him. He slots into the seat next to me with a *humph*.

'It's busy, isn't it?' he says.

I don't even answer him. It's the kind of thing that strangers would say to each other.

I continue to look out of the window as the train pulls slowly out of the station. Being so close to Steve makes me feel uncomfortable, like I can't quite stretch out or something. There's a knot in my back that won't leave me.

'Are you hungry?' Steve asks.

'A bit,' I reply through a half-closed mouth.

'We'll get something to eat before we change trains. See if we can make the best of Paddington Station restaurants, shall we?'

'Okay.'

I can feel him still looking at me. I know that he wants to talk.

'What did you think . . .' he starts to say, but then something catches in his throat and he starts coughing. He goes a bit red-faced and then finds a water bottle in his bag to drink from. 'How do you feel after seeing your mum?' he says, in the end.

I shrug for an answer.

'I think she was pleased to see you,' he says quickly. 'I mean, I know she was asleep, so it might not seem that way, but I'm sure she knew you were there and was really happy. The nurses told me she's been talking about you non-stop. But, Billy, I hope that you could see what I mean about your mum needing rest and help?'

I can feel myself growing hotter and hotter with every word he speaks.

'She's got a way to go before she recovers.'

'She spoke to me,' I say, staring hard at the pattern of the seat cover in front of me. Steve's wrong about Sylvia. She understands what is happening and I can't stand to hear him keep talking about her like she's not really all there. 'She told me to keep practising.'

'What? When? She was asleep the whole time.'

'She woke up, before you came in the second time. And then she . . . she pretended to be asleep when you came in. So she didn't have to speak to you. She told me that I'm going to really need the survival training we did.' I take a deep breath before adding: 'And she believed me.'

'Believed you about what?'

'About the fallen man. Sylvia knew I was telling the truth.'

'Billy, that's enough.' The look on Steve's face tells me that he doesn't even believe that Sylvia actually spoke to me. 'All those things your mum taught you were because she wasn't well. She was wrong when she told you that you should miss school, not have any friends, move around all the time. She thought that the survival stuff was more important than anything else.'

'It is important,' I say.

'No, it's not, okay? It's not important.' Steve's voice grows into a shout. I see people looking over at us. He notices and drops his voice a little, but he's finding it hard to contain his anger. 'You have got to stop this. I don't want you going down the same path as your mother, I just won't let that happen. You have to move past this, Billy. See it for what it really is. Just plain nonsense. Sylvia is not well and she's filled your head with rubbish. The sooner you can believe that, the better.'

'And what if I don't?' I say. 'What if I won't believe that?'

Steve flounders for an answer.

I stand up and start to move past him.

'Where are you going?'

'I don't want to sit with you,' I say simply.

'Billy, come on. Don't make a scene.'

But I barge past his knees, his water bottle falls to the floor and rolls down the aisle, and I go and wedge myself into the seat that he was sitting on before, with the woman with the tiny puppy and the two businessmen who don't even look up from the laptops that they are tapping on loudly.

I don't speak to Steve again the whole way home.

HOW TO MAKE A POCKET SURVIVAL KIT

I go to Anwar's house early before school the next day, but before I leave I look through *How to Survive* and collect up a few things that we have around the house to take with me.

Anwar's sister Nadifa opens the door to me. Her face is painted like a zombie, with dark shadows beneath her eyes, a trail of blood dripping from her mouth.

'Hello, Billy,' she says, smiling, as though she's completely unaware of her make-up.

'Is Anwar here?' I ask her.

She doesn't answer but runs off into the flat and so I follow her in.

Anwar's standing on the sofa, putting the finishing touches on his other little sister's face. Taifa stares over at me, her face a ghostly white, her lips grey and blood-stained.

'Billy!' He sounds surprised to see me, mixed in with something else that I can't quite put my finger on. He doesn't stop painting Taifa's face, keeping his back to me so I can't see his face. He carries on talking but his voice sounds a bit funny.

'They have to dress up as book characters for school but they both wanted to be zombies. There's probably a book that's got zombies in it.'

'I'm sorry about yesterday,' I say quickly. We got back so late last night and I was still so cross with Steve, that I didn't have the energy to explain in a message all that had happened in the day. Instead I sent Anwar something short just saying I was sorry I couldn't meet up and that I didn't get the chance to tell him.

'Were you with Angharad?'

'No. It was . . . actually . . . Steve took me . . .'

I start to speak but I'm reluctant to, in front of Taifa.

'Go away, then,' Anwar says to his sister. She launches herself from the sofa and runs after Nadifa, a low-deep howl emerging from her bloodied lips.

We start to speak at the same time.

'I saw Sylvia yesterday,' I tell Anwar, just as he says: 'I thought—' but as soon as I mention her name he stops himself.

'What? How?'

'I think Julie told Steve to take me. They think that Angharad and I made up seeing the . . .' I trail off as I remember all that has happened since I saw Anwar on Friday. The fallen man infecting Ted, seeing the people who'd got sick on the news, knowing Sylvia really does believe something bad is coming, my argument with Steve. This weekend has felt like a lifetime.

I go back to the beginning and try to tell Anwar about what I saw with Angharad in the alleyway and all that's happened since. I don't think I do a good job of it. I can't fully explain how weird and terrifying it was all at the same time; what it sounded like to hear the fallen man and Ted shrieking.

'It was as though his voice had been completely broken into pieces and then sewn back together with everything in the wrong place. It was horrible – I can't explain it properly. And their skin was grey, but it was more than that, it was like all the shades swirled up together.

'And there's something else . . . I remember that Sylvia had these diagrams in this emergency shelter she was preparing. They were of people that were grey, I'm sure of it. I asked her about it but she didn't explain what they were. But I think she knew about them somehow – something to do with her old job, I think.

'She told me that if I needed to, I had to get to the tower, that she would meet me there.'

'Where is it? The tower?'

'It's on the Kent coast. A place called Sandgate. Hold on, I'll show you.'

I tap at the map on my phone and zoom out further so I can see what other areas are close by to it. I see blue – the tepid, bland blue that depicts the roar of the sea – on the map. It's by a little jagged part of the coast. I can imagine the Martello tower standing there, close to the sea.

'This is it,' I say, pointing at the screen. 'She only took me once.'

Anwar examines it closely.

'Do you think Sylvia knew about it all the time?'

'She always said that we were getting ready for something,' I say. 'We had these survival rules. One of them was all about only trusting yourself, following your instincts if you think something is wrong – even if everyone is telling you not to. I think this was what she meant.'

'How was your mum?' he asks.

'Umm . . .' I feel hot all of a sudden. 'Well, Steve says that she's . . . she's still . . . not well. But she spoke to me, only me, and I think she's . . .' I don't know how to put it into words.

I look up and see Anwar's face, his steady brown eyes hold mine in his, and in that moment, I'm suddenly so sure of a truth that until that moment I had not fully realized. I know that if I don't want to say anything then Anwar won't push it. But, if I do, then there's someone who will listen.

I take a deep breath and tell him more. 'Sylvia was pretending to be asleep when Steve was there – I guess so she didn't have to speak to him. But we just had a few minutes together alone when I was able to tell her about the fallen man and what happened at the garages.' I remember it now as though Sylvia is right in front of me. I feel my arm strain to reach out and touch her. 'She said that I knew what I had to do. And there was something she wanted to tell me about heliographs.'

'Heliographs? What about them?'

'I don't know. Steve came back in and she pretended she was asleep before she could finish. But I wanted to ask you if you can help me make something?'

'Of course,' Anwar says, packing up the face paints carefully, screwing on the lid to the bottle of fake blood. 'What is it?'

'A personal pocket survival kit. It's from my mum's book. It's things that you might need if you are caught out with nothing else. I've got some of it already.'

I hadn't stopped thinking about it since I'd seen Sylvia yesterday. The more I thought about what she said, the more it made sense. She just wanted me to be ready, to remember everything that she had taught me; she knew I understood what I needed to do.

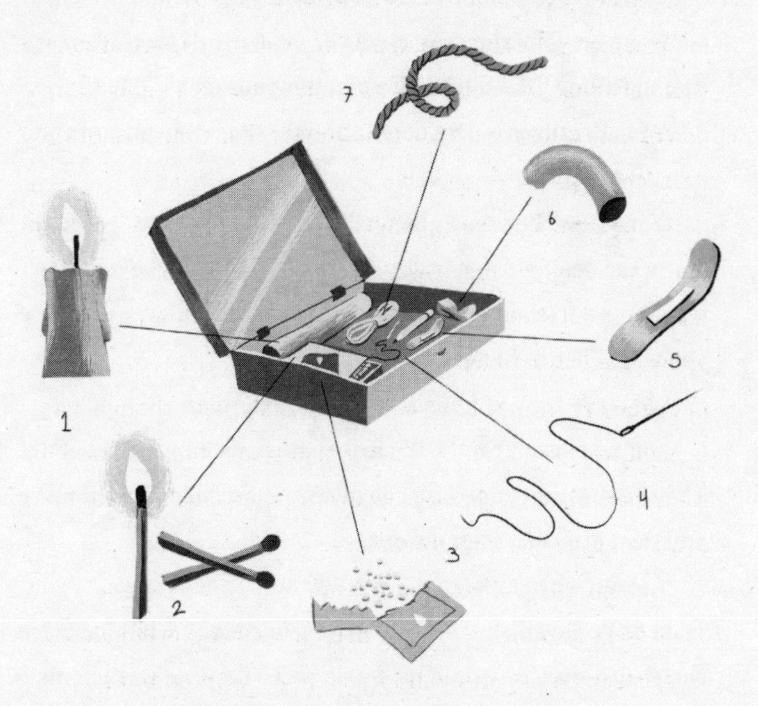

Fig. 9. – How to make a pocket survival kit

I open up the bag I have with me and show Anwar the matches and the candle, the tubing and the string, the whistle and the safety pins.

'I need to waterproof the matches,' I tell him. 'And there's a few more things that I have to get.' I show him the list.

He nods and disappears off.

I think: this is what friends are to each other – someone who knows, without you having to explain, that right at that moment all you need is their help. I've not really had that before. I like it. It makes me wonder if Sylvia's rule for not trusting anyone is completely right; surely it's better when there is someone on your side, someone you know you can rely on. It's a good feeling, like solid ground under your feet.

Anwar returns with a needle and thread, a few plasters and a small pencil.

'You know,' he says as he walks back towards me, 'I thought you were seeing Angharad yesterday – that maybe you don't want to be friends with me so much any more now. Because you've got her to hang out with.'

'No way!' I say in a rush. 'Why'd you think that?'

'Oh, no reason really. It's just that that's happened before. They've met someone else they want to be friends with more and then kind of . . . left me out.'

'Anwar, it's not like that at all. I wanted to see you yesterday. I just forgot my phone in the morning because we left in such a rush – otherwise I would have told you where we were going – and then I was really tired when we got home.'

'It's okay.'

'And I'm not sure I'll be seeing Angharad that much any more because Steve and Julie probably think I'm a bad influence on her for making things up.'

'Okay,' says Anwar, more cheerfully. 'What else do we need?' He looks at my list. 'Condy's crystals,' he reads. 'Where are we going to get those? What do they do, anyway?'

I consult the book. 'You can use them for lots of things. A little bit will sterilize water or if you use them in a more concentrated dose then they can be used as an antibacterial wash if you get cut or something. You should be able to get them from the chemist.'

'Maybe we could ask Diric to get us that?' Diric, an older cousin of Anwar's, helps Anwar buy things he can't get sometimes.

I feel myself get calmer at the thought of collecting all the things on the list. Of getting ready, being prepared. I hear Sylvia's voice again, like I did yesterday at the hospital. *Master your fears. Always be prepared: have everything you need ready and with you at all times.*

'We also need a box that we can put everything in that can also act as a heliograph. It says in the book something like a small tobacco box, but I don't think you can get them any more. I wonder what it was that Sylvia wanted to tell me about heliographs?' I think aloud.

'It doesn't have to be a tobacco box though, does it?' Anwar asks. 'Just something that is that kind of size that's a tin and has a shiny lid.'

'Yes – anything like that.'

Anwar rummages through one of the cupboards in the kitchen and produces a small tin with a purple-flowery design on it.

'It came with chocolates in it but it's the same kind of thing, isn't it?'

I smile. 'It's just right,' I tell him.

HOW TO SHARE (AGAIN)

As Steve and I walk over to We The Curious, the science museum in Bristol, I can feel the weight of my pocket survival kit swinging in my jacket.

Anwar and I punched a hole in the top of the lid so it could be used as a heliograph, and filled it with almost everything from the list.

When the box was full, we sealed the edges with electrical tape so it was waterproof and covered up the hole in the lid with a little more.

I can't really explain it, but gradually filling the little tin box with the odd bits and pieces made me start to feel a lot better.

I wonder if this is how Sylvia felt when she learned how to make fire using a firebow, or when she stocked up with tins from the supermarket – each small bit of preparation adding up to make her feel a little more relaxed and settling the desperate beating inside of her.

'Here we are,' Steve says with a triumphant grin and holds the door open for me. I was wrong about not seeing Angharad as much any more. When I got home from school on Monday, Steve told me that we were going to spend Wednesday evening together and that I had to come home from school straight-away and not 'dawdle back with Anwar'. It has been strained between me and Steve since we got back from seeing Sylvia and I can't help but wonder if he wants us to spend time with Julie and Angharad so it's not just the two of us, unable to speak or understand each other properly.

'Steve! Billy! We're over here,' Julie says. I'm not sure whose idea it was to meet at We The Curious but I wonder if Julie and Steve think it'll make us not want to talk about men with grey skin. It's a special evening at the museum where they only let a small number of people in after opening hours and so you can have more of a go at everything.

'Hey, Billy,' Angharad says and then when Julie and Steve are greeting each other and not looking at us, she mouths, 'I need to speak to you' in an exaggerated whisper.

I nod back. I need to tell her about the people who fell sick and see if she can remember any of the people from the day the man fell, too.

As soon as we are wrist-banded, we tell Julie and Steve we'll meet them later.

Steve starts saying, 'But shouldn't we go round togeth—' but Julie puts her hand on his arm to stop him.

'We're trusting you to be sensible,' she says. 'We'll meet at the way we came in if we can't find each other at the end, okay?'

Angharad and I both nod.

'Okay?' Julie says again in a louder voice.

'Yes, Mum.'

'Yes, Julie.'

'So what did you want to tell me?' I ask Angharad as soon as we're out of earshot.

'I found this,' she says, swiping on her phone and handing it over to me. It's about Ted, he's been reported missing by his wife. It's an article on a local news site and there are photographs of Ted, wearing a T-shirt in front of bright blue sky, squinting into the camera, and another from his wedding, grinning in a blue suit. I suddenly remember the way his ginger hair fell from his head and I feel as though I can't breathe. I hand the phone back to Angharad.

'There's more,' she continues. 'There's been a rise in missing people reported in the last few days. It's not a huge number but there's definitely more than normal.'

'I've got something too. Did you hear on the news about that group of people who got really ill all of a sudden and no one knows what's wrong with them? Well, I think that they might have been the people who were on the street that day and helped the fallen man. I recognized one man who was definitely there and then there's two paramedics in the group. Here, look, maybe you'll remember someone?'

I find the website on my phone; I'd found the news article online after I saw it on the television in the hospital. She scrolls through. 'That woman looks familiar,' she says, 'but I can't be completely sure because I wasn't really watching for long.'

We hear the sound of someone whooping loudly and look over to see Julie and Steve on one of the exhibits, releasing miniature parachutes into the air.

'Let's go upstairs,' Angharad says.

We find a quiet corner we can talk in.

'There's something else,' I tell her. 'Steve took me to see my mum on Sunday. I got to speak to her alone for a little bit. She completely believes us about the fallen man.'

'Were you able to ask her about those diagrams you mentioned?'

'No, there wasn't time – we only had a few minutes before Steve came. She told me that I needed to get ready though. I think she thinks that things might get a lot worse.'

'Really?' Angharad says, her eyes widening. 'So, what have we found out . . .' she says, twisting one of her braids round and round and tugging on the bright-pink bead at the end of it, 'that people are being changed, that people are getting ill and dying. And no one thinks it's serious, not really.'

I nod.

'And we know that we have to keep away from anyone who's infected in case it happens to us.'

'Although it doesn't seem like the people that just got sick are making other people ill, unless they haven't reported that in the news,' I say. 'We can't trust anyone. Sylvia taught me that. It's Rule three.'

'What do you mean – Rule three?'

'It was just something me and my mum did,' I begin awkwardly, but there's no trace of judgement on Angharad's face and Anwar has been fine about the survival stuff, so maybe she will be too? 'We just had these rules that we needed to follow,' I finally say.

'Trust no one? What about each other?'

I falter. Really the rule meant that Sylvia and I should only rely on the two of us, but surely now I could include Angharad and Anwar too? 'Well, I guess we can trust each other,' I say. 'I think.'

'I don't think they would be able to keep that secret, that there were a lot more people who were ill in the hospital. But I suppose there's only one way of finding out – we'll have to go to the hospital,' says Angharad.

'Angharad! Billy!' Julie calls over to us in a sing-song way. 'There you are! Come and see this – it's really fun.'

There's a dark wall laced with a chemical that reacts to light and so you can use the torch on your phone to write words and draw pictures that fade away as soon as you have made them. It's like having a sparkler that you can use over and over again. Julie and Steve are drawing squiggles and lines and laughing away.

'Come on, you two,' Steve says. 'Have a go!'

Angharad looks over at our parents and then back to me, with a small smile on her face.

'What do you think – shall we have a break from predicting the apocalypse for five minutes?' she asks.

'All right,' I say, smiling back. 'But only for five minutes.'

We draw swirls and scribbles with our phones and draw large looping lines around each other. I'm having so much fun that I start to forget myself and everything that's happened, but then I think I see a flash of grey. It rushes past us, in the distance.

I drop my phone as I spot it but when I look around there's no one grey, it's just normal people with normal-coloured skin doing normal things. I try to push the thought of the fallen man out of my mind.

Angharad hands me my phone from the floor.

'Are you okay?' she asks me. 'Did you see something?'

'No, I don't think so. I'm not sure.'

We step out from the photon wall and I spot immediately what I saw. There's a dressing-up stand and someone's wearing a sort of cloak made out of a dull silver material. I point it out to Angharad. 'It was only that,' I tell her.

I try to take a deep breath but something inside me won't completely relax.

'How about we get some pizza?' Julie suggests when we get outside and we all murmur in agreement. We drift from the museum towards the harbourside walking as a pack: Steve and Angharad lead the way, Julie and I walk at the back.

'Did you enjoy that, Billy?' Julie asks me.

I nod, trying not to remember the feeling of dread as I glimpsed the grey body rushing past us. Instinctively my hand reaches for my pocket survival kit in my jacket but my fingers close around nothing; the solid shape of the tin is missing.

I check the other pocket, I check again. I look on the ground, I look behind me.

'Have you lost something?' Julie asks.

'I've got to go back,' I say.

'Steve – wait up – Billy's left something at the museum.'

'What is it, Bill?' Steve says. 'Maybe we can go and pick it up tomorrow. We're almost at the restaurant now.'

'No! I need it now,' I say. I search again through my pockets even though I know they are quite empty. I hear the heavy exhale of a sigh, and without even having to look up, I'm sure it's coming from Steve. I feel it too. It snakes around my shoulders, an ache I cannot ignore.

'Billy, what is it that you've lost?' Steve asks.

I can't tell him.

I can't let him know about the survival kit.

My mind races with what else I could have left there which would be so important.

But then Angharad makes the decision for me. She simply pulls me along with her and starts running back.

'We'll see you at the pizza place,' she shouts over her shoulder. 'Get a table!'

When we get back to We The Curious, they're starting to close up but they let us dash up to the photon wall where I am sure I dropped it. Angharad points at the tin lying on the floor at an angle.

'Is that it?' she asks.

I run forward and grab the pocket survival kit and shove it deep into my pocket.

'What is it?' she asks, breathless from running. 'What's so important?'

'You won't tell my dad? Or your mum?'

'I won't,' she says straightaway.

'It's a pocket survival kit. I just made it and it's got things we might need for an emergency.'

'What kind of things?'

'Like . . . matches and fishing line . . . just some things . . .'

Angharad wrinkles up her nose just the tiniest bit, making me think she thinks I'm crazy for doing it. 'Why can't you tell your dad?'

I take a deep breath.

'Steve's funny about things like this because of my mum. She's the one who taught me about this kind of thing and he thinks it's bad for me. He thinks that she's made up why it's so important – because she's sick. It's like that book that I was hiding on the first day we met – I have to keep things secret from him because he won't understand.'

'Your dad did go a bit funny when you mentioned your mum the other day.'

'Yes – he doesn't believe in any of it. He hates me mentioning it because he thinks that it means I'm sick like he thinks my mum is. She's . . . she's in hospital, you see. That's where we went to see her, on Sunday.'

The words catch in my throat and I suddenly feel tears

building out of nowhere. I blink them furiously away.

'Well,' Angharad says quickly, taking care not to look at me in the eye. 'I think it's good to be ready. Especially if we're right about the fallen man and people getting sick. I won't say anything to anyone. But we're going to have to come up with an excuse for coming back.'

I haven't got an answer.

'Money!' Angharad says all of a sudden. 'Say that you dropped ten pounds or something and you were really worried Steve would be cross. They won't ask you any more about that.'

'Do you think that will work?'

'I'm certain of it. Adults worry about money.'

I try to tell myself that everything is going to be all right as we walk out of We The Curious. But then I catch sight of the grey sweep of the dressing-up material as we pass it.

Be ready, I correct myself. Always be ready.

HOW TO GET INFORMATION (FROM MEDICAL STAFF)

Anwar and I see Angharad locking her bike up just outside the hospital. I told Anwar that Angharad and I were going to try to find out more. We'd made a plan on our way back to the pizza place last night to meet here after school. Anwar insisted he come along too.

'That's her,' I tell him.

'Hi,' she says shortly when she sees us. Her eyes look a little puffy, and she's not standing as tall as she normally does, as though the air has gone out of her a bit.

'Are you okay?' I ask.

'Yes,' she says in a short sort of way which I know means that she's not really.

'Did something happen . . .'

'I'll tell you later,' she says to me, glancing towards Anwar.

'Um, okay. Well, this is Anwar,' I tell her and then I turn to Anwar. 'This is Angharad.'

They eye each other up but don't actually say hello. Then Anwar looks past Angharad as though she's not even there and

Angharad's eyes are on the floor, blinking something away. They're both acting so differently to how they are when I normally see them that I don't know what to say. But when neither of them speaks, I try to fill the silence.

'So . . .' I say. 'Shall we just go in then?'

There's another awkward pause.

Finally Anwar speaks. 'So do you have a plan then? Does anyone know which ward the group of people were on?'

Angharad and I both shake our heads.

'We really just want to see if there are more sick people than normal,' I say. 'If the group of people that met the fallen man can make other people ill, that should be spreading through the hospital pretty quickly.'

'Well, maybe we don't have to go in to see that,' Angharad says, pointing to the hospital entrance.

There are a few people waiting outside in wheelchairs and a couple of nurses wearing blue overalls walk through the doors chatting. There's nothing to suggest that things are out of control.

'But now that we're here, we should take a closer look, shouldn't we?' I say. I look over to Angharad. Something's wrong with her. This was her idea and she's been the one pushing me to do things all along, but now it's like she doesn't even want to be here.

'I guess . . .' she says and then, as though she can't help herself, she starts suggesting ideas. 'We could try and find the doctors and nurses who looked after that group. Maybe even find out if *they're* okay because they would have been with them the most. If anyone's going to have been infected, it's them.'

'But we mustn't get too close to them,' I remind them. 'In case they *are* infected and they infect us.'

'Maybe we don't have to go inside,' Anwar says quickly. 'Maybe seeing the hospital is just like normal, is enough.'

'Why don't you stand watch outside?' I suggest. 'We won't be long.'

'Stand watch?' Anwar says.

'If loads of ambulances turn up,' Angharad says. 'We'll need to know so we can get out. Or if you see a Grey.'

'A Grey?' I question.

Angharad turns towards me a little. 'That's what I thought we could call them. Greys. The people that are transformed, when their skin turns grey.'

'Yeah, if you see any Greys, then ring us straightaway,' I say to Anwar.

'How will I know if I see one?'

'You'll know,' I tell him.

The hospital hums with beeps and the steady rhythm of low-toned voices.

'It all looks pretty normal, don't you think?' I say to Angharad quietly as we walk by the person on reception who yawns loudly as we go past.

Angharad nods.

We head for the lifts and when we're in there we look at the long list of names for all the different wards and floors of the hospital.

'Where do you think we should go?' I say. I want to ask her if she's okay but she's studying the map of the hospital, her hair swept over her face, and so I get the feeling she doesn't want to talk.

'I'm not sure.' Angharad reads the list. 'Maybe Intensive Care . . . does that sound like where they would have been taken?'

'Let's try it,' I say, jabbing the lift button.

When we get to the right floor, we follow signs and walk down corridors. I try not to think about the last time I was in a hospital, when I saw Sylvia, but it keeps returning to me. My stomach twists and turns at the thought.

'Are you all right?' Angharad asks me when I stop walking all of a sudden.

'Yes – it's just – being here, in a hospital, makes me think about my mum.'

'Do you want to go back?'

'No, it's okay. Let's keep going,' I say. We continue down the corridor.

'I tried to tell my best friend at school about the Greys,' Angharad says suddenly. 'But she didn't believe me. She told everyone else that I make things up to get attention. That's why I'm feeling funny today. Sorry if I'm being weird with you.'

'I guess it's hard to believe it when you haven't seen it,' I say gently, although I can't stop thinking of how Angharad backed me up to Julie and Steve when she hadn't actually seen the fallen man.

'But Anwar believed you right away, didn't he?'

'Well yes . . . but Anwar's my . . . I mean he would always believe me because . . . you know he's my best . . . Maybe this girl isn't really your best friend?' I end up saying.

Angharad scoffs and wipes something from her eye.

'Maybe. She's definitely not as good a friend as Anwar is to you. I need to find someone like Anwar, perhaps.' When I look again, she's staring steelily into the distance. 'What was it your mum would tell you? Trust no one?'

'Yes. But then you said that we should trust each other.'

'So maybe it's more, trust the people you can trust,' she says, screwing her face up. 'That sounds so cheesy. But I should have known better than to trust her, you're right – I don't think she is my best friend. Maybe I don't have one.'

I don't know what to say, so I'm a little bit relieved when I see that we've arrived at the Intensive Care Unit.

But the double doors are locked.

'Now how are we going to get in?' Angharad says, but I think it's more to herself than me.

Just then, some staff come out through the doors. A man and woman deep in conversation. They rush right past us.

'Let's wait until someone comes out who looks like they will talk to us,' Angharad says.

The doors swing open and a short man wearing a white coat marches out. 'Not him,' Angharad whispers.

After that a younger nurse walks out of the doors. She smiles when she sees us, the only one to have noticed us.

'Are you two all right? Are you looking for someone?' she asks.

Angharad speaks up straightaway. 'Our uncle's in there. Our parents said we couldn't come to see him but we just wanted to try.'

'Oh, I'm sorry, love, there are quite strict visiting hours for ICU. Maybe when he gets a bit better and he's moved to another ward, you could come back all together.'

Angharad goes on. 'It's just that we were worried because of those people who all got sick. The ones we saw on the news? We thought our uncle might have the same thing as they had.'

'Don't you worry about that,' the nurse says. 'That was all a bit of a mystery but touch wood – ' her fingers lightly touch the fuzz of her hair – 'we haven't had any more cases. What's your uncle's name?'

Angharad falters for just a second.

'Bob,' I say quickly. 'Bob Belvedere.'

'Hmm, I don't know him,' says the nurse. 'Maybe he's been moved out of ICU already. Come back with your parents during visiting hours and you might be able to see him.'

'Thank you,' we chorus as she walks away.

We turn to each other.

'So – no more cases,' says Angharad. 'Yet.'

HOW TO GET IN TROUBLE (AGAIN): PART I

My arms are outstretched and Bob runs from one hand, all along my arm, across my neck and across to the other arm.

Anwar and I have snuck in to visit him again because we want to try him on one of Anwar's new inventions for him. It's a sort of maze made out of different-sized tubes. It's massive and bulky and Anwar's dad had to drop us off at school in his taxi because it was too heavy to walk with. Our teacher Miss Watson tutted and raised her eyebrows when it kept toppling off the shelf we placed it on in the book corner. In the end she moved some things off a side table so we could store it there. It took both of us to carry it to the Year 3 classroom where Bob lives.

We hear someone's footsteps coming down the corridor and I freeze, bracing myself for a telling off like we had from Mr Belvedere on my first day, but it's the Year 3 teacher, Miss Pennyworth. She's carrying a huge pile of books that she drops on to one of the low tables with a thump.

'Can't keep away, Anwar?' she says when she sees us, smiling.

'I just miss Bob too much,' Anwar says back.

'You are his most devoted servant,' Miss Pennyworth says. 'I mean . . . apart from the time you tried to drown him.'

'He was never in danger, miss, honestly! Mr Belvedere just hadn't appreciated what a brilliant boat it was.'

'Well, no more watersports, okay? Now what have you made for dear old Bob today?' She seems genuinely interested in the maze and suggests that we time Bob to see how fast he does it in and then we can see if he improves with practice. She even gives us a stopwatch to use.

'I'll be back in ten minutes,' she tells us. 'And then you'll need to go outside, okay?'

'Yes, miss,' we mumble.

We try Bob in the maze a few times. The first time he doesn't seem that interested at all but when we drop some treats down he soon gets the idea. He scuttles along the tubes, his nose twitching this way and that.

'So what are you and Angharad going to do next about the Greys?' Anwar asks me, out of the blue.

'I don't know,' I say. 'I guess right now we just have to be prepared in case things get worse.' Then I say, a little awkwardly, 'Anyway, it's not just me and Angharad, it's you as well, you know.'

'I don't know. You were right about what you said when you first met her – she's not very friendly, is she?'

'She's a bit like that at first. And yesterday she was upset. Her best friend from school didn't believe her about the Greys and told everyone that she made up stories. She asked whether you believed me straightaway—'

'Of course I did!'

'I know, that's what I told her. I said you believed me, because you're . . . you know . . . you're my really good friend.'

Anwar punches me lightly on the arm. 'Billy,' he says, a wide grin spreading over his face. 'We're best friends, man.'

I can't stop myself from grinning. I feel a lightness growing inside me, I've never had a best friend before.

'And Angharad's okay, I suppose,' Anwar says, scooping Bob out from the end of the tube and delicately placing him at the beginning again. He disappears down a toilet-roll tunnel. 'I think I just thought you might prefer hanging out with her . . . than me.'

'No way,' I say. 'But it's nice to be friends with both of you . . .' As I speak the words I realize how much I mean them. Sylvia's drilled it into me for so long that I shouldn't trust anyone but finding people who want to support you feels so different. Unknown, but also kind of wonderful.

'Maybe Angharad can help out with one of our experiments too. We could do with someone else around if we're going to try and do the rocket launcher.'

'Yeah, I'll ask her,' I say. I can't stop a smile creeping over my face. I'm glad that Anwar and Angharad are getting on better now. It's weird to think that not that long ago even having one friend seemed impossible, and now I have two.

We're so lost in our conversation that we don't hear the sound at first.

It's a scratching sort of sound.

A clawing.

A scraping.

We think it's just Bob's paws scampering along the cardboard.

Then I glance up towards the window.

'Anwar!' I shout.

'What is—' He stops as he looks up at the window.

He sees.

He sees them.

I've never seen Anwar speechless before. His mouth drops open wide as he takes in what's causing the scratching noise.

They don't look quite human, their arms are elongated and spiral out from their bodies in all different directions. Their skin is dulled like leaden metal.

It's a group of Greys.

And they're clawing at the glass to get in.

HOW TO GET IN TROUBLE (AGAIN): PART II

'We have to go,' I say and start to stand, walking backwards to the door, not turning away from the window, not able to tear my eyes away from their sunken, steely faces.

But Anwar hasn't moved a muscle.

'Anwar, Anwar!'

'I have to wait for Bob,' he says. 'I'm not leaving him.'

I glance towards the cardboard maze and see that Bob's disappeared into a long tunnel section. I hold my breath.

One of the Greys closes its giant, clawed hand into a fist. It pulls its arm back slowly and then in one supple movement, pounds its fist hard on the glass. The window does not break but it rattles in its frame.

They strike the glass again. And again.

The Grey that's hammering on the window looks right at us.

Its face is puffed up, and deepens in shade as it looks at us. Then it opens its mouth and a terrible shriek is roaring from somewhere deep inside it. It's strangled and fierce and raw. I look again as the Grey plunges its fist against the glass once more and emits another screaming cry.

At first I can't see it but in the next moment, it is unmistakable: who the Grey used to be. It's lost most of its hair, but there are still the remnants of a bushy moustache above the grey arches of its lips. Its eyes peer out from hollow sockets, glinting stonily.

It's Mr Belvedere. He has been turned into a Grey.

I remember from this morning's assembly that he wasn't in and his class had a new teacher, a young man with floppy hair who didn't know which way the hall was. My eyes quickly scan over the other Greys but I don't recognize any of them, only Mr Belvedere.

On his fifth hit, the glass splinters. It's carved with cracks.

I turn desperately to the mouth of the tunnel, willing with everything for Bob to appear.

Mr Belvedere hits the glass again. This time it gives.

The sound of glass shattering across the floor rings in our ears just as Bob's twitching whiskers emerge from the end of the tunnel. Anwar grabs him and holds him close to his chest with both hands.

We run.

We almost collide with Miss Pennyworth who's running back towards her classroom.

'What happened? Did I just hear glass breaking?' Her eyes are wide with worry.

We yell at her to stop. We try to stop her going in, we tell her not to, but she runs past us anyway.

She disappears into the room.

I look at Anwar and he looks at me. Without us having to say anything we turn back and follow her in.

I don't know what we were expecting to do. I don't know how we thought that we could help. But when we rush back through the door, we only see Miss Pennyworth staring out at the broken wreckage of her window. The sunlight streaming past the jagged shards.

There are no Greys in sight.

'What happened?' she asks again.

'Did you see them?' I ask.

She turns to face us. 'See who?'

'The Greys,' I say and then I remember that this is just the name that Anwar, Angharad and I have made up. 'People who look like their skin's turned grey and they can't speak any more.'

'What are you saying?' she says. She sounds confused and lost. 'Boys, why did you break my window?'

'It wasn't us, miss, I swear,' Anwar says. 'There were these things outside, they were trying to get in, they broke the glass.'

'Things? And now these "things" have gone away? Anwar, I know you don't mean to get into trouble but you really don't help yourself when you make things up. And Billy . . . I don't know why you let him drag you into these things.'

'No, Miss Pennyworth, it's not like that,' I begin to say.

'Enough,' she says. 'Just enough. I should never have let you stay in the classroom by yourselves. I can't believe I thought that I could trust you. You are absolutely forbidden from being in here again. Put Bob back in his cage. I'm going to have to speak to Miss Watson and Mr Belvedere about what we need to do about this, but damaging school property is a very serious offence. And so is lying about it. Very serious.'

I raise my head when she mentions Mr Belvedere.

'I don't think Mr Belvedere is in today, miss,' I say.

But what I want to tell her is that Mr Belvedere is no longer Mr Belvedere any more.

HOW TO MAKE A PLAN

Angharad insists on writing everything down in the small spiral notebook that she now carries around with her all the time.

She's ripped out all the pages she'd written in before, so now it's just about the Greys and everything we've learned about them.

'Tell me again,' she says.

'So the Greys were scratching on the window—' Anwar says.

'How many?'

'Four?' I say.

'Five, I think,' Anwar says.

'Okay, I'll write four or five,' says Angharad. She jots it down in her notebook and then makes us repeat every detail of what happened at school, asking lots of questions along the way.

Steve has banned me from seeing Anwar because of what happened to the window but when we came to see Angharad and Julie today, I told Angharad about the ban and she said she had an idea.

'Mum, Steve,' she said. 'Would you mind if I showed Billy the city farm? He says he's never been.'

'Why don't we all go?' Steve suggested.

Angharad fixed her mum with a look and some sort of unspoken conversation passed between them.

'Actually, it would be nice for them to go together, don't you think, Steve?' Julie said. 'Good for them to have some time to get to know each other, without us getting in the way.'

Steve looked a bit disappointed but he agreed without a fight.

As soon as we left the house, Angharad turned to me and said, 'Okay, let's meet Anwar. I'll not say anything to anyone.'

I messaged him and he answered straightaway. We decided to meet in the main city library which is halfway between Anwar's house and Angharad's. We had to catch a bus to get there but Angharad said she'd keep an eye on the time so it doesn't seem like we've been gone for too long.

So now we're sitting across a table from each other, in a little corner that's hemmed in by bookshelves to avoid being overheard.

I'm glad that Angharad and Anwar seem to like each other much more now. It might have something to do with the fact that I told Anwar that it was Angharad's idea to come and meet him and Angharad saying, 'Well, we're a kind of team now, aren't we?'

Anwar smiled his big old grin when she said that.

'A team,' he said back, in agreement.

He doesn't even seem to get annoyed that she's asking so many questions.

'Interesting,' she says once she's satisfied she knows everything there is to know, peering down at all the tiny notes she's made. The words are cramped and filling up the page.

'So what shall we do next?' Angharad looks towards me. I can feel Anwar's eyes on me too.

I take a deep breath. 'Well, we've got to be vigilant. Really vigilant. I mean it's probably better that we avoid public places, really.'

'We can't not go to school though,' Anwar says. 'There's no way our parents would let us stay home.'

'You're right,' I say with a sigh. 'Until they understand how dangerous it is. I mean they just have no idea. We know they don't believe us at all at the moment. But if we have some—'

'Evidence!' Angharad finishes the sentence and slaps her hand on her thigh. 'We need some video footage of the Greys or something so we can show them!'

'But we don't want to get close to them, remember,' Anwar says. 'In case we get infected. So how do we video them?'

'Right,' I say.

'And we don't really know *where* they are,' Angharad adds.

'We could try the garages again? And if they are there, we could film them on our phones and keep as far away as we can?' I suggest.

'Let's go!' Angharad says, standing up. 'I'll text Mum and tell her that we're going to have lunch in the café at the farm or something, to buy us more time. Come on!'

Anwar stands up too and they both look over at me.

In that moment, despite the worry and feeling scared, a rush of excitement comes over me. It's a bit like I'm on one of my first adventures with Sylvia again, just the two of us, before things started to go bad.

'Let's go then,' I say and we rush from the library.

HOW TO COLLECT EVIDENCE

As we walk towards the garages, I can feel a prickling sensation climbing up my back. I can't stop looking around me in every direction, my eyes darting from place to place. Some old rubbish – a crisp packet and a balled-up chip wrapper – rustles in the long grass and my head jars at every sound. I feel hyper-aware of everything around me, like it's in full colour that I've never seen before.

We all have our phones out, ready to record, and we walk slowly in a line. Angharad had a few missed calls from Julie and so she texted her to say we'd run into her friends from school.

'That should buy us a bit more time.'

'Make sure your phones are on silent,' I say. 'We have to be quiet.'

We set off. Me in front, Anwar behind me and Angharad at the back, walking as quietly as we can. On the bus on the way here, I'd explained how Sylvia had taught me to walk so you make as little sound as possible. You have to walk in a slightly crouched position, and then place the toe of your foot down first. Then slowly, slowly you gently roll your foot towards your heel and on to the ground.

Fig. 10. – How to walk silently

Angharad takes some puffs of her inhaler before we set off, so her asthma won't start up again. We agreed not to speak from when we turned down the passageway and Anwar and Angharad know to mirror my every move; if I stop, they'll stop, if I yell run, they'll run. We've agreed to head back to Steve's, because it's closest, if things get out of hand.

We walk on in silence around the corner towards the old garages.

I stop for a moment and strain my ears to listen for any sound out of the ordinary. I can hear the wind in the trees from the gardens and there's something that's making a creaking sound but nothing to signal that we are not alone.

I take a few steps forward and then do the same again – just stop and listen and look.

It takes us a while to make any progress, moving like this, but I know it's not worth the risk to move any quicker.

I look back towards Anwar and Angharad. Their faces are drained of colour but they continue to fall into step behind me, holding their phones high in the air.

I face forward again. We're just a few paces away from where I saw the fallen man and where Ted was changed, so I move even more slowly. I'm just about to take another step when suddenly I hear a crackle, a footstep, the definite sound of something ahead of us.

As if they are just a blur, or a shadow, a Grey darts out in front of us.

'Run!' I roar. 'Run!'

HOW NOT TO BE BELIEVED

We sprint away from the garages without looking back. There are moments when I think that I feel a claw closing around my arm, something's breath hot on my neck. But it's only when we're back on the street that I let myself look back. It's only my imagination; there's nothing behind us.

We run to Steve's house and once we all tumble in I slam the door behind us.

It takes us a few moments to be able to speak. Angharad's breath comes in shallow, quick gasps.

'Did you see it?' I say.

Anwar nods but Angharad shakes her head.

'I was too far behind,' she says. 'When will I ever see one of them properly?'

'You don't want to,' Anwar tells her.

'Let's look at our phones,' I say. We examine the videos from all three of us, but only my phone caught it.

Except, well, it looks like what it is – a grey haze.

'It's a bit . . . blurry, isn't it?' Angharad says, scrunching her nose up as she plays it again.

'It was fast,' Anwar says. 'That's why it was a blur. I'm just glad that it didn't follow us.'

'Do you think it was Ted? Or the fallen man? Or someone else?' Angharad asks.

'I couldn't tell,' I answer.

At just that moment, there's the sound of a key in our front door and suddenly Steve is filling the doorway, blocking out all the light.

'I just can't trust you, Billy,' Steve says. He wrings his hands together and pulls his hair back against his skull. 'I told you I didn't want you spending time with Anwar, and you disobeyed me. Worse still, you dragged Angharad into this, too.'

'Mr G—' Anwar starts to say, but Steve cuts him off immediately.

'Please go home, Anwar,' he says in the coldest tone I've ever heard him use. 'Leave before I say something I'll regret.'

'It wasn't his fault,' I argue. 'Anwar's my friend. He was being my friend.'

'A fine friend,' Steve says. 'All he seems to do is get you into trouble.'

Anwar's large eyes are like puddles when he looks at me, I send him a silent apology with my eyes, and then he slinks out of the living room. A second later I hear the front door open and then close.

'Angharad, you're not blameless in this either,' Julie says.

She looks at Angharad and shakes her head. 'You lied. You didn't go to the farm. We went down there to surprise you, to buy you lunch, but when we checked with the staff, no one had even seen you. We even asked to look at their CCTV! We were about to call the police.'

'But Mu-um.'

'No, don't you "Mum" me,' Julie says in a bluster. 'You can't keep making these stories up, Angharad.'

'Show them, Billy. Show them your phone,' Angharad says, turning to me.

'What's on your phone?' Steve asks.

'Well,' I start. 'Anwar, Angharad and I all think something is happening, something big.' Steve opens his mouth to object but I rush on in a loud voice. 'And we know that you don't believe us, so we thought the best thing would be to try and catch one of the Greys on film so you could see for yourselves. That was what we were doing today.'

'A Grey?' Julie asks.

'That's just a name I came up with for them,' Angharad says. 'Because of their grey skin.'

Julie and Steve exchange a look, but Steve reaches out for my phone. They watch the video and then they look back at us.

'Do you see now?' Angharad says.

'To be honest, Angharad,' Steve says, 'all I can see is that you two are getting very good at making things up. But this elaborate game is over. We're out of patience.'

'We'd better go home,' Julie says. 'I don't think we'll be doing any of the things you wanted for your birthday now, Angharad. Liars don't deserve treats.'

Angharad opens her mouth as though she is about to scream but before any sound comes, fat tears spring from her eyes. They're so large, it's almost as though I can hear them slowly sliding over her cheeks.

I feel a heat growing and bubbling up in my body. It almost feels like vomit, stinging, hot and lashing.

'Why don't you believe us?' I want to shout at them, but instead my voice breaks and I realize that I'm crying too.

I'm angry but more than that, I'm upset that even now Steve thinks I'm lying. And now I understand why Sylvia felt she had to stop Steve visiting me.

Because what's the point of trying to get someone to believe you over and over again when they just won't listen?

HOW TO LOOK AT THE STARS

It's a clear night.

On a clear night, you must look at the stars.

That's what Sylvia always told me.

It says the same thing in *How to Survive*. That you need to look out on clear nights so you know the sky inside out, and then, when it's cloudy and you only see a few stars you can still use them to navigate.

On a clear night, you can trace the shape of the Big Dipper and find the two pointers of it, the stars named Dubhe and Merak. They point roughly towards the North Pole. Or you can look for the constellation Cassiopeia. It looks like an upside down 'W' and the star in its middle also points to the Pole Star.

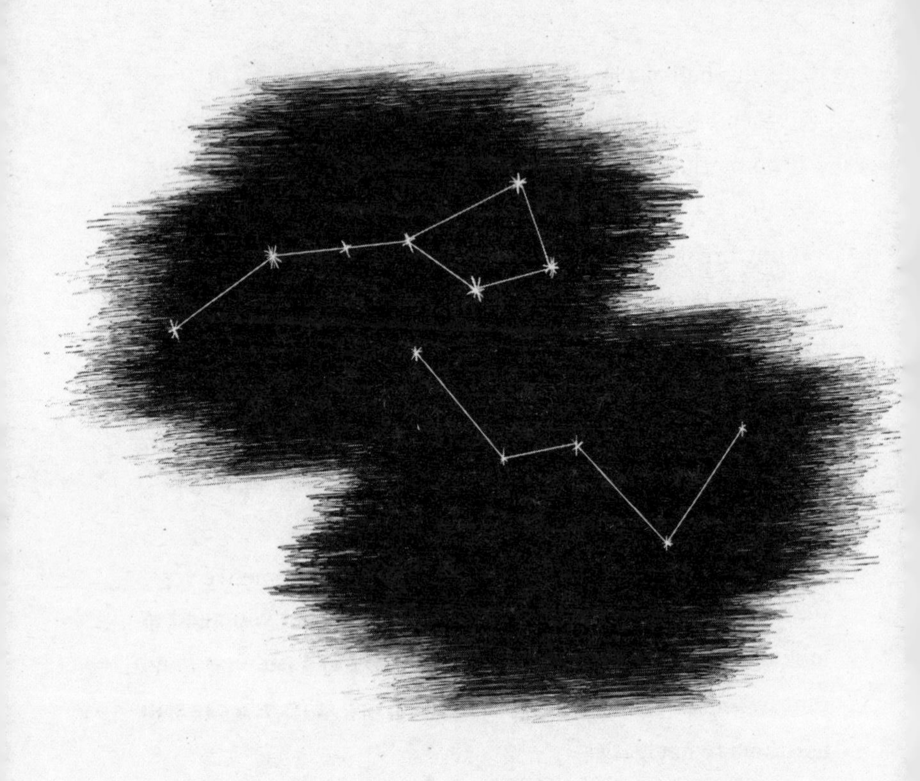

Fig. 11. – How to navigate using the stars

It's like I can hear the quiet, clear night ticking over outside and it's calling to me. I venture from my room and go quietly down the corridor, passing Steve's room as I do.

His bedroom is dark. I will probably be able to hear the whistle of his snores if I stay here long enough. I am just about to pass his doorway when I hear a voice coming from his room.

It's Julie. She's speaking quietly but in the still house, I can hear her clearly.

'Don't be too hard on him. Or yourself. I mean, Billy's been through a hell of a lot.'

When I hear my name, I can't help but lean into the door a little more. I hear the rustle of a duvet, the sound of Steve sighing.

'But breaking a window, being suspended,' Steve says. 'I mean he's been in trouble at school since day one. I wish he'd never met that Anwar. It's just one thing after the other.'

'I can't imagine what it's been like for him,' says Julie. 'He must miss his mum all the time. And be worried about her. How was she when you saw her? We haven't had the chance to talk properly about it.'

'Not good. She wasn't even awake the whole time we were there. Billy said she spoke to him when I wasn't there but I'm not even sure if that's true. She looked really out of it. I don't think she's even any better than she was when Billy first came to live here. At least she's safe there.'

'I'm sorry, love. It's hard on you, too.'

'I think I was in denial for a long time. Maybe I still am. Sylvia changed, I mean, she really changed after Billy was born.' Steve tries to keep his voice low but I hear it rising, almost in panic. 'I mean she was transformed.'

Change. Transformation. I think of a werewolf in a full moon. I think of skin ripping and turning inside out into chunks of dense grey fur.

'Everyone changes,' I hear Julie say. 'I mean, that's the deal . . . being a parent, it's life-changing.'

'But I don't mean like that,' Steve continues. 'Not like in

the normal way of becoming a parent – it was like Sylvia was possessed by it. By a single idea. By the thought that the world as we know it would end. I knew it was getting worse, each time I came to visit.'

'And she convinced Billy that it was all true?'

'He completely adores her. He'd believe Sylvia if she said the moon was made of cheese. But I thought he was getting better by living here with me, I thought he was starting to leave it behind him. But sneaking off, videoing "evidence" and personal survival kits! I *knew* it wasn't money he dropped at the museum. He was too frantic about losing it.'

'Angharad asked me not to tell you that. Billy told her that he knows he has to hide it from you.'

My hands had closed into two tight fists. All I needed was something to hit.

'You never really talk about her,' Julie goes on. 'Didn't she do all the survival stuff before Billy was born? Or did it all start afterwards?'

'Sylvia was always interested in it, liked being outdoors and camping, that kind of thing, but nothing like it turned into,' Steve says. 'I mean, she was just a different person before Billy was born, it took over somehow. But it wasn't that bad. I thought she was fine. That Billy was okay with her. It was when she lost her job at the lab that she really went into overdrive. It was like I didn't know her any more. She was a stranger. It had been hard to see Billy before, but then she cut me out completely. Talking about such crazy nonsense you wouldn't believe.' He sighs and the duvet rustles again. 'I think that's why I'm so worried about Billy. Hearing him talk like this, about people being infected, monsters lurking around garages – he sounds just like Sylvia.'

I think I hear Julie take a breath as though she is going to say something but at just that moment, the floorboard below me squeaks as I shift my weight ever so gently.

'Did you hear that?' Steve says.

As quickly as I can, I turn back to my bedroom and throw myself into bed. I don't hear Julie and Steve get up, in the end, but I don't go back to listen again.

I don't want to hear any more.

I don't want the knowledge that rolls around my head now:

I can't trust Angharad. Sylvia was right, you can't trust anyone but yourself.

And that I am the reason. I am what made Sylvia sick.

PART 2

DAY 1

HOW IT BEGINS

We can see everything.

We are high up, in Cabot Tower, and we can see everything.

It's red brick, the tower, up on a hill in a park right near the centre of town. It used to be closed but they reopened it on some days and you can climb up it and see the view.

From up here you can see the river that snakes round and the boats sitting tall within it. What Steve likes best about Bristol, he tells me, is that even from the centre of the city, where we are now, we can see the edges of it – we can see where the city turns to green – fields and woods and countryside and space. He loves the tower because from up here, you can see it all.

Julie and Steve have clamped their arms around each other as they look over the view. I wander round and round the small walkway and Angharad trails behind me. She's been trying to talk to me all morning. Each time I've ignored her and get as far away from her as I can, but in the confined space of the tower there's nowhere to hide.

'Billy!' Angharad hisses. 'What's wrong? Has something happened?'

She won't give up asking me.

'Fine then,' she spits. 'If you won't speak to me then I won't speak to you.'

But in a few moments, she's back beside me. 'What is it?' I won't look at her face but her voice sounds shaky. 'Has something happened to your mum? I *have* to tell you something.'

I stomp away to another corner.

We had to climb many narrow steps to get to the top. Voices echoed in the winding stone corridor and some boys behind us started shouting as though to test how loud their voices would go. I tried to ignore the fact that Angharad jarred at every sound.

I look over at Julie and Steve. They hold hands as they peer out over the side of the tower, they could be one being, the way they are pressed into each other.

I try to walk away so I don't have to look at them but then I almost run into Angharad. For a moment, I see her face light up, thinking that I'm coming over to speak to her but then, when she sees my face, hers falls too.

'How are you two doing?' Steve says, suddenly appearing next to us. 'It's beautiful up here, isn't it?'

'It really is,' says Julie, materializing at his side.

'Shame that the weather isn't a bit nicer,' Steve says, leaning into Julie. We were the only people up there now; the other people had already made their way back down the teetering staircase. 'We'll have to come back another time, when it's sunny.'

'Can we go home now?' Angharad asks through clenched teeth.

'In a minute,' Julie says. 'Just take a look at it, will you? People have been waiting for this view for years, all the time that the tower was closed. Sometimes you have to take opportunities that come your way.'

'That's right,' Steve says, and he reaches for Julie's hand and grins at her.

Angharad makes a face and starts to walk away from them, to another corner, but as she turns to go, she suddenly stops.

She stops with such a jolt, I think that something has fallen in front of her and she's had to freeze to avoid being hit.

But in the next moment, Angharad sticks out her arm and points desperately to something in the distance.

'Look! Can you see it?' I hear her say, although her words are so garbled that she can barely get them out of her mouth. 'There's a Grey—'

Before I can answer, before I can even look, the sound of a scream splits through everything.

It cuts through Julie and Steve who release each other in a beat and look frantically over the side of the tower. Angharad sways a little as she hears it but then she's by my side and I'm glad she's next to me because the scream pierces through me too. I feel suddenly empty and yet at the same time, it's as though every thought I've ever had is rushing around my body;

I'm spinning and I'm toppling over inside of myself.

As quickly as it started, the scream dies away, disappearing into the distance, as though it never was. I let myself think, for just a single second, that perhaps the scream had nothing to do with what we've seen happening. It could have been to do with something else – a car almost hitting someone perhaps, a small child running into danger. It might have nothing whatsoever to do with the Greys.

But then there's another scream.

And then another.

'Look!' Angharad points. 'Over there!'

There's a surge of people running along the street. They are running as though they are a wave that is growing and gathering water, surging and rolling and falling forward under its own weight. Some people fall amongst them. They don't get up.

'Steve.' Julie's voice sounds like something sinking. I turn and follow her gaze.

There are people who are spasming violently on the ground; they move as though they have volts of electricity moving through their bodies. Their limbs extend and drop as though they are something separate to them.

It's what I saw happen to Ted but it's more violent and furious this time – and it's everywhere.

Their hands grow out like claws, grasping and slicing through the air. The people grow pale, and paler still, and then a surge of grey flushes through their skin. When they move, their whole body undulates and their legs seem to flow beneath them. And when they make a noise, it's as though their vocal chords have been torn out and what is left is ragged and broken.

We all look away as they jolt and shudder, as though if we can't see it, then it will stop happening.

But when we look back, all we see is grey. This is definitely happening. And, deep down inside, I can't help but think that at least Steve will believe me now.

HOW TO FIND A WAY OUT

We didn't bring a car. We'd caught a bus into the centre.

And as we stand at the top of the tower and watch the scene below, the running people, the mayhem, the transformations, that's what I can't help thinking about. We don't have a car. If we leave the tower now we will be out in the open, out in the screams, with nowhere to hide. We aren't prepared . . . we aren't prepared. I have failed to follow the first Rule.

The others have slumped down behind the pillars of the walkway. Julie's sitting between Steve and Angharad and she holds one of their hands in each of hers. Angharad sees me staring over the edge and lets go of her mum to come over to me.

'Don't look any more,' she says and pulls me down so I too am sitting with my back to all that is happening beneath us.

'I know you're not speaking to me because . . . well, I don't know why . . . but what are we going to do?' she whispers to me and when I look at her face, I realize that she really thinks that I might have an answer.

'I'm not speaking to you,' I whisper back, still angry despite what's going on beneath us, 'because I know I can't *trust* you.'

Angharad thinks for a moment and then she speaks very quietly. 'You know I told my mum about your survival kit – she promised she wouldn't say anything.'

'You promised *me* you wouldn't say anything.'

'I'm sorry, I know.'

'You gave me such a hard time about how important your word is to you – remember, you said that you'd never speak to me again if I ever shouted at you. You said that when you promised something you meant it.'

'I know. It's just, Mum was going on about you getting in trouble at school and Steve being so worried about you, I was trying to . . . I was just trying to stick up for you. I tried to tell her that stuff with your mum wasn't exactly how Steve was saying it, and it just kind of came out about the survival kit and that time at the museum. I'm sorry, I really am. I shouldn't have told her, but I thought it would help. I'm on your side, you know.'

We're silent for a moment.

I look around. The four of us are alone. It is fairly safe being up here, I think – unless the Greys start to climb up the winding staircase.

'I'm really sorry I told my mum, okay?' Angharad continues. I can feel her reach out and take my hand in hers. It feels warm and solid and for a moment, it makes me think of Sylvia's hand in mine. 'You can't keep being angry with me. Not now. Not with what's happened. I promise if you tell me a secret again, I'll keep it.'

I raise my eyebrows and Angharad says quickly, 'I know, I know. I know you don't believe my promises any more. But Billy, please. We have to get out of here and that means we have to work together.'

'I know,' I say quietly.

'We can't risk being down there, wandering the streets,' Julie says, her voice getting higher with every word. 'If we meet someone who's . . .' She doesn't finish the sentence. Julie and Steve are trying to decide what to do. They're trying to keep each other calm. I can't help but notice the fierce way their hands clench each other but listening to them run through their options, the terrifying realization that they have no plan, that they don't know what to do, is quite clear. I can't help but think of Sylvia who would know what to do, who would have a clear plan.

'Is this what you saw before?' Julie asks us. 'The man by the garages? The . . . Grey?'

'Yes,' Angharad says. She actually stamps her feet as she says it. 'We *don't* make things up. Billy saw them at his school too.'

'The broken window,' Julie says quickly.

'We didn't break it,' I tell her. 'Anwar and I were attacked in the classroom by Greys. They smashed the window trying to get in.'

I'm aware that Steve's staring at me but I don't want to meet his gaze.

'Why didn't you tell me that?' he asks.

When I don't answer, Angharad speaks for me.

'Would you have believed him if he had? No, because you haven't believed *anything* he's told you about the Greys this whole time. You just think Billy makes stuff up.'

Steve looks like he wants to speak but there's something that's stopping him. Perhaps he can't find the right words.

'Listen,' Angharad says all of a sudden. 'It's stopped, it's quiet.'

I stand and look over the side of the stone railing. Angharad's right: there's no commotion, there's no shouting or screams. There's no one to be seen.

The silence feels more terrifying than the panic.

At least when we heard the noise, we knew where the Greys were but now nowhere feels safe. There is no marker of where anyone or anything is.

'I'm going to call the police,' Julie says and she reaches for her phone. 'Maybe they can come and get us.' She raises her eyebrows hopefully at us.

She dials three nines and holds the phone to her ear, but we can hear the dull bleeping tones. She tries again and again.

'I can't get through,' she says.

'We could go out to the square and break into one of the cars there,' Steve suggests.

'Do you know how to do that?' Julie asks.

'I – I – I've seen it in movies.'

'Right... so maybe we need to work out the best way we can

walk home?' Julie says.

They start discussing a route that should be quieter – a back road where we might find cover – but their voices tremble a little as they picture it.

I think of Sylvia again and I can almost imagine she is here, I can almost see her profile shimmering in the air. I picture her face as it would whir through different possibilities, weighing up what to do. This is what she taught me to do. All the Survival Rules reverberate round my head but I distil them down into just one: *take action.*

I reach for my phone and send a message to Anwar. If he gets it, then I know he and his dad will come in the taxi. I slide the phone into my pocket but I keep a hand resting on it so I will feel the vibration if he writes back. I don't mention what I've done to the others, I'm not sure it will work and I don't want to get their hopes up yet.

Angharad shivers although it's not cold. She looks pale and tired. I want to tell her that it will be okay, but I don't know if it will. I could ask her if she's all right but it's clear that she's not. So instead, I say nothing.

Then I feel the buzz of my phone in my jacket and I'm reading it, I'm reading how we will be saved.

Steve and Julie are so engrossed in their debate over the best route to take, that even when I approach them, they don't break off. Their voices are becoming higher and higher, more ragged with every breath.

'Steve?' I say. 'Steve?'

'Hold on, Billy,' Steve says. 'Just wait a minute. Julie and I are trying to work out how to get us out of here.'

'I know a way,' I tell them. 'I know a way out.'

HOW TO USE A HELIOGRAPH: PART II

Angharad leans out of one corner of the tower. Her braids fall forward making her beads clatter into one another and I'm reminded of the first time we met.

'They're almost here,' I tell everyone, reading the last message that Anwar sent me. 'They've just turned off Park Street.'

'Ask them to beep their horn, so we know when they arrive,' Steve says.

'No,' Julie says quickly. 'We don't want to draw attention to where they are.'

My phone buzzes again with a new message from Anwar.

'They've had to move somewhere else – there were people in the square or something – they're going to come in from another direction.'

'Why would people stop them from parking?' Julie says.

'Maybe they want to get into the car?' Angharad suggests.

'We don't know what's going on down there right now,' Steve says.

Suddenly a shriek fills the air. There's the sound of a police siren. It blares and pierces but its everyday familiarity is comforting, it's a sign of life. But then we hear a crash, a sharp defeat, and once again, there's silence.

I check my phone but there's no message from Anwar. My fingers fidget. I want to ask him – Where are you? What's happening? – but I know that he will message when he can.

Moments later, my screen lights up.

'What does he say?' Steve asks.

I read it twice through so I don't misunderstand it.

'They've had to park a little way away. Anwar is coming to get us to take us to the car.'

'Anwar?' Steve repeats. 'No, tell him to stay with his dad. It doesn't seem safe down there, so he shouldn't get out of the car. We'll find another way.'

I write back immediately, I tell him to stay, I tell him to go home, but he doesn't reply.

Steve paces the small area at the top of the tower. There is nowhere to go.

Julie, Angharad and I keep watching from above, our eyes searching for any sign of movement.

Then, I see something flashing from one of the windows of a building a little way away.

'That's him!' I cry and point to the light. 'That's him!'

'How can you be sure?' Steve asks, striding back to us. He peers at the flashing from the building.

'He's using his heliograph,' I tell him. 'We made them together – I taught him how to use it.'

'Heliograph?' Steve says, but his face drops as he says it. I can tell he knows the word, but I guess the last time he heard anyone use it, it was coming from Sylvia's mouth.

'What's a heliograph?' Julie asks me.

'It's a way of signalling using sunlight – I taught Anwar how to use a mirror to do it,' I tell her.

'But why doesn't he just message you?' Steve asks.

'I don't know – maybe his phone ran out of battery or maybe it's easier to show us where he is this way . . . I don't know, but that's Anwar, I'm sure of it. Let's go.'

Angharad is the only one who is listening to me. She looks at me expectantly and walks over to the stairs. She seems so anxious to get off this roof that I wouldn't be surprised if she just kicked off from the ground and flew away.

'Come on, Mum,' she says. 'We can't stay here. Anwar is down there, just like Billy says.'

Julie looks at Steve whose forehead is ridged.

'Anwar is here and his dad can drive us out of here,' I urge. 'They are our only chance to get away without meeting someone who's been infected.'

'Billy's right. We've got to go now,' Angharad says.

Steve and Julie look as though they are searching each other's faces for another answer but when they find none, they turn to follow us.

We walk down the steps of the tower silently. There's none of the shouting and shrieking that we heard on the way up. Those moments feel a long time ago, so long ago that it's difficult to imagine that they even happened. The steps twist round and round, on and on, in a spiral of darkness. Though I know it has an end, I wonder, as we take those steps, if we will ever make it to the bottom.

I'm leading the way and Angharad falls into step behind me. I know that she's watching me carefully because each time I stop if I hear the slightest sound, she freezes too and warns Julie and Steve in a quiet whisper.

'Almost there,' I murmur behind me when I can see light ahead of us.

I feel Angharad's hand reach out and touch my shoulder.

'Let's stop for a moment,' she whispers. 'In case there's anyone there.'

I nod back at her.

We hold our breath as we look out through the doorway.

The day outside looks both sunny and dull all at once; dark clouds hang down low but a bright sunshine beats, almost as though it is a spotlight and the city, its stage.

There's no sign of movement.

I look over to Angharad. She gives me a small thumbs-up and signals to Julie and Steve to follow. They shuffle behind us, their faces pinched and scared in a way I have not seen before. It doesn't feel like they are the grown-ups any more.

I lead the way from the tower and then we are out, we are out in the park, the silent, deserted park that looks sunny and cheerful but feels anything but.

I am missing the sounds of other people – the couples who chat non-stop and preen each other like birds, the child that screams with glee and then just as suddenly from fright. All the talking on the phones about nothing really at all.

I can't see Anwar's flashing any more. Hoping that this is because Anwar is still directing his heliograph towards the top of the tower, rather than anything else, I make my way to the building that we saw his signal from.

'Are you sure it's this way, Billy?' Steve asks, drawing up next to me.

I don't answer him and just beckon everyone on. I know we don't have much time, that we can't stop to talk.

When we reach the building I speed up a little more, I hear the others do the same. When we get to the door we run in without looking back.

The building feels deserted, everywhere feels like that really, but I think there must be many pairs of eyes watching us, that the city must now be full of waiting and hiding and wondering and hoping.

'Anwar!' I call out up the stairwell. 'Anwar! Anwar!' After the silent walk from the tower, my voice comes from my mouth like a siren.

At first there is no sound other than the echo of my voice. We are in what looks like an office building. Its reception is laid in creamy, shiny marble and my shouts bounce off the walls and back towards us in a loop.

'Anwar!' I shout again. 'Anwar!'

But there's no answer.

I feel Steve's hand on my shoulder. I turn to him and see his face is set in lines. Behind him, Julie stands defeated too. Their shoulders have drooped, their feet turned inwards and their faces are masks of what they once were. They won't look at me. Their eyes stay fixed on the ground as though they are looking for something they have lost there.

'It was a good try,' Steve is saying. 'We had to try.'

But then Julie starts to cry. She tries to hold it in, but it's like she can't help it.

'What are we going to do?' Her voice is full of worry and fear and despair all mixed up together. They bleed into each other, feeding one another, growing larger and larger and larger.

'It's okay, Mum,' Angharad says, going to her. But I see from the way her eyes dart around the empty room that she thinks that we've made a mistake too. Have I let them all down?

Steve goes to comfort Julie too, stretching his arm around her.

'I'm sorry,' I say, but I am speaking too quietly or perhaps everyone else is too loud because no one hears me. No one can hear me.

'I was sure . . .' I begin to say, but I don't want to keep speaking. What I want to say doesn't matter any more, it won't change anything. It won't move the slippery guilt that coils around me, that is tightening around my heart. It won't alter the fact that I've exposed us to more danger with no clear escape. My mind races with this single thought, that after all my training I've got it wrong. I've let Sylvia down. I've let everyone down.

'Should we hide here? Or should we leave?' Julie's voice is shaky and her breath is catching in a frantic, darting way, although she tries to conceal it. 'Steve? What do we do?'

Steve takes a deep breath.

'I hear something!' Angharad says suddenly. 'Someone's coming!'

There's the sound of footsteps squeaking on the stairwell. We have no time to hide as they thunder down towards us.

'Billy!' I hear. 'Billy!'

It's Anwar, he's flying down the stairs and past us.

He moves so fast, his feet don't seem to touch the ground.

He moves so fast, I wonder if I am imagining him.

'Come on, we've got to get to my dad!' he yells. His eyes are fixed ahead of him in a way that makes me think that he doesn't want to look back, that he can't possibly turn to see what's behind him.

He grabs on to one of my hands as he passes me, to jolt us from our stupor at seeing him. I'm relieved to feel that he is real. But then I feel a cold dread stiff in his fingers, I can feel his fear and suddenly I'm afraid too.

So we run with him. We run from the office building, out again into the silent, sunlit streets. The guilt that hung over me shrugs off me with each step we take towards safety. I wasn't wrong. Anwar came. My best friend came as I knew he would.

Anwar streaks ahead, turning down alleyways and through back streets. We've let go of each other now, running as fast as we can, our arms pumping at our sides. I take no notice of where we are going or what we are passing but just follow his snaking back and so when he stops quite suddenly at the end of an alley, I almost crash into him.

I'm about to ask him why he's stopped, because I can't see his dad anywhere, when I see it.

There, just lying ahead of us.

A body on the floor.

HOW (NOT) TO LOSE IT WHEN THERE'S A GREY RIGHT IN FRONT OF YOU

'Don't move,' Steve says, although no one is even considering taking a step further. All of us stand paralysed.

The body is quite still – it's lying face down on the ground – and if it weren't for what I've seen of the Greys, I wouldn't fight the urge to run up to whoever it is and help them up. But I know that just because this body is on the ground, doesn't mean it won't get up and be a Grey after all.

Julie takes a few steps forward and I see that she is fighting this impulse too. Her fingers quiver and her eyes fix upon the body, as she decides whether to help or not.

'Julie – no,' Steve hisses. 'Come back.'

She looks back at him. 'It's all right,' she mouths and takes another step forward.

Suddenly there's a hand in mine, gripping it tightly. I look down and see it's Angharad's. It makes me feel a tiny bit better to feel her fingers clasped around mine. I am able to look at the body without feeling that I might fall over; the world has been able to right itself a little.

The body is blocking our path out of the alley to the road. We would need to walk right next to it to keep going.

I scan our surroundings. I have to make sure that I don't miss a thing. When I turn to look behind us, the only way out without passing the body, I see there's a shadow approaching in the distance. Another Grey headed right for us.

'Behind us,' I manage to say. 'There's one coming. We don't have a choice. We have to go forward. We have to go round . . . the body.'

I force myself to take a step forward.

The person was once wearing a fuchsia-coloured suit but it's been torn away from behind and so we can see bare skin and the nodules of their spine rising almost like spikes from their back. The flesh has lost its pinkness, its shade is somewhere closer to grey. It looks cold to touch. As soon as I think this, it's almost like it grows colder as I watch, that the grey is sweeping across the surface and becoming harder and duller and darker.

Julie takes another few steps forward. She's right next to the body now.

'Keep going.' The words are on my lips as the body suddenly convulses in an almighty jerk.

It is so violent that it's as though it is levitating. It rises off the ground for just a few seconds and then crashes down with such force that I wonder if it will simply break.

Then it does it again.

Julie watches in horror as the body flails beside her.

Someone whimpers. I'm confused because it's coming from the wrong direction; that sound, laced in pain, should be from the mouth of this person who's thrashing in front of us, but it's coming from beside me. It's Angharad, who now looks away and cannot bear to watch what we are witnessing. I grip her hand even more tightly and feel hers, in return, clamp into mine.

The body is now shuddering in deep, jolting waves. An arm flails out and almost hits Julie but she moves out of the way just in time.

I turn. The Grey down the alley has moved closer still. It seems to flow towards us, supple and sinuous. I can't stop myself from thinking of a dancer propelling itself through the air, there's something so graceful and agile about the way the Grey moves. Anwar spots me looking and notices it too, although everyone else is fixated on the body blocking our path.

'We have to go round,' I say again but even though I know that's what we need to do, I can't make myself take another step forward. Each time I try to plot a path past the body, it flails in another direction, blocking me completely.

'Get behind me,' Steve says. He stands in front of Anwar, Angharad and me and pushes us back. Julie steps next to Steve, joining him in making a wall. 'Run,' Steve tells us. 'Hide. We'll follow on.'

'There's a Grey coming,' Anwar says. 'There's nowhere to run. We're trapped.'

'I'm not leaving you,' I hear myself say to Steve. I know it doesn't make sense, because as Anwar has pointed out, there's no way out, but I need to say it anyway.

'Then we have to go this way. Make a run for it,' Steve says, pointing past the body to the road as he finally sees the grey shape behind us approaching like a shadow. He takes a shaky step forward but it's too late.

The body, the person, the half-person, the half-body, it has started to rise.

It curls up to standing. I think of a fern leaf unfurling, the shell of a snail uncoiled.

One moment, its head is thrashing on the ground and the next it's upright and tall. I watch the body in front of us inspect their hand, their arm, the crook of their elbow, as though it's only seeing them for the first time.

For a few moments, it doesn't seem to even really notice us. Then it takes a step towards the road, extending its leg outwards in one single graceful movement. Maybe it hasn't seen us and it will keep going, keep moving away from us. My eyes are fixed on its legs, willing them to extend out once more towards the road. We hold our breath, we don't move an inch. Our only slight movement is that of our fingers as we grasp one another's hands tightly. My other free hand is back in Anwar's, who looks at me, his eyes wide and buggy. I can read his thoughts from his face: he can't believe that this is happening, he can't believe this is real. We had both seen the Grey in the garages, but this is something else. I feel the same myself and staring at this being doesn't make it seem any truer.

It takes another stride away from us so it's standing on the road now. If it keeps moving then our way out will be clear.

Steve turns round to me and makes a gesture with his hand to follow him. I shake my head furiously, trying to tell him not to make a move yet, it's too soon. But he steps forward. Even though I can tell he's trying to step gently, his foot lands heavily on the ground, it grinds into the stone just a little. Enough to make a sound.

Then the Grey looks up. It sees us.

The skin around its face has grown haggard now, making folds around its eyes. Its eyes peer out at us and make me think of endless, bottomless holes, a tunnel that I could fall down but never exit. All I see is emptiness.

Now it takes a step back towards us and when it opens its mouth, a sound that isn't human pierces the air. Angharad releases her grip of me to clamp her hands tightly over her ears.

We huddle together. We grow closer and smaller.

The Grey moves towards us again and then reaches out as though it is pointing us out. It bellows another noise that I feel as a shudder, ridged and sharp as though it is something I can touch.

We turn away from it but now the Grey coming down the alleyway is almost on us. We shrink back into each other as much as we possibly can but there's nowhere else to go. When we turn back to the first Grey, its clawed hand is still pointing towards us.

'We can't let it touch us,' I hear Angharad whisper through clenched teeth.

It leans forward, it's only steps away from us now, and I close my eyes.

I wait for the feel of its touch.

I can sense it amongst us, landing like stones: the realization that it's too late, that here, we have reached the end. The infection will be in us and we might die from it.

Or we will never be the same again.

HOW TO SAY GOODBYE TO THE FIRST FRIEND THAT YOU'VE EVER REALLY HAD

We hear the car before we see it.

It roars towards us.

For a second I wonder if it will hit the edge of the wall, but then it careers off at an angle and runs straight into the Grey blocking our path. The body disappears in front of us as it is bulldozed by the bonnet of the car.

The driver yells something to us but it's in another language and only when I see Anwar rushing to the door, do I realize that it is Anwar's dad, come to rescue us.

'Get in! Get in!' I yell to the others.

For a moment they are too stunned to move. It's Angharad who tugs at her mum and it's as though that begins a chain reaction: Angharad darts to the car and Julie runs after her and Steve follows Julie. We all tumble into the car.

Before we have even closed the door, Anwar's dad starts to drive. The car swerves violently to one side and Steve almost falls out of the door. Julie, Angharad and I are all clinging on to him and that's the only reason he stays in.

I just notice through the triangle of the window the grey figure looming. Like the body on the ground, its arm is reaching out for us, pointing towards us, and in that split second I see that it doesn't just remind me of the fallen man, it *is* the fallen man.

I can tell by the arched hunch of his back, the cap that shades his face. His skin is greyer and more mottled now and his legs still flow beneath him. In a single movement he springs up and lunges towards the car with a jump.

'Shut the door!' Anwar yells.

Angharad reaches round Steve, her fingers splayed and stretching for the handle, and in that moment I know that if she keeps reaching, the fallen man will have her. His fingers will close around hers and drag her from the car. I pull her back so forcefully that she cries out in alarm and then, holding on to the seats, I kick my legs towards the open door with everything I have.

My feet touch him. He feels like stone, like a wall, but I kick again and again and finally he loses his grip on the car and as Anwar's dad swerves again, he falls away.

I see his face though just before he lets go. There's not just the emptiness that I saw before. I see something else pass through his eyes as he loses his grip and falls away. I think it's fear, although how can it be when we are the ones running from him?

I try not to think of it and slam the door shut.

We are a heap in the back of the car, on top of each other, gasping for breath like fish that have been pulled from the sea.

Anwar and his dad speak to each other rapidly in Somali. They both sound angry, although when I look over at them I can see that Anwar's dad has pulled him close, that he is crying.

The car veers round corners. Anwar's dad doesn't slow down until we are out of the centre of the city. There are cars left abandoned on the road; their doors are wide open but there is no sign of anyone who was in them.

'Where do you want to go?' Anwar's dad asks us.

'Our house is closer,' Julie says. Steve nods and she calls out the address to Anwar's dad.

Her face is white with shock. 'Thank you so much,' she manages to say.

Our voices unite as an echo of Julie's. *Thank you. Thank you. Thank you.* Those two little words can hardly express all that we feel.

Anwar's dad looks over to his son. 'It was Anwar,' he says. 'He persuaded me. To tell you the truth, I didn't want to come. He made me.'

Anwar doesn't say anything. He just keeps looking ahead out of the windscreen.

'Anwar?' Steve says. 'Billy's very lucky to have a friend like you. You really are the best friend I could ever hope he could have. I'm sorry I didn't see that before. Thank you for being there for him and for all of us.'

I think Anwar is going to make a joke, that he'll call Steve 'Mr G' in the way he always does but when he looks back at Steve, he doesn't say a word. His face is tearstained and he just looks at Steve and Steve looks at him and without them speaking, I can see that they understand each other.

When we pull up outside Julie's house, we all get out of the car and just stand there. The street is eerily empty but then we hear what sounds like gunshots in the distance and our bodies shake as though we can feel the bullets inside of us.

'We'd better get inside,' Julie says. 'Thank you both again, so much. We owe you our lives.' She nods towards Anwar and his dad.

Steve looks like he is about to shake Anwar's dad's hand but then he leans in and hugs both of them tightly.

'I hope we see you soon,' he says, and he and Julie disappear into the house.

'See you, Billy,' Anwar's dad says to me, just like he always does. 'Don't be too long,' he says to Anwar. He starts the engine of the car and leaves it running, the door open for Anwar to jump straight in.

'So,' Anwar says.

'So,' I say back.

'Oh, you two!' Angharad says. She reaches for Anwar who looks surprised when she hugs him closely. 'I hate to say it,' she says. 'But we were totally, completely right.'

'Yeah,' Anwar says. 'I hate being so right all the time.'

They catch each other's eye and smile. Then Angharad takes a deep breath. 'I kind of wish that we hadn't been.'

We stand in silence for a moment. No one wants to move.

In the end Angharad just pulls Anwar in for another close

hug. 'Thanks. Thanks for coming to get us. Now take good care of yourself, Anwar.'

Anwar smiles at her. 'You too,' he says. She walks away into the house.

Now it's just the two of us, we are both quiet. What's just happened feels too big for us to even talk about.

'You saved us!' I say eventually. 'You totally saved us. You and your dad. Thank you.'

Anwar looks at his trainers.

'At least,' he says, 'at least your dad doesn't think I'm so bad any more.'

I start to laugh. I can't stop. And then Anwar looks up and grins at me.

'Anwar! Come on!' Anwar's dad calls out sharply.

'Give me a minute, Dad,' Anwar shouts back. 'He wants to leave Bristol straightaway. Get out of the city,' he tells me.

'Sounds like a good idea.'

'So – I'll be seeing you, Billy,' he says. His warm eyes lock with mine. It's what he always says after school when we reach his block and I turn down the road towards Steve's house. Like this is the same as every other normal day.

'Wait! I've got something for you,' I say and I dig around in my backpack. I've been carrying it around with me, waiting for the right moment to give it to him – it's another pocket survival kit that I made just for him. I found a mint tin that Steve had that was the right size and packed into it all the things the book listed you should carry in one.

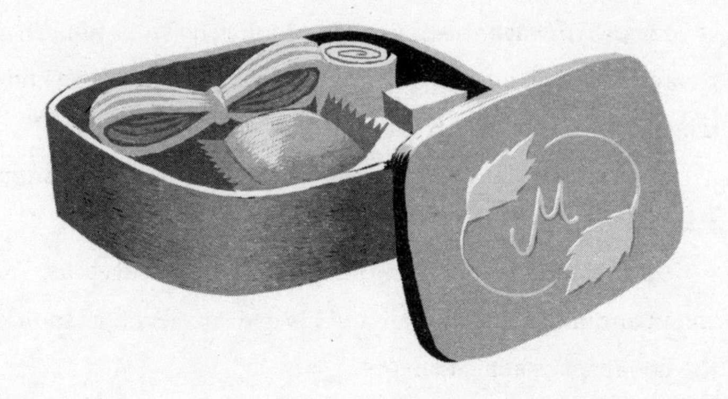

Fig. 12. – How to create a pocket survival kit for a friend

'I made one for you – a pocket survival kit – like the one that you helped me with. It might come in useful.'

Anwar thinks for a moment and then he shakes off his yellow rucksack.

'Take this,' he says and thrusts a plastic bag into my hand. 'It might come in useful too.'

'Shall I open it now?' I ask.

'Look at it later . . . it's nothing really.' I stuff the bag into my own rucksack.

'I'd better go. See you soon, Billy.'

'Wait,' I say. 'Remember when I showed you where Sylvia's Martello tower was on the map? A place called Sandgate. If you need somewhere safe to go, remember you could go there. I don't know what we're going to do but I think Sylvia would want me to go there. She'll be there too, if she can. She's been preparing for this all along.'

'I hope . . .' Anwar begins to say, but then he stops himself as though he has changed his mind about something. 'I don't know where Dad wants to go but I remember the place. Thanks.'

'Anwar!' his dad shouts again. He sounds like he is angry but his eyes reach out in concern.

'Gotta go, man!'

Anwar jumps into the car and his dad speeds off as soon as the door slams shut.

I wave and I can't really see him any more but I imagine that Anwar is waving back at me.

I wave and wave until the car is out of sight.

HOW TO (NOT) FALL ASLEEP

It's been hours since Anwar and his dad left us, and we haven't moved from Julie's living room. We just watched the television churn out more and more information.

There were endless reports about the infection spreading, on every channel, and the internet was full of videos of people's transformations into Greys.

'Though it is fatal for most people who are exposed, some seem to be carriers of the virus, transforming and seeming to live on. There is no evidence to show that after the transformation there are any human qualities left. They do not seem to respond to pain, to language,' a man on the screen is saying. He has rolled his sleeves up to his elbows and is leaning into the camera as he speaks. 'Those infected must not be seen as people any more. They must be avoided at all costs.'

The news keeps cutting to government warnings that you should stay inside until further notice, but there are news reports of people saying that they are going to ignore the advice because it isn't safe to stay in one place any more.

My mind turns to Sylvia. Whatever Steve said, whatever the doctors thought, she was preparing for something, even if that meant she sometimes went too far . . . I remember the diagrams of the grey people in the tower again, had she known what was going to happen? And, if so, how? But more importantly, is she still at the hospital, or have they closed it? Maybe she is already at the tower? The questions rush around my head but all I know for sure is I have to get there. If there is a chance she is waiting for me, I have to meet her.

Julie turns off the television.

'That's enough of that,' Julie says. 'We all need some sleep. Billy, are you okay on the sofa?'

'I was thinking,' Angharad says. 'We should all sleep together, don't you think? In the same room? For safety?'

Julie thinks for a moment and then she is all action, giving us instructions.

'This is the biggest room and so we'll sleep in here. Let's bring down some of the mattresses from upstairs and we've got an inflatable one too. Steve? Can you help me move them? Angharad and Billy, you go grab duvets and pillows and any blankets you can find.'

It almost sounds like we are just making plans for a slumber party – if it wasn't for the way that Julie's voice wavers as she speaks.

We gather up bedding from upstairs and by the time that we've set up the beds, there is hardly any floor space left.

'We just need a campfire and some marshmallows now,'

Steve says cheerfully but no one is really convinced. We all lie down on our makeshift beds, not speaking. It takes a long time for everyone else to fall asleep, but eventually I can tell it is only me still awake. I run through survival techniques in my head to try and keep myself distracted from the memories of the day, the look on the man's face as he dropped away from the car, the body transforming in front of us. When that doesn't work, I get up, careful not to make a noise, to find my rucksack. I reach in gingerly and my hand closes around the edge of *How to Survive*. I turn to the cover where Sylvia made me write down the five Rules for Survival and read them to myself over and over. I can't even properly see the writing in the darkness, but I know them so well I don't really need to – just tracing my fingers over them makes me feel calmer.

DAY 2

HOW TO LEAVE

The next morning, I watch everyone still asleep beside me. Julie next to Steve: they lie turned towards one other, their legs curved up slightly, their hands just touching. They are mirrored images of each other. Angharad frowns as she dreams and kicks out her legs but then her breathing grows heavier again and she does not wake.

As slowly and quietly as I can, I rise from the sofa and escape the fuggy, warm sitting room, its air thick from sleep.

I try to message Anwar, but it doesn't send. The mobile networks must be down. I find the Wi-Fi box back in the sitting room and put the password into my phone as quietly as I can, but all I can hear is soft snores from everyone else.

Then I look up the name of the hospital that Sylvia was in and find the phone number. I use Julie and Angharad's landline to try to call it but I just get a blank-sounding tone. Though I hadn't really thought that I would get through to Sylvia, I can't ignore the feeling of disappointment welling up inside me. I just hope she's escaped from the hospital and is on her way to the tower. She said that I would know when it was time to meet her there. She was right.

When I peer out of the kitchen window, lots of people down the street are loading up their cars. Filling them up with suitcases and bags as though they are going on holiday. What do you take with you that is truly precious? Because we're at Julie's all I have is the clothes that I am wearing, my phone, my pocket survival kit and my rucksack.

I hear voices: Julie's, Steve's and Angharad's. They've woken up.

'I think it would be a good place to go,' Julie is saying. 'It's remote, but it has resources. He stockpiles, my dad. There'll be enough food to keep us all going for a while. I mean, it's almost like he's been preparing for this for years. It won't take us that long to get there, either.'

'But the news is saying that the government advice is to stay inside,' Steve argues.

'Looks like most people are leaving,' I say as I walk back in. 'Anwar told me yesterday that was what his family were doing, and a lot of the neighbours are packing up.'

Julie walks over to one of the windows at the front and peers out.

'I think we should go too,' I add. 'If we weren't in a city, maybe it would be best to stay where we are, but there could be too many of them here.'

'I agree,' Julie says quickly. 'We have no idea how many of the, what did you call them, you two – the Greys? – are here. We should leave as soon as we can.'

'Where did you want to go?' I ask. 'I heard you talking about your dad?'

'His farm is quite remote. I think we would be safer there.'

'Where is it?'

'In Wales,' Angharad says.

'Just a few hours' drive away,' Julie adds. 'I can call him and let him know we're coming.'

Steve shakes his head but says, 'If that's what you want to do—'

I start speaking at speed before he can finish, it's the right move to leave and I don't want Steve to talk Julie out of it.

'Right, pack only the things that you really need,' I say to Julie and Angharad. 'And we'll need to take food and water.'

For a moment no one moves, as though we don't want to leave, but then we all scramble into action at once. Angharad stumbles from the mattresses covering the floor, Julie runs upstairs and Steve and I rush to the kitchen.

It's the first time that I have been alone with him since it all began.

'We don't need to go back home, do we? There's nothing that we really need to take from there?' Steve mutters to me as he pulls open the kitchen cupboards. 'I'm sure this won't be for long.' He doesn't sound certain. 'And Julie's dad will have clothes that we can borrow for the time being.'

'It's okay,' I say, thinking of Sylvia's book tucked carefully into my rucksack. That's all I need. I feel stronger just knowing that I have it with me.

Steve continues to rummage through cupboards.

'So, aren't we going to talk about it?' I ask.

Steve looks up. 'What?'

'That Sylvia was right to get me ready for something big happening. Despite everything you said.'

Steve closes one of the cupboard doors with a slam.

'There's not much to talk about,' he says shortly.

'But—' I start to protest.

'Billy, look. This is just a completely crazy thing that happened. No one could have predicted it. I know you think it aligns with some of the things that your mum said but it doesn't mean . . . it doesn't mean . . .' He runs out of words like he's not even sure what his point is, so instead he gives up and starts pulling at food packets in one of the cupboards.

I start to feel a wave of anger rise up from the pit of my stomach to the back of my throat. I try to say something back, like how can he say that, or he was wrong to have Sylvia sent away, but the rage chokes me and I let out a cry of pure frustration.

Steve looks at me in shock and finally I find my words: 'Why won't you admit she *was* right?'

He ignores me and keeps sorting out the food packets in front of him.

'I don't want to talk about it any more,' he says, almost to himself. Then he says it again, louder: 'I don't want to talk about it any more.'

'You can't just pretend that she doesn't exist,' I say, the sound of my heart pounding in my ears.

But he doesn't answer me and won't meet my eye.

We go through the rest of the cupboards in silence. I feel myself prickling with resentment and when he asks me about what food I think we should take, I just shrug. When Julie sees the stash that we've collected she says, 'I was just about to do a supermarket shop . . . Sorry there's not more.'

When neither of us answers her, she looks from Steve to me.

'Everything all right?' she asks.

'Yes,' says Steve at the same moment that I say, 'No,' and walk out of the room.

Suddenly we can't leave quickly enough and with every small thing that slows us, I feel a stomach ache growing inside me. Julie makes us all go to the toilet before we leave, even if we don't need to go. I avoid Steve as much as I can and busy myself with filling all the large bottles that I can find with water, and then ask Angharad to dig through their recycling and wash out old milk bottles and sparkling water bottles to use those too.

Angharad and I start to pack up the car. It takes several journeys to load it up with all the things that we want to take. The next-door neighbours are doing the same thing. They have two young children who are grasping soft toys and playing on the pavement. The younger one, a boy, is holding a floppy-eared rabbit in one hand.

'But I don't want to go,' he protests in a small voice, over and over. The parents smile over at me as they see me heave the heavy water bottles out and struggle to pack them into the boot, and I hear them say to him: 'See, they're going on an adventure too.' I hear the fake cheerfulness in their voices.

'That's right,' I say back as lightly as I can. 'We're going on an adventure.'

When I head back inside, Julie suddenly seems reluctant to leave and starts to grab blankets off the sofas.

'We should really get going,' I tell everyone.

'Come on, Mum,' Angharad says and gently takes the blankets out of Julie's hands. 'We need to leave now.'

Angharad hasn't brought much with her but I see the sharp, pointed corner of a photo frame sticking out a little from the top of her bag.

We slam the car doors shut, one after the other. There's stuff everywhere in the car, we can't put our legs down and are squashed up next to each other.

I look over to the neighbours and see that they, like us, are about to leave. The children are sitting in the back of the car, the father hunched into the driver's seat, and the mother is dashing back into the house, presumably to grab the last of their things. The boy carrying the worn-out rabbit raises his hand and waves at me. I wave back and try to smile, although it feels like it's cracking my face.

'Right, here we go,' says Julie as she starts up the ignition.

'Did you speak to Granddad?' Angharad asks.

'I couldn't get through, but I'm sure he'll be expecting us to come. He'll know that I'll think of it because there's no one who lives that close by – it should be a safe place to go.'

'Granddad won't be trying to come to us?' Angharad asks.

'No way – he'd never leave the farm unless he really had to—' At just that moment, Julie brakes suddenly as a car comes tearing round the corner. We jolt to a stop and everyone is thrown forward.

'Sorry, everyone. I didn't see him coming.'

I see Julie's gaze follow the disappearing car that careens out of sight.

'We're all okay,' Steve says. 'You're okay, guys, aren't you?'

Angharad rubs her forehead a little, which collided with one of the front seats.

'We're fine,' she says.

I turn over in my mind whether I should suggest going to the tower instead of the farm but after what happened with Steve in the kitchen, I keep it to myself. I want to make sure they are all safe, but I know now that I have to find Sylvia on my own. Steve will never understand – he probably wouldn't even believe me if I said she's waiting there for me. I'll get them to the farm and then I'll go to the tower as quickly as I can. There's a big part of me itching to get away, that feels sure Steve doesn't really want me around anyway, that he'll probably be relieved if I go. But I can't abandon Angharad.

We don't meet many more cars at first, but when we reach one of the bigger roads we end up in a traffic jam, full of people leaving Bristol, just like us. They've packed their cars up too. Everyone is getting out of the city and no one knows when they will be back.

I try to text Anwar again but my messages still won't send. Steve tries to call Julie's dad but there is only the monotonous dial tone I got when I tried to call the hospital. It's like we're cut off from the world even though we're surrounded by people.

Our car edges forward slowly.

'We should have gone last night,' Julie says under her breath.

Dark, voluptuous clouds gather over us.

'Feels like it's going to storm,' Steve says, peering up.

I see other kids through car windows looking out miserably back at me. The engine ticking over, the stale, warm air of the car, the stuff all squashed around me makes me want to get out of the car, throw open the door to the air.

I'm not the only one who is thinking this. As the jam crawls to a stop, we see some families get out. They stretch out, making wide star shapes with their bodies.

'Do you want to get out, too?' Julie asks us.

'No,' Angharad and I say together.

'It's probably better that we stay in the car together,' Steve says quickly.

I close my eyes. Watching the other families standing outside is only making me feel hotter and more cramped than before.

Most of the people around us have stopped their engines. If they haven't got out, they have opened up their doors. They sit on the side of the seats and dangle their legs out. I can hear people chatting to each other, laughter even. It almost feels like we're just stuck in a traffic jam on a bank holiday, trying to get out of the city. After our frantic departure, it feels too relaxed now, too normal.

'I'll open my window,' Julie says. 'Let in a bit of air.'

'Not too much, Mum,' Angharad says sharply.

Julie opens the window a small amount. I can't even feel any difference that it's making.

'Maybe we should turn the engine off?' Steve says. 'We'll save on the fuel.' We haven't moved forward in ages, not even by a couple of centimetres.

Julie's hand moves to the key, her fingers are just about to touch the edge of it, she is only seconds from turning the engine off when it happens . . .

That's when we hear the first gunshot.

HOW TO HAVE A NEAR MISS

Everything happens at once.

Everything happens in just one moment.

There's the sound of the gunshot.

It rings through the air, silencing the gurgle of chat that had been bubbling away.

It seems to come from behind us, from somewhere in the distance.

Then there's footsteps. Desperate running.

Like a wave that's mounting, the sounds of panic rise up. They grow and grow, folding in on themselves to make something larger.

It is all around us. It is everywhere. It comes from every direction.

I look around at the faces of panic. People start scrambling into their cars, but then they stop, staring at something in the distance. Their eyes widen, they point, they shrink away, but before I can see what they are seeing, Julie is driving away.

We are propelled forward, jerked by the sudden acceleration.

Julie pulls around the car ahead of us on to the small space on the side between the barrier and the cars. It doesn't look like we can possibly fit.

In places, we don't. The sides of our car scream as it grates against other cars and the concrete barrier. The doors shake as though we are being squeezed smaller. Angharad and I bundle into the middle of the car to move away from the trembling doors.

Steve looks round. He sees us, squished together, terrified but all right, and then back to Julie who is hunched over the wheel, her body strained forward as though she can make the car go faster just by her will.

Other cars are starting to pull out now, but so many of them are stuck in the lanes of traffic. It was only a moment ago, I remind myself, that everyone was standing in the sunshine. It does not feel possible that this is true.

We speed past the traffic jam.

The screaming continues behind us. It's almost like it's getting closer and part of me worries that the screaming will pick up our car, that it will carry us with its force and discard us to one side when it's done with us. Greys appear from every angle.

I can see people falling. They are running away or trying to throw themselves back into their cars but then a Grey catches up to them and they jolt, they stop, they fall.

The Greys weave through the traffic jam – a silent tide only marked by the screams of those they meet.

'Come on, come on, come on,' I hear Julie saying urgently.

She has leaned forward even further over the steering wheel. She keeps her gaze fixed on what is ahead of her: there is a split in the road – the turning that we were heading for. More cars are moving here – they are screeching as they pull away. They catch the light as their wheels fly and then disappear.

'Your window!' Steve says, as he spots one of the Greys take a jump towards us.

Julie hits the button to make the window go up but the Grey pushes its gnarled, hooked claw through the disappearing crack before she can close it.

It's stuck there, half of its hand out of the window, the other half twisting and writhing just centimetres from Julie's face. The Grey looks at its hand for a moment as though it's puzzled at what has happened.

You can tell that it used to be a man. There's the shred of his shirt and his tie still hanging from him, like he was a business-man or something like that. I imagine him in another life, carrying a briefcase, his slightly rounded belly tucked into dark trousers. Drinking a coffee, always being in a hurry, catching a train. But now all he cares about is trying to break into our car.

The Grey's fingers are splayed and stretching towards Julie. With every second that passes it looks like his hand is squeezing further through the gap, getting millimetre by millimetre a little closer to her.

She leans away as far as she can while still trying to hold on to the steering wheel. She doesn't stop herself from sobbing as she drives, as his twisted fingers stretch ever closer towards her.

Ahead of us, I see a truck in the jam to the side of us and without thinking too much about what I'm doing, I throw myself forward to the front of the car.

'Billy!' Steve shouts out in alarm.

I ignore him and reach for the steering wheel, pulling it down sharply to one side, so that we almost swerve into the traffic.

The Grey crashes into the truck.

There's a terrible cracking sound.

A sound that is both hollow and sharp.

A sound of splitting and splintering.

It feels as though it could be coming from inside me. Like something inside me has broken in two, although I know it's not me, just that I'm the one that caused it.

The Grey is crushed in between our car and the truck. I look away, not wanting to see what I've caused, but then I make myself turn back to make sure it's no longer trying to get into the car.

Julie pulls the car away so sharply that we all tumble to one side; I see the Grey's bashed body almost embedded into the truck. As we drive off, the arm that had been reaching through the open window tumbles back through the gap, leaving the Grey collapsed on the road.

It looks like a shadow, lying there.

I can't take my eyes from its shape, studying it for any movement, any sign that it might follow us, but it does not stir.

'Are you okay? Are you okay?' Julie cries out as we drive on.

'We're all right, Mum.' Angharad reaches out for Julie and places her hand firmly on her shoulder. 'We're all okay. Just keep driving. Don't stop. You're doing so well.'

Our moving car is attracting more Greys. They are rushing towards us, they are running to keep up with us and the remarkable thing is that they are somehow able to. Their legs are circling so fast they look like a blur, they are coming at us from every direction; it won't be long before they jump on the car, before they bring us to a stop.

'Please, please, please.' Julie is begging but I don't know to whom – the car, the Greys, the road. 'Come on, come on, come on.'

We are almost at the split. We are almost there.

The sides of the car screech as they scrape past a narrow gap. We knock a car on one side that spins out slightly from where it was.

I watch as another car pulls out behind us. A man is driving, there is a woman in the passenger seat.

The man looks steely, his expression grim. The Greys that were following us spot them and as we accelerate on, they fall back to this new car, this car that they have more chance of reaching.

I look forward, we are almost at the split. I look back . . . and then I have to look away.

The car is no longer following us.

It is engulfed with Greys.

I can't see the man and the woman any more.

HOW TO START A JOURNEY

We do not speak.

Julie drives, still sitting in the same hunched over position. Steve stares out at the road. Angharad leans forward, so she's as close to her mum as she can be without climbing into the front.

My fists are clenched. It takes me a while to notice. I wonder how long they have been like that because when I try to unclench them, I find that I can't.

We cross the bridge into Wales in silence. I realize I'm holding my breath until we cross it. It feels like something might stop us again but Julie keeps pushing down on the accelerator and we speed onwards, untroubled.

I look out of the window, at the trees and bushes that blur together in a green that races past me, at the sunlight hitting a field and illuminating every ridge of its earth. It looks so idyllic, so tranquil, that it does not seem possible that this place can exist in the same world as the one we just left.

No one speaks.

I hope that Anwar and his family got out of the city okay, that they are safe, wherever they are. For a moment, I imagine what it might have been like for them if they'd been attacked by the Greys as they left, like us. I can see Nadifa and Taifa's scared faces so clearly and I can picture Anwar desperately trying to distract them even though he would be feeling terrified himself. I turn my phone over in my hands. Although I know there is no way he can receive a message, I type one out anyway, telling him what we're doing, hoping that he is okay. It sits, unsent, on my phone.

As we drive on, I spot on the dashboard that the petrol gauge is steadily swinging to the left. It is moving closer and closer to the red line, showing that the tank is almost empty.

No one speaks.

There are cars that are driving like us. We all drive faster than the speed limit; we are driving as fast as our cars will go.

There are other cars too, ones that have been abandoned – often on the side of the road but sometimes left in the middle at an angle. Julie has to swing our car to the side to avoid them.

We don't see any sign of the people that once drove them.

We've made really good progress, but then we spot a queue building up.

Cars are stopping ahead of us. We all sit up, really alert now, and look round.

Julie points to the sign that reads 'Services' and I realize that the people in the queue are stopping for petrol – they are probably running low, like us.

But Julie doesn't slow as we reach the queue. She pulls around and carries on driving. It doesn't feel safe to stop here. In these new times, seeing lots of other people means trouble. Today, seeing a queue of traffic means danger.

No one questions her when she does this.

No one speaks.

One moment the car is racing ahead, pushed on, almost, by Julie leaning into the wheel. Her need for it to go forward fuelling the car alone.

Then its power dies. The engine cuts out. Julie pushes uselessly against the accelerator.

The car rolls to a stop.

Julie turns the wheel hard to try to bring the car to the side of the road but we don't quite make it – we come to a halt at an angle on the outside lane.

She turns the key in the ignition over and over but the car does not make a sound. After a few minutes of trying, she stops.

'Right.' Steve breaks the silence finally. He turns to look at Julie. 'Are you okay, love?'

'Yes,' Julie says in a very small voice. She sounds weary. Her face is drained and white. Like the car, she's empty, she has nothing more to give.

No one moves. Julie's hands remain gripped on the steering wheel.

I look around us. The number of cars on the road has lessened as we've gone further and I can see no one else around us, at that moment. We're surrounded by green here, now we're even further into Wales.

'How far are we from the farmhouse?' I ask.

'About an hour's drive. Maybe a little less,' Julie says.

'How long would it take us to walk?'

'I don't know . . .' Julie's answer seems to wither away.

'We should get off the road and start walking. Carry as much as we can,' I say. 'I'll take the water.' I unlock my door and push it open. It takes a few shoves before it will budge because of the damage done to it when we squeezed in between cars. Finally it swings open with a creak.

My feet land a little unsteadily on the warm tarmac of the road. For a moment I'm not sure if my legs will support me and I have to hold on to the side of the door until I feel calmer. Then I turn to the boot of the car to haul out the first of the water bottles and that's when I notice that I'm the only one who's made a move.

Julie is still staring at the patch of road in front of us, clenching the steering wheel. Steve's eyes are glazed and he sits forward, frozen still. Angharad is still bent in between the space of the two front seats.

'Angharad,' I whisper and then I say it louder: 'Angharad.'

She flinches, as though she's just waking up.

'We've got to get off the road,' I tell her. 'We've got to get moving.'

She nods but does not answer me. I cannot tell what she is thinking but I can see her mind ticking over, lingering over something, or someone. But then she pats Julie's shoulder and tells her gently, 'Mum, we've got to go.'

'Yes,' Julie says. It sounds like an exhale. She still makes no sign of moving.

Angharad looks over at me a little hopelessly and I jerk my head towards Steve. I haven't spoken to him since our argument in the kitchen and I can still feel resentment ticking over inside of me. Angharad seems to understand that I can't speak to him at the moment.

'Come on, Steve,' she tries. 'We've got to go.'

But still neither adult makes a move.

'We've got to get off the road – before anyone finds us,' I repeat.

The words sink in. Steve opens the door on his side in a sudden movement; he winces as it rasps and scrapes open.

'I think we should stay in the car,' Julie suddenly says. She speaks almost with a shout, each word increasing in volume, and then almost pleading. 'We can lock the doors.'

Angharad and Steve exchange a look.

'Come on, Mum, we can't stay here,' Angharad says. She almost sounds like she's the mother, the one who should be comforting and solid.

'We've got to get to the farm, love,' Steve adds.

'I know,' Julie says. 'I think . . . I think I'm just . . . I don't know. I can't believe it.'

'We'll be okay,' Steve says and then he repeats it, as though he really wants to believe it. 'We'll be okay.'

I put down the heavy bag of water bottles from the boot. I won't be able to carry it that far, I think. Its handles are already cutting into my fingers. The bottles make a sort of thump as I drop them on to the tarmac. One of them falls on its side and out of the bag.

At first I think it's just the movement of the bottle rolling away. I tell myself that that's all I'm seeing because I so want it to be true. I want us to be the only people on the road.

But when I make myself look, there is no denying that we are no longer alone.

The figures look like shadows in the distance. There are two of them and from far away, they look like little more than small dots. They could just be normal people, people who are looking for help, people who are just like us. But we can't find out. We can't take any risks.

'We have to go,' I tell the others. 'Someone's coming. We have to leave now.' I speak like I want to move: rushing through the words, sprinting from sentence to sentence. There's no time for fear any more.

We break into movement then, even Julie. We grab what we can. Some of the food. The bag with the bottles of water. We leave behind most of the things that we brought with us.

There's a parting in the bushes that we run towards.

I can't see anyone following us, although it's too early to tell.

We run, we scramble, we don't look back.

HOW TO WALK (AND START RUNNING)

We agree to keep quiet as we walk and though it makes sense to do this, I wish that we were able to talk. I wish that it was different.

I imagine that if we were walking together through the countryside in a different time, on a different day, that we would play games as we walked. Steve and I would be speaking to each other; we wouldn't have fallen out. He'd be able to look me in the eye again. Maybe we would start with something like I Spy and then move to Twenty Questions, taking turns to guess. We would break off when someone spotted something that they wanted to share – an interesting snail shell or a view through the trees.

It's funny that I can imagine us so easily doing this. I almost feel sick for it, as though it's something that I am actually missing, although we have never spent time together like that before.

'I think there's a village coming up ahead,' Julie says.

We've tried to look up a route on our phones but there's still no signal. Julie thought that it would take about twelve hours if we didn't stop at all.

'Should we go round it?' she asks.

No one answers and I wonder if everyone else is thinking the same thing as me: I'd like to go there, I have a need to see other people all of a sudden. It's as though I want to know that we are not the only ones left. I know that we are not, but I want proof.

'It's probably best we avoid it,' Steve says and Julie nods and makes a right turn where the path forks.

'Look!' Angharad hisses, suddenly. She points to the sky and we see a trail of smoke rising steadily in the air. 'Is that where the village is, do you think, Mum?'

'Yes, it looks like it,' Julie says. Her face grows fixed and unreadable and then she looks down to the ground and walks on and I can't see her expression any more. 'Let's stop for a break for a moment, shall we?' She puts down her bags and gestures to Steve that she wants to talk to him. I can't hear what they are saying, only their muttering from behind a tree.

'They're worried,' Angharad says to me.

'Steve's always worried.'

'Why do you do that?'

'What?'

'Call him Steve, why don't you call him Dad?'

'Sylvia called him Steve,' I say back, although I know that doesn't really make sense.

'So why do you call your mum Sylvia?'

'She wanted me to call her by her name,' I say. 'She said that if there was an emergency and people were calling out for their mums, she wouldn't know if it was me. But if I said her name, then she would always hear me.'

Angharad considers this. 'Wouldn't she just know your voice?'

'Of course – but in a real emergency, every small thing counts. You might not be able to hear someone's voice clearly if everyone's shouting.' I hear my voice rising as I recount the explanation that Sylvia herself had given me. There's something about it that makes me feel funny. It makes sense for me to call her by her name but as Angharad pointed out, wouldn't she be able to tell my voice over everyone else's? Isn't that what a mum does?

'Maybe I should ask Mum if I can call her Julie.'

'I don't think it would work – she knows that you call her Mum now – she wouldn't think it was you if you said Julie.'

'I guess so.'

We've headed on again, Julie still leading the way as we follow in a single line. Steve insists on going at the back. It's slow going because we are carrying so much and because we stop to drink water fairly often, in the beating midday sun. After each of those stops, my bag is not quite as heavy to carry.

It feels as though it will take us much longer than twelve hours to get to the farm at the speed we're walking and with the stops we're taking.

There is little shelter from the sun on the path we're on. Angharad raises a hand to try and shade her face. I can feel my skin burning too but I have to use both hands to carry the water bag. My mind races over the Rules and then it's like I'm reading *How to Survive*, turning the pages and poring over every word and diagram. As the sun beats down, I remember a section about the different kinds of exposure to the weather you need to be wary of.

'We need to stop,' I say.

'What is it?' Angharad asks.

'Has anyone got any T-shirts or shirts or anything like that? We've got to make sure that we don't get heatstroke being out in the sun like this. We need some protection.'

I think I hear Steve make a scoffing sound but I don't look over at him.

Julie throws off the rucksack that she is wearing. 'Good idea, Billy. How about these?'

She pulls out some T-shirts from her bag.

I tie one of them around my head.

'You look ridiculous,' Angharad says.

'I'd rather look ridiculous than get heatstroke.'

'Quite right, Billy,' Julie says. She starts to tie a T-shirt around Angharad's head, although Angharad tries to bat her away.

'Mu-um,' she says, in that same tone she used when they first came round for lunch at our house.

'Hold on,' Julie says. 'Almost done. You'll feel cooler in a moment.' When she's finished, it looks like Angharad is wearing a lumpy-looking turban but it shades her face.

'Steve? Do you want one?' Julie asks.

'Ah – I think I'm okay without . . .'

'Come on, Steve!' Angharad says and touches the T-shirt on her head gently. 'Don't you think it looks good?'

'If you get heatstroke, you'll slow us all down,' I say quietly.

'All right, all right,' Steve says, holding his hands up in defeat. 'The sun's gone behind a cloud now anyway,' he mutters but he lets Julie wrap a shirt around his head. It's much bigger than the T-shirts so she has to coil it round and round him until it bulges out.

'There,' she says when she is finished. 'That wasn't so bad, was it? You look, you look – really good.' She almost finishes the sentence without laughing, but not quite.

Angharad starts to laugh too, so much so that her shoulders begin shaking. I don't want to look over but I sneak a peek. He looks ridiculous and I can't help but smile for a moment.

Steve catches me looking and he begins to grin and strike a pose with his funny, lumpy turban that makes Angharad and Julie laugh even harder. I look resolutely away.

'Stop it! Stop it!' Julie is saying. At first, it seems like she is saying that because she is laughing so hard but then her voice changes. 'Stop it. Stop it,' she commands.

Steve whirls round.

We spot what Julie has seen. There is a blur of Greys moving together like a pack on the path ahead of us.

And they are coming straight for us.

HOW TO BE MUCH CLOSER TO GREYS THAN FEELS COMFORTABLE OR DESIRABLE

'This way,' Steve says. We dart off the path into the bushes.

They've all pulled the T-shirt turbans from their heads now and Angharad's braids sweep out behind her in every direction.

'Leave it!' Julie shouts when she sees me struggle to run with the bag of water bottles. I hesitate for just a moment but then I let the handles go.

The bottles tumble from the bag and roll off down the path.

I almost fall as I leap across the uneven ground. It feels as though we are making no progress at all as we scurry through the bushes; the landscape is impossible to sprint through. There are too many obstacles in the way, too many holes in the ground.

We run until we can go no further.

The vegetation grows so thickly we cannot pass through it.

'Hide!' Angharad cries. I duck next to her, behind a tree trunk, and Julie and Steve crouch behind some large bushes.

Now that we have stopped running, I can hear the sound of the Greys stumbling and tripping towards us.

I can hear the rustle of bushes as they pass them, the grass that is crushed under their feet, their stampeding legs whipping through the undergrowth. But more than anything else, I hear their terrible moaning; something like grinding, something like pain, all at once.

They are getting closer.

I am aware of every breath that I take. Each one seems too loud, sure to give away where we are.

I close my eyes. I try to slow my breath down and calm myself. I am sure that they were attracted to the sound of our laughter and only if we keep absolutely quiet will we be able to escape them.

I motion to the others, placing my fingers on my lips, and I think that they understand this. Angharad looks like she is holding her breath.

Then I see Steve beckoning us over. He points to a small gap he has spotted in the hedge beside them. Julie has started to edge towards it. I can hear every rustle, each leaf that she brushes past. The sound seems to grow louder as she moves through the gap and the Greys move closer still.

But before I can say that I think we should stay where we are, Angharad begins to crawl over to follow Julie. Steve waves at me frantically to follow.

He mouths at me desperately: *Come on, come on!*

Then, Angharad cries out.

Her cry slits through the air. It rises up above us like smoke streaming from a fire, a beacon of where we are.

We freeze.

Angharad is hunched over her leg, it looks like she's hurt herself. When I turn back, I see the Greys amassing. They flock towards us.

They know exactly where we are now.

I see Steve's face change as he notices the Greys approaching.

It's almost as though he himself is going through the transformation. His eyes dull, his skin turns ashen and pale.

The bushes and the trees seem to shiver and then shake as the Greys move past them, as though they too are afraid of them.

Steve looks over at me. He's metres away, but with that look he's right beside me. His eyes reach out to me as if he were reaching out with his arms to pull me close in a tight hug.

I think of her then too. I see flames, I see the light and the warmth from them cast upon her face. I see her despair and I see her joy and I hope, I hope with everything that I am, that she is safe.

I wonder if she will know when the Greys reach us. I imagine she will sense that I am gone. I can't explain why, but I just can't believe that she wouldn't know that I was not in the world – it feels impossible, somehow. Just like it's impossible for me to think I wouldn't know if she were gone.

Steve's eyes have grown large and bright. There are tears gathering in the corners. He looks at me with an intensity that seems to be able to speak. He is saying sorry, perhaps; he is saying he wishes things were different.

The echoing bellows of the Greys surge around us.

HOW TO USE FUN SNAPS

I know that we have little time.

I reach for the reassuring lump of my pocket survival kit. In my head I run through what it contains, if there's anything of use, but I draw a blank. I feel a surge of panic, but then I hear Sylvia's voice: *Never stop trying – you must never give up.* Rule number five.

Then I shrug my rucksack off my back in one movement and yank it open. There's some food in there, a bottle of water, Sylvia's book wedged between the food, its front cover ever so slightly bent over in a triangle, but not much else. Only the bag that Anwar gave me.

With everything that's been happening, I haven't thought to look at what he'd given me but I pull it out now, not caring any more about the rustle the plastic of the bag is making, and unwrap it quickly.

It's a small box, light in my hand, covered in orange paper.

Fun Snaps.

It takes me a moment to remember what they are. Anwar

had mentioned them to me before – little bundles of gravel combined with a tiny amount of explosive wrapped up together in paper. If you throw them on the ground or any hard surface they make a loud cracking bang.

I look round the tree trunk to see the quivering bushes that mark out the Greys heading in a straight line towards us.

There's a beech tree that's just a little distance from us, but I think it should be far enough away. I tear off the wrapping of the Fun Snaps box and reach inside. They are packed with sawdust that flitters away through my fingers. I take a handful of them; they're shaped like little cherries.

I know that I'm going to have to throw them hard to make this work, that I'll have to do it at exactly the right time.

The Greys grow closer.

The seconds count down.

They are almost at the beech tree.

I lob the Fun Snaps high into the air so they sail over the undergrowth. At first I'm worried that I did not manage to get them far enough. I've never been very good at throwing, but as they soar through the air, they fall against the trunk of the beech tree with a splatter of bangs.

They crack one after the other, exploding as they hit the trunk in a burst. The sound halts the stampeding Greys for just a moment.

'Stay absolutely still,' I mouth to Steve as quietly as I can. 'Tell them, too.'

Steve nods and relays the message to the others. I see Angharad bite down on her lip. Julie's face is flushed with concern but she remains silent.

The Greys scatter around the beech tree. They are looking for what it was that made the explosion; they are looking for who is there.

All that we can do is wait.

'Do you think they're gone?' It's Angharad who speaks first.

Her voice is so quiet it sounds like it could be a ripple of breeze through the trees.

I look around the trunk I'm hiding behind. The sun is blinding in its heat again and I can't see any sign of the Greys.

'I think so,' Steve says, just as quietly. 'Shall we keep moving? Are you all right?'

'She's snagged her leg on something,' Julie says. 'It's nasty. We need to wash it and dress it. I can't believe that I left the first aid kit in the car.'

'I have some Condy's crystals,' I say, pulling out my survival kit from my pocket. 'They work as an antiseptic.'

'Condy's crystals?' Julie sounds disbelieving.

I unpeel the tape from the tin and find the small sachet. I use one of the water bottles from my rucksack to mix a little in the tin. It's bright pink which I know means it's the right colour to use.

'Billy,' Julie says. 'This is great – really great . . . I don't know what we would have done if you hadn't . . .'

Angharad tries to smile at me and I think she would have spoken if she weren't in so much pain.

'It's nothing,' I say. 'It's just in my kit.'

'It's not just the Condy's crystals,' Julie says. Suddenly she leans towards me and hugs me tightly.

'It's true,' Angharad says in a tight voice, her teeth clenched together. 'If you hadn't distracted them, then they would have come right for us.'

'It was a hell of a throw!' Steve says.

'It was amazing!' Angharad says. 'Where did you get them from? The banging things?'

'Anwar gave them to me.' I smile. I can't wait to tell him how I used the Fun Snaps, although at the same time, I wonder if and when I will see him again and a cold feeling of dread washes over me.

But Julie is continuing to beam at me. 'And now you've magicked antiseptic out of nowhere . . . I don't know what to say.' She looks like she wants to reach out to me and in the next moment she does and we end up in a slightly awkward hug.

'What else have you got in that tin?' Angharad asks, peering at the matches that have been dipped in wax so they're waterproof.

'Just survival stuff,' I say quietly. I shrug my shoulders and try not to notice that Steve has looked away, but Julie draws him in.

'Steve? Billy's really saved the day with his survival kit,

hasn't he? There's lots of useful stuff in there that I'm sure we will need.'

'It's nothing,' I say again.

Steve looks over. He bends down and for a moment, he inspects the contents of the kit. I hold my breath.

'We'd better get moving,' he says. 'Can you walk, Angharad?'

He turns his back to us and looks into the distance. 'I think we can go this way,' he says, not really speaking to us.

'He doesn't want to admit my survival kit is good, because he still won't believe that anything Sylvia taught me was worthwhile,' I say loudly.

Steve turns to me in a flash, his voice raised. 'It's not as simple as that, Billy. It's just not as simple as you think.'

'How is it then?'

He starts to say something and then stops himself. 'You're just like her. You push and you push and you push,' he says, looking right at me. 'But sometimes people can be pushed too far.'

I try to swallow down the huge lump that's suddenly grown in my throat. I blink desperately, trying not to cry.

Julie and Angharad look awkward, not sure what to do.

Steve walks a few steps away and as though we haven't spoken at all, he peers down one of the tracks and says again, 'I think it's this way.'

I do not sleep very much.

Julie and Steve insisted that they would stay up and keep

watch and that Angharad and I should sleep, but when I wake in the night, I see that they have both fallen asleep so I make myself sit up and stay awake, my ears pricking for any noise.

Angharad had tried to talk to me after what happened between me and Steve, but I'd walked on ahead, alone, trying to untangle the mix of feelings wriggling inside me. There was the frustration that Steve refused to acknowledge Sylvia might have been teaching me the Survival Rules for a reason, plus the constant worry about whether Sylvia was safe or in danger somewhere, but both were then mingled with something that I kept backing away from: the thought that if Steve really didn't like Sylvia, then he couldn't like me either, because I was, after all, half of her. And it's that thought which swirls in my mind as I finally close my eyes to sleep.

DAY 3

HOW TO GET LOST AND FIND YOUR WAY AGAIN USING THE SHADOW-STICK METHOD

I feel my legs twitching to move as soon as the sun rises early on the horizon. We didn't make a fire last night in case it drew attention and though I tried to find a shelter that was as comfortable as it could be, it was not dry and it was not warm.

I found us a fallen log which we lay beside for a little shelter. I showed Angharad and Julie how to position their bodies so it would protect them as much as possible, but Steve said he was fine where he was and settled just next to us.

'Breakfast!' Steve injects some fake cheer into his voice as he passes around the broken-up oat bars that we took from Julie's cupboards. Angharad passes me a piece when I refuse to take any from Steve directly. They taste just fine but they are rather dry and because I left the water bag behind when we were running from the Greys, we only have a little left, so we have to ration how much we drink.

Angharad can't stop her face from grimacing whenever she moves her leg, although she says that it doesn't hurt that much. Julie rebandages it and washes it again with the Condy's crystals.

'Thanks, Mum,' Angharad says. 'That's much better.' But I notice that she's limping as we all start walking.

'How are you doing?' she asks me as we fall into step together.

'I'm okay. How's your leg?'

'It's fine.' Angharad says it so quickly that I know it's not true. 'It's a pain though . . . I mean – it doesn't hurt that much, it's just annoying!' She laughs a little to herself. 'I wish I'd spotted that metal thing I cut it on.' She readjusts her bag and I see the shape of the photo frame that I spotted yesterday jutting out against the fabric. 'But really, how are you? That stuff with your dad, it's just . . .'

'There's nothing more to say about it,' I say shortly. 'He didn't believe Sylvia, he didn't believe me. I'm not even sure if he likes me.'

'No, that's not true,' Angharad says, but I think I can hear the doubt wavering in her voice.

'I just wish,' I start to say, 'I just wish that Sylvia was here.'

It's only as I say it aloud that I realize how true it is.

'We've been this way before, I'm sure,' Steve says. 'I remember the shape of that bush.'

'And I'm sure we haven't,' Julie is saying back.

We are all thirsty and tired and hungry and even just speaking seems to take up precious energy that we do not have. The more we've walked, the thirstier we've become, and as the morning passes to midday, the sun's heat pulses down and grows fiercer with each passing hour. Our phones still have no signal and Steve's has already run out of battery.

My mouth feels dry and parched but the more I try not to think about it, the more I find myself dwelling on it.

A dull pain blossoms behind my temples.

'Let's face it,' Julie says. 'We're lost.'

As soon as she says it, she shakes her head, like a dog drying itself of water, and looks over to Angharad and me.

'I didn't mean that,' she says quickly. 'I'm sure we'll get to the farm okay . . . it just might take us a bit longer than we thought.'

'I'm sure we should have taken that track I saw,' Steve starts saying and then they are off again, arguing about which way to go, on and on.

I find a straight stick and bore it into the ground so it stands upright. I clear the ground around it and place a stone in the line of its shadow.

'We should sit down and have a break,' I tell Angharad while Julie and Steve bicker. I offer her the small water bottle that I have in my rucksack. She hands me a banana in exchange.

I don't like bananas and, worse still, its skin is bruised and brown and its flesh feels powdery in my mouth, but I make myself eat it anyway. We sip at the water.

'Are you all right?' I ask Angharad. She hasn't spoken very much in the last few hours.

She looks pale and drawn and her hair hangs limply over her shoulders.

'Just-thinking-about-my-dad,' she says in a rush.

I don't know anything about her dad – where he is or even if he was still alive before any of this happened. She reaches into her bag and pulls out the framed photo. I recognize her and Julie in the picture, although she looks much younger and Julie looks different, with darker, longer hair. There's a smiling man with a domed belly standing between them, with both arms around them. It looks like he might lift them up into the air in the next moment.

'He works on an oil rig so I don't see him very much,' she says. 'An oil rig – it's pretty much the safest place he can be, really. But . . .'

'You want to see him,' I finish for her. 'You want to be sure.'

Angharad nods. 'You know what it's like,' she says. She tucks the picture back into her bag. 'Do you think your mum's okay? Have you heard anything from her?'

I shake my head. 'I tried calling the hospital the night before we left yours, but I couldn't get through.'

'Have you got a photograph of her?' Angharad asks.

I shake my head. For a moment I hesitate but then I reach into my rucksack and pull out *How to Survive*.

'This belongs to Sylvia,' I tell Angharad. 'She found it in a second-hand bookshop when she was a child so it's really old, but all the stuff in it, it's really good.'

I pass it over to her and she reads through the blurb on the back page and examines the cover. 'This is the book that was under your bed, wasn't it? The first time we met?'

I hear Steve trudging towards us and I quickly grab it from

her hands and stuff it away into my rucksack. 'He still doesn't know I have it,' I say under my breath and give her a look that I know she'll understand: please don't tell him that I do.

'How much water have you got left?' Steve asks us.

'That's the last of the water in my bag,' I say, without looking at him.

'Then we're almost completely out.'

Steve gives a long sigh and then turns away.

Julie sits down next to us and takes a piece of banana that she chews mechanically, her eyes fixed somewhere in the distance, somewhere on the ground. Steve doesn't stay with us; he continues to examine the path we have just taken and the one which Julie has suggested we go down next.

After a little while, I look again at the stick that I placed in the ground. The shadow has now moved so it's no longer in the path of the stone marker. I pick up another stone to mark the new shadow line and take the stick away. Angharad watches me.

'What are you doing?' she asks.

'I'm finding out where north is,' I tell her.

I place my left foot where the first stone is and the right where the second is. I look up.

'North's that way,' I tell them, pointing ahead of me.

Julie sits up.

'How do you know that?' Angharad asks.

'Because of the shadow. The sun rises in the east and sets in the west, so I put the stick in the ground because its shadow moves as the earth rotates around the sun. These stones are marking out the east–west line. The first stone is showing west and the second east, so that means that north is that way and south is behind me.'

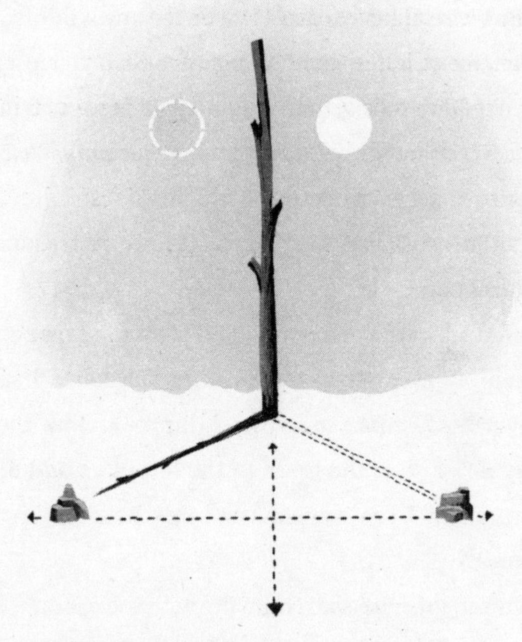

Fig. 13. – How to find North using a shadow-stick

'Which means,' Julie adds, jumping to her feet, 'that if we need to go northwest, it would be that way!' She points to the direction halfway between where I am facing and my left-hand side.

'Exactly!' I say.

*

The sun beats down. I can almost hear it humming around us as we walk in a line along the narrow path.

I strain my ears to listen out for the sound of water but I can't hear anything. Sylvia told me that the best way to find a stream is to watch out for animals or birds who can lead you there. But when I look around I can't see any wildlife.

When we stop for another break, we all collapse into the shade. We don't talk about how many stops we're making or how our water bottles are now completely empty. We can't even shake out a last drop from them any more.

I hear Steve ask Julie how far she thinks we are now and she looks uncertain.

'I'm not sure we'll make it today,' is all she says back.

I keep my eyes glued to the skies and when I spot some birds overhead – small sparrows, I think – I follow their flight. They fly down over the trees to the left of us and disappear. Moments later, I see some other birds heading in the same direction.

Steve and Julie are searching through the contents of all the bags we brought with us. They've spread everything across the ground. They don't say it but I know they are looking for a non-existent bottle of water that we haven't yet realized we have. They won't find it.

'I'm going to look for water,' I tell Angharad who's lying flat on the ground with a T-shirt covering her head.

My voice sounds hoarse from the dryness in my throat.

‘Water?’ Angharad croaks, and lifts her head. Her cheeks are flashed-pink-red, burnt from the sun.

‘I’m going to look for some. I’ll be right back.’

‘Wait, I’ll come with you,’ she says, pulling herself up unsteadily. I can see her leg is still giving her pain.

‘You need to rest,’ I tell her.

‘We’ve got to stick together. My leg’s okay. Where do you want to look for water?’

‘I’m not sure . . . but I think there’s a stream close by.’

Steve overhears us. ‘I don’t think it’s a good idea for you to go wandering off by yourselves.’

‘We won’t go far,’ Angharad says.

That’s what we tell them.

We won’t be long.

Be right back.

See you soon.

We have no reason not to believe it.

HOW TO FIND WATER

We start to follow the flight of the birds that I saw.

I tell Angharad why we're looking for them.

'There's another,' she tells me each time she spots one. 'Is this something from the survival book?' she asks.

As we're alone, I show her the page.

'It says here that we might see birds flying from water too, but they might be flying slowly after they've had their fill,' she says. 'But if it's flying . . .'

'Straight and fast then it's probably flying to the source,' I finish for her. 'Looks like they're flying to it, to me.'

There are more and more each time we look for them, drawing straight lines through the sky.

'Can you hear that?' Angharad says all of a sudden. 'Can you hear it?'

'This way,' I say, following the birds through the trees.

We almost tumble into the stream when we reach it. We lap the water up in handfuls that never seem quite enough. We fill up our bottles and then slug them down greedily, so water trickles from the sides of our mouths. We don't care. We let it trickle and then pour more over our faces.

The water is icy cold and even though it's delicious, it almost feels as though it is burning my throat as I swallow it because of the greediness of my gulps.

'We'd better go back and tell Mum and Steve,' Angharad says.

I lie on my front by the edge of the stream and let my hands dip into the water. I like the feeling of it flowing past me.

'Billy,' Angharad says suddenly, sharply.

I'm not sure what it is that I sense first.

Whether it's the faint whiff of soured milk.

The very soft bleating of a baby beginning to demand food.

Or whether it's the dark shadow of the gun.

The gun is long, with a stick-like barrel. It's pointed right towards me.

'Please,' I hear Angharad say.

I look up.

There's a couple standing just by me. They look like a family that I might pass on any day, on any street. There's a very young baby strapped to the father in a stripy, colourful sling. It's murmuring a little and nodding its head ever so slightly. They look just like a normal family. Only their eyes are lit up: furious and blazing. Only the mother is pointing a gun right at me.

'Get away from the water,' the woman says. My legs feel useless, heavy pieces of flesh that are not connected to me. The baby opens its mouth and cries and the mother jogs it on the spot to shush it. But then it cries out a little louder.

'Go!' the man says. He takes a step closer – the gun moves a step closer to me – and I am frozen all the more.

'Billy,' Angharad begs, but when I don't move, she tries to talk to the family. 'We just wanted some water. We'll go . . . we just wanted water.'

'How do we know that you're not one of them?' the woman says tightly. 'You might have infected the water supply now.'

'It doesn't work like that,' I say. 'You'd know if we were infected.'

They can't hide a puzzled look creeping over their faces although they keep the gun fixed upon us.

'I don't want to have to use this,' the man says. I don't believe him. I don't think that he *wants* to hurt us but I can also hear it in his voice, see in his face, something that's more terrifying: he's scared. He's the one holding the gun but he's the one that's scared. And that means he's dangerous.

'We're going,' Angharad says. She pulls me up to standing and without turning our back to them we stumble away.

The couple don't speak.

The baby continues to cry. It makes ragged bleats that feel unfinished, somehow.

They keep the gun focused on us.

HOW TO (MAKE YOURSELF) LEAVE

When we get back to the clearing where we left Julie and Steve, our belongings are still spread out all over the ground.

'There was a couple with a gun,' Angharad gasps. 'We've got to go.'

Julie looks up, astonished, but starts stuffing things into bags straightaway.

Steve stands up and looks hard in the direction that we've just run from.

'Steve!' Julie shouts. 'Help me.'

We grab at everything we can but then we hear a rustle in the bushes that makes us pick up our feet and start to run.

I keep looking over my shoulder to see if anyone is following us but all I see is a blur of trees and bushes; all I feel is the stamping of my feet and the beating of my heart.

When we are a little distance away, Julie turns to us both.

'Are you all right? What happened?'

'They had a baby,' Angharad says. 'A really little baby.'

'They were afraid but they thought that we were infected.

I don't think they'd actually met any Greys.'

'That's good,' Julie says. 'Maybe that means that there aren't very many around here.'

'What did they say to you?' Steve asks.

'They just told us to leave the stream,' Angharad says. 'They thought that we were contaminating the water. We told them we weren't but they didn't want to listen.'

'Let's keep walking for as long as we can,' Julie says. 'We should be able to make it to the farm first thing tomorrow if we make good progress today. Maybe . . . maybe . . . we'll make it all the way there.'

We keep walking until it gets dark. We ignore the blisters. We try to forget about the ache in our legs and the weariness that hangs like low clouds in our brains.

When Steve stops walking ahead of us, I can see that he is straining to see the path.

'Maybe we should stop now while we have just enough light to make a camp,' I suggest loudly. We're still not talking to each other and I'm glad of it; it's easier this way. Since I had the thought that Steve can't really like me, everything he does gives me more reason to believe it.

'Yes – good idea,' Julie says straightaway, but Steve says, 'I think that we should go on a bit further,' at exactly the same time.

'The light's going now,' Julie says. 'I think we should stop.'

'Me too,' chimes in Angharad. 'What do you think, Billy?'

I look around at the darkening countryside. I can't see any other lights. For that moment, it looks peaceful – the grass and trees wrapped in a velvet twilight, the fields rolling on to one another like silent waves of a silent sea.

'It doesn't seem like there is anyone else around here,' I say. 'But who knows about Greys?'

'There is something that worries me,' Julie says. 'There should be a small town over there. I mean, I might be wrong, but I would expect to see its lights in that direction. And well, there's . . . there's nothing.'

We all stare together where Julie pointed. The quiet, dimming countryside no longer seems tranquil – it is full of shadows and dips and humps that we cannot see properly. We don't know what's out there; we don't know what might be hiding.

'Let's keep quiet,' I say.

In the last of the light, I find us a spot that is a little sheltered and off the track. There isn't a tree trunk to shelter beside and I worry at first that we will get too cold here, that we might be too exposed. But then as I unwrap the tarpaulin for us to lie upon, I feel Angharad and Julie beside me. They help me to pull the sheet so it is as wide as it can go. I hate every crackle that it makes, it's too loud, but I know too that it will protect us from the cold that rises from the ground in an ever-increasing swell.

Julie and Steve pile all of our bags together. I suggest to Julie that they check on how much food we have left for tomorrow and the pair of them check through our supplies. I check on the water although I know how much is left; just the couple of bottles of water at the stream that we managed to fill before we met the family. When I hear them stop talking, I look up and see them, their arms wrapped so tightly together that I can't see where one body ends and the other begins.

I feel a stab as I see them together. I can't remember Sylvia and Steve ever holding each other like this, not so tightly, not as though they were joined together by something physical.

I know in that moment that I have to get to Sylvia. Steve and Julie have each other, Angharad has her mum but Sylvia has no one, only me. I will get them to the farm and when I know that they are safe I'll leave to find Sylvia, at the Martello tower.

'Come on then, everyone, we should try and get some rest,' Julie says as she and Steve finally let go of one another. It's hard to see each other properly now that the darkness is falling around us, I can't see their faces.

'I'll do the first watch,' Steve says. 'Goodnight, everyone.'

Julie and Angharad mumble goodnights; I stay silent.

'I'll sleep next to you,' I hear Angharad whisper to me as she shuffles up next to me. Julie joins us as Steve keeps a look-out.

Julie and Angharad sleep around me, one on either side, and that night, despite all that has happened, I drop off to sleep soundly.

I fall into a dream before I know it's a dream.

DAY 4

HOW TO GET TO SAFETY

Steve wakes me.

It's still darkish but I can see the soft light of dawn creeping across the sky.

'Time to go, Billy,' he tells me.

I can't believe that I slept so long. I look over to Angharad who lies still beside me, emitting soft, wispy snores. Julie gently shakes her awake. She looks startled at first and looks all around her, looking, I think, for danger, for Greys. Then she sees me and she relaxes.

'Are you okay?' I whisper to her.

'Bad dream,' she mutters.

We ration out the last of the oat bars for breakfast. Then we begin walking.

We're quiet as we go; there's a feeling hanging in the air that this should be the last leg of our journey, but it's edged with another thought too: that if the farm is not safe then where will we go?

After an hour or so, Steve starts singing quietly to himself as we walk along.

'You've got a good voice,' Julie laughs.

'I was in a band at university.'

'Were you really?'

'Yes, I was the lead singer.'

He bursts into a loud chorus of a song I don't recognize.

'I think it's best that we keep quiet,' I say. 'We don't know if there are any more Greys around.'

'We haven't seen one for ages,' Steve says, a little petulantly. 'I think we're safe now.'

'Billy's right,' Angharad rushes in. 'We need to be careful.'

I see Julie and Steve exchange a look with raised eyebrows.

'How can you do that?' I say. The words spit from my mouth.

'What?' Steve says.

'Make that look, like you think we're being silly – with all that has happened.'

'Billy, no one's suggesting that,' Julie says quickly.

'I saw the way you looked at each other – like you think I'm overreacting by saying we need to be quiet.'

'Well, maybe you are a bit,' Steve says. 'Billy, there's no one around. We've not seen any sign of anything since we set off this morning and you even said that the couple you saw didn't know what the Greys were like. It's okay to relax a bit, you know. We can't be on high alert all the time.'

'We can't relax,' I say. 'That's the whole point. Sylvia always said—'

'Billy! Enough! Your mum is not here.' There's a sharpness

to his voice that makes me draw back. He says it again: 'She's not here. I am, and that means you have to listen to me and not always argue back. I know you think that all this proves that Sylvia was right all along, but it doesn't. The sooner you accept that, the better it will be for all of us, including you.'

'If she hadn't taught me anything, then we wouldn't have made it this far. You know it – and the sooner you accept *that,* the better it will be for all of us – including you.' I don't quite recognize my own voice twisting away as I spit his own pompous words back at him, but it's like I can't control the anger, hurt and fear any more.

Our eyes meet for just a single moment. The way he looks at me makes me feel like I'm broken.

I look away first, staring at the blades of grass that look more grey than green, that look sharp to the touch and shadowed.

As we walk on, no one says another word.

When Julie first spots it in the distance, she makes a sound like a whimper or a cry.

'There!' she says and points.

It's nestled into the top of the valley: a few white, low buildings sitting on the green of a hill.

'I can't believe we made it,' Steve says. 'We should get there in a couple of hours if we don't stop.'

'I can't wait to eat something proper,' Angharad says.

'Me too,' Julie says, giving Angharad a quick, tight hug. 'Granddad will cook us up a storm.' Then she looks over at

Steve and me. 'I can't wait for you to meet him.'

Steve swings his hand into Julie's and they lead the way, their locked hands rocking with every step. It makes me once again so certain that I need to get to Sylvia. I can't stop thinking of her alone, in the tower, waiting for me, wondering where I am.

'What are you thinking about?' Angharad asks me as we start to follow Steve and Julie.

'What?'

'You've got a faraway look on your face.'

'Nothing,' I say. 'Just – you know – thinking about getting to the farm.'

'Granddad can be pretty grumpy and stubborn sometimes but I can't wait to see him.'

'Oh, so you take after him, do you?'

'Something like that.' Angharad grins over at me.

We speed up our pace as we get closer to the farm. It feels almost like we're stumbling towards it. My legs no longer feel tired now that we're almost there. I feel like I could just keep on walking and walking for ever.

As we approach the farm buildings, my eyes scan over every inch of the surroundings. Rule number two: pay attention. It's quiet and there's no sign of life at any of the windows, but then I spot a curtain swishing closed at one of the top windows.

'Stop,' I tell everyone.

'What is it?' Julie asks.

'Did you see a Grey?' Angharad says, a tremor in her voice.

'Someone behind that curtain,' I whisper.

Only Steve carries on walking.

The front door swings open and a small, grey-haired man rushes out. Julie runs towards him and they fall into each other; it looks like they are two pieces of a jigsaw puzzle slotting together perfectly.

'Granddad!' Angharad squeals, running towards him.

'Why, look at the state of you!' Julie's father exclaims. He cups his hands around Angharad's cheeks and I can't imagine a trace of grumpiness lining his face which is creased into a huge smile.

'See, Billy,' Steve says to me. 'I told you we would be safe here.'

DAY 5

HOW TO LEAVE

A whisper in the darkness.

'Billy? Are you awake?' The door to the bedroom I'm in creaks open.

'Yes.'

'I thought I heard you get up.'

'I'm just – I was just going to the toilet.'

In truth, I was packing my bag. I tried to move silently but the floorboards of the old farmhouse groaned and squeaked beneath me. I quickly shove it behind me, hoping that Angharad can't see it in the darkness.

'You're not really going to the toilet, are you?' she asks gently.

'What? Yes, of course I – I am – I'm just—'

'It's your mum, isn't it? You want to go to her?'

'How did you . . .' My voice trails off.

'Because I see you, Billy. And I know you. You get a look in your eyes, when you're thinking about your mum. I know it because you look how I feel about my dad. I miss him so much.

I wish he was here. Although he'd drive Mum completely up the wall.'

'I was thinking about your dad on the oil rig,' I say. 'It's definitely the safest place to be right now. I am sure that he will be all right. He'll be thinking just the same about you as well, you know. Missing you and wishing you were with him.'

Angharad speaks in a quiet voice: 'I hope so.' Then: 'Where do you think your mum is? How will you even find her?'

'I know where she is. When I last saw her in hospital she told me that she would be waiting for me. It's a type of tower – a Martello tower, have you ever heard of them?'

Angharad shakes her head.

I continue in a low voice: 'It's an old fort, built a long time ago. Before she got taken away, Sylvia had been breaking into it and storing food and other things there – everything that we might need in case something like this would happen.'

'Did she really know that this was going to happen?'

'Sometimes I think that she didn't – that everyone was right to think that she has . . . that she has problems in her head. When I was living with her, before all this, I know she used to scare me sometimes because she acted . . . not okay. But now this has *actually* happened, we did need to prepare and everything she taught me has helped to get us here. So maybe even if she didn't always get it right, she was trying her best to keep me safe? I mean, if it weren't for Sylvia, we might still be going round in circles, not knowing which way north was.'

Angharad nods as though she agrees with me. 'Where is

this Martello tower? Is it close by?'

I shake my head. 'It's on the other side of the country. A place called Sandgate. On the east coast.'

'How on earth are you going to get there?'

'Any way I can. If I have to walk it will take me a long time. But I'm sure I can do it – I'll just have to do as much as I can in a day. I'll get there in the end.'

Suddenly Angharad lights up with an idea. 'My granddad! He has a Land Rover!' she whispers excitedly. 'We could take that. We could *all* go.'

I shake my head. 'They'd never let us. Steve would never let me go,' I say. 'He'd think it's too dangerous. That it's not worth the risk. You've seen how he reacts when I mention her.' I can hear my voice turn in on itself as I imagine his furrowed, disapproving face.

Angharad slumps a bit and I know that she sees it's true.

'Thank you, though,' I say.

'I don't want you to go,' Angharad says in a very quiet voice. 'It feels too dangerous. Especially on your own.'

'Maybe I'll come back,' I tell her. 'Maybe I'll bring Sylvia with me.' I try to sound cheerful although I can't truthfully imagine that will happen. The distance that I need to travel to get to the Martello tower feels like a gulf, a hole that I will need to fall into and then climb my way out of.

And I don't really know for sure that she is there. What if something happened to her on the way to the tower? What if she wasn't able to leave the hospital? What if I travel all that way only to discover that she's not there, after all. I dismiss the thought from my head; all I can focus on is getting there.

But then another thought comes to me. What if she is there and she won't leave the tower? We're stuck there, just the two of us. I remember the dank, mushroom-smelling room with the two sleeping bags laid out on the floor, the way that Sylvia's moods would rise and fall as quickly as the wind picking up. I can barely admit how uneasy it makes me feel to remember. I quickly try to stuff the feeling away, somewhere inside where it can't reach me.

'I'd better go,' I say. 'Before anyone else wakes up.' *And before I change my mind*, I add silently to myself.

'Are you sure that there's not another way?' Angharad asks. Her voice rises steadily, panicking.

'I'm sure,' I say. 'Please do something for me? Don't tell Steve or your mum where I've gone. I don't want them to follow me. Steve will know that I've gone to Sylvia but he doesn't know about the Martello tower. Don't tell him. He can't know where I've gone. Do you promise?'

'I promise,' Angharad says.

'Really promise?' I say. 'Not like last time.'

'Yes. Really promise.'

'If Steve knows where I am, he might think he has to come after me, but I'll be fine with Sylvia and he's better here on the farm with you guys. He does really love your mum, you know.'

Angharad looks like she is about to ask me a question but she doesn't say any more and just nods her head a little.

'Let me help you get the stuff that you need,' she says. 'I know where all the good food is in the larder.'

We pad downstairs in the silent farmhouse and Angharad raids the kitchen for me. When I've stuffed as much as I can possibly carry into my bag, we turn the large iron key in the old door and I step outside.

The moon must be hidden behind clouds but I can just about make out the shapes of the trees around me, and for a moment I just stand there and listen. It sounds like there is nothing to hear but if I really listen, I can hear a breeze shaking a tree, a small creature, possibly a mouse or a vole, scurrying through the undergrowth.

'Billy?' Angharad whispers.

I turn back to her.

'Yes?'

'Be careful,' she says. 'I hope you find Sylvia. And stay safe.'

I nod because suddenly speaking words seems like a difficult thing to do. It feels like they would get stuck in my throat if I tried to say anything.

I rummage in my bag and pull out *How to Survive*. 'I want you to take this,' I say.

I hold the book for a moment. Even in the darkness, it feels so familiar to me. It's been my one link to Sylvia while I've been living with Steve, an invisible connection between us that's been all mine. When I found it under the bin on the day she brought it to me, it felt like more than a book, it felt like trust, like belief, like something more than could ever be expressed in words. I know that Sylvia gave it to me because she wanted me to remember – not just everything that she had taught me – but to remember the two of us, together, as well. I want to pass that on to Angharad, in the same way that I wanted Anwar to have a pocket survival kit. I want to give them something to show how much they have taught me, how much I don't want them to forget me and the friendships that have grown between us. I press the book into Angharad's hands. 'Just in case. It's got everything you'll need to know in it, just in case.'

'I can't . . . Billy . . . it's your mum's . . .'

'It *was* Sylvia's, and then she learned everything she needed from it and so she gave it to me. Now I've learned everything from it and so I'm giving it to you. I really want you to have it.'

'Are you sure?'

'Yes . . . and if Steve asks where you got it from, just tell him the truth. Tell him I got it from Sylvia. Tell him I've been hiding it from him, all this time.'

'Thank you, Billy,' she says and she throws her arms around me. 'Remember when we said that we could trust the people we could trust? Well, I trust you, Billy Weywood, I trust you with everything. Let me get something to prove it.'

She dashes back inside before I am able to stop her. She's gone for just a few moments and then she's back, thrusting something into my hands.

'I want you to take this with you.' She's holding out the heavy picture frame and the photograph of her with her mum and dad. 'This is *my* most precious thing. Maybe you can use the glass of the frame to do something survival-ly with. I don't know. But please take it.'

'No, no, I can't,' I say. 'It's yours, it's too special.'

'You gave me this.' She holds up the book. 'It can't be more special than this. Please, I want you to have it.'

'Okay,' I say, looking at her smiling face in the picture. 'Thank you.' I push the frame into my bag.

I have been waiting for this moment for the last few days but now that it's here, I find myself immobile. There's a part of me that does not want to leave. I want to turn again to Angharad. I'm sure that she will still be standing at the doorway, hugging *How to Survive* to her, watching my every movement.

But I am certain too that if I turn around and see her just one more time then I will never leave. I will throw my bag down and retreat into the farmhouse. I feel like a magnet drawn to metal just thinking about it.

And so instead I force myself to put one foot in front of the other and walk away.

Only in this way, by thinking about just one step at a time, am I able to leave.

HOW TO START A JOURNEY (BY YOURSELF)

I don't look back.

I try not to tell myself that what I am doing is stupid, that there is almost no chance on earth that I will be able to make it. That what I am doing is dangerous and every step of my journey is taking me further and further from any kind of safety.

I try to forget that the Greys exist. I try to shake them from my memory, for if I think about them for too long, I am sure, too, that this will bring me to a halt.

After a while, there is a rhythm to my footsteps. After a while, I know that I have walked far away enough now and if I did turn back I would not be able to catch sight of the farm. When I go further still, I lose the expectation that I had been carrying with me that Steve might catch me up and demand that I come back with him.

I try not to think about Steve and what he will think when he finally wakes up and discovers I'm gone. I'm guessing he might be torn for just a few moments between wanting to follow me and wanting to stay with Julie and Angharad, but then reason will win out. He doesn't know where I am going; there would be little hope of him finding me. The only choice he has is to stay at the farm, as planned; he can hardly abandon Julie now.

There's another voice inside me that's asking if he would even think about following me – that's saying maybe he will be glad that I have gone. I know that I'm the reason that Sylvia became so ill which means I'm the reason that Steve left. Whatever he's said about wanting things to be different, he probably never wanted me to live with him. He never really wanted me. That's why it's been so hard for him to believe me when we first discovered the Greys, because he didn't really want me.

I look to the stars. I identify the Big Dipper and from there, I find north. I check it constantly to make sure that I am heading east, even when I am sure that I am walking in the right direction.

It comforts me a little to plot the shape of the Big Dipper. My eyes travel from star to star and then back again, over and over. Maybe it's because their position doesn't change, maybe it's because the stars are beautiful. Maybe it's because I sense Sylvia so strongly when I look up at them, it is as though she is standing beside me. Guiding me towards her.

As my eyes grow more accustomed to the dark, I stumble less but the more I detect the shapes of the trees and bushes around me, the more my fear grows. I start to wonder about the detail of their outlines. My mind begins to rush with the thought that perhaps there are Greys all around me. The shadowy trunk is actually a Grey, the dip in the ground is hiding another.

I want to freeze when I think these things; I feel my footsteps begin to slow, but I push myself onwards and onwards and I try to forget. I try to forget all that I have seen.

I try to forget that I could be surrounded by them.

Suddenly I hear the sound of something rustling in the undergrowth from behind me and my breath sticks in my throat. I force myself to turn around.

I trace the outline of a dark shadow moving steadily in my direction.

My eyes strain to identify them, trying to spot any marker of who it could be: the way that they walk or an item of clothing. I realize that I actually want it to be Steve, that I want him to have come after me, to stop me, to protect me. To want me.

But I know it's not him.

When I look again I see that there's another figure behind the first, and another behind them, and another behind them. I stop counting how many there are.

They could be an army.

An army of Greys.

I skitter through the trees as lightly as I can but when I turn, the Greys are getting closer. They've broken into a loping run now they've heard my movements.

I run as fast as I can. Roots trip me up, brambles claw me as I pass them. It's as though I'm stumbling, almost falling, into the mouth of a cave. And I have no idea whether there's another way out or if I'm trapping myself in a corner.

I reach a steep bank that I scrabble to climb up. I worry with every step that I will fall, that I will tumble backwards, but I press forward, I don't look back.

I slip, and claw my fingers into the undergrowth to regain my balance, only to slide down a little further still.

'Hold on!' My voice no longer sounds like my own, words no longer sound like words; it's all feeling, it's all fear. I throw an arm forward and my fingers close around a root. I pull myself up with all my might, just enough to find footing so I can clamber up the slope.

The sound of the Greys behind me is like a drum. With each beat I propel myself on.

When I reach the top of the bank, there's a low metal barrier and once I'm over that the soles of my shoes slap across hard tarmac in echoing, smacking steps.

A road. I've reached a road.

I'm exposed here, so I dart across it to the other side, looking for any place that I can hide, anything that will conceal me, but as I'm halfway across, I hear something approaching in the distance.

A noise growing louder as it grows closer. But for once it's a welcome noise: the whining of a motorcycle's engine.

I don't think. I throw off my bag and desperately search

through it until my hand closes around the hard, cold cylinder of the torch I found in Julie's kitchen. It's small, but powerful, although it feels quite light in my hand.

The headlamps of the motorcycle are flooding the road now; it will be past me, if it does not hit me, in the next few moments.

But I stand there, my feet rooted, in the middle of the road.

I turn the nozzle until the beam is as bright and as strong as it can be. I wave the torch as the motorcycle approaches me and I hold up my other hand, as though whoever is driving the motorcycle might be able to see me waving. Like I am an old friend, as though I am expecting them. For a mad, fleeting moment, I imagine that it will be Anwar. I picture him atop the bike, comically too small to be driving it, but hunched over the handlebars nonetheless, come to rescue me. But the truth is that I can't see the driver in the darkness, I can only hear the roar of the bike and all around me, I am surrounded by shadows.

The motorcycle is almost upon me and is not showing any signs of slowing. The driver must be able to see me because there are no other lights. I think about this for a second as I look up to the streetlamps on the side of the road – I hadn't realized when I first got here that none of them were on.

The engine whines and roars in alternate beats. It sounds as though it is speeding up, not slowing down. As it nears me, its light blinds me. I screw up my eyes and keep them shut as it passes me. I feel a rush of air whip my cheeks as it flies past me.

My heart sinks. It's gone. The Greys will get me for sure now . . .

I almost don't believe it when I hear the screech of its brakes.

I turn to see the motorcycle has stopped just a little distance down the road.

I run towards it.

HOW TO FIND HELP (WHEN YOU REALLY NEED IT)

The figure on the motorcycle is clad all in black. They wear a helmet so I can't see their face.

A great, tall figure on a motorcycle: so huge they have to hunch over to hold on to the handlebars. A giant, almost.

I can make out the width of their shoulders – massive and broad – and I find myself thinking of the trunk of an oak tree.

I want to shout out – *Please help me, can you help me* – I can feel the words bubbling up inside me but they are stuck.

As I get closer, as I approach the ticking, grumbling motorcycle, my throat closes up. I can hear thundering steps striking the tarmac behind me. The Greys have reached the road.

The motorcyclist is shouting at me now: 'Get on!' They reach out a huge, strong arm towards me to swing me up on to the narrow seat behind them.

In a beat of a moment, I am up there, on the quivering motorcycle that feels, sitting upon it, as though it's alive.

Just as the Greys are almost upon us, it bursts forward with a growl and a pounce and as I cling on to the bike, to the motorcyclist, we rush away.

I try not to look at their splayed, bent fingers, like twigs of a branch, reaching, growing towards us. They almost scratch at my arm; they are only millimetres away.

I screw my eyes tightly closed.

But the motorcycle leaps forward again with another sudden bolt of power and we are away, untouched.

We roar down roads. When I open my eyes, I can see we're passing fields that are lined with darkness and trees that make shadowy, leering shapes. Their branches look like they might reach out at any moment and scoop us up.

It doesn't take long before I start to feel stiff and uncomfortable, sitting on the back of the motorcycle, clutching on fiercely for fear of falling off.

It's not until the sun has started to rise that the motorcyclist pulls into a smaller road, and then a lane and a lay-by. He pulls it into the clearing. The engine dwindles for a moment and then is still.

I almost fall off as I try to climb off. We are both getting off at the same time and it's as though we are trying to untangle ourselves from each other.

The motorcyclist reaches up for his helmet.

The face in front of me is creased with lines, like a paper map that's been folded and folded in on itself in all the wrong ways so it's no longer neat, and is made into a completely different kind of shape.

When he speaks, it's low and gruff but it also sounds a tiny bit like Julie – a voice that almost sounds like singing, in the up and down way of a Welsh accent.

'So who've we got here then?' he says.

'I'm Billy,' I say.

'Billy,' he repeats, rolling each syllable. 'I'm Len. You gave me a bit of a turn when I saw you on the road like that. Though I suppose nothing should surprise me. Not any more.'

'Thank you for picking me up,' I say. 'If you hadn't come, or if you hadn't stopped, the Greys would have . . .'

'But I did,' Len says gently. 'Greys? That's a good name for them.'

We fall silent for a moment, remembering them.

'Where are you going to?' I ask.

Len scratches his beard. It grows out in white patches, spikily. 'I'm driving to Folkestone.'

'That's not too far from a place called Sandgate, is it?' I ask.

'Not too far. You know someone there?' he asks.

'My mum. I think my mum's there,' I say.

'I won't be able to take you all the way but I could get you pretty close.'

'You'll take me?' I ask, unbelieving. Sylvia appears in my mind as I imagine getting all that way closer to her.

'Can hardly leave you here, can I? What are you doing out here all on your own, anyway?'

'I live with my dad but he wouldn't want me to go to my mum. He would never let me go to see her.' The words come tumbling out. 'So I had to run away . . . to try to get to her. Because she'll be waiting for me. She needs me, my dad doesn't.'

Len looks like he's going to say something but then changes his mind.

'It's a bit difficult to explain,' I add. 'They separated and then . . .'

But Len just nods his head. 'It's all right. Life can get mighty complicated. I'm going to see my old mum too, as a matter of fact,' Len says. 'She lives in a nursing home in Folkestone. I'd been trying to get her moved to be closer to me for years but, well, it didn't work out. And now, I have no idea if she is safe. I can't get through to the nursing home. And she would have no idea anyway – she has dementia. Her memories – her memories are going, going, gone. She doesn't recognize me any more.

'You might think what's the point going across the country to see someone who doesn't even know who you are? But I've got to go. I've got to get to her. I think that she knows I'm familiar, even if she doesn't know me, right? And she must be confused with all that's going on. Who knows what state the place will be in? I don't know if the staff will have stayed with them. Or maybe they will have jumped ship to be with their own families? I wouldn't blame them.

'This thing happening, it shows us the things that are really important. The things that really matter. Everything else . . . everything else just drops away.'

'Yeah, it does,' I say.

Len suddenly looks startled, as though he'd forgotten I was there.

'Sorry,' he says. 'There's me jabbering on when we really should make a move. You're the first person I've spoken to for a couple of days now. But it doesn't do to stay in one place for too long. It doesn't do at all.'

Len uses a petrol can hung on the back of the motorcycle to refuel.

'If only we knew more about the . . . what did you call them? . . . the Greys,' he continues.

My mind swarms with everything that I know, each encounter I've had with them. I can feel a fragment of a thought rising. If I can just let my brain track back over all that has happened, it might just turn into something fully formed.

'Have you noticed,' I suddenly say, 'that whenever it's been really sunny, they're not around as much. I've seen them in the daylight . . .' I let myself wonder back to that first time I saw the fallen man on the street: it was raining and grey and after that it was night-time. It was overcast at the garages too. The day that the infection seemed to break through when we were up the Cabot tower, it was cloudy. 'I've not seen them out and about when it's been really sunny,' I say.

Len scratches his beard. 'I'm not sure,' he admits. 'What do you think that would mean anyway?'

'That they don't think they like sunshine.' It sounds a bit absurd saying it aloud and maybe it's nothing at all but I feel myself storing it away, that little piece of information, as though I were writing it down. *Greys – can they come out when the sun is shining?* I ponder.

Len empties the petrol can into the tank, giving it delicate little shakes so every last drop is used, and ties the empty can back up onto the back of the motorcycle.

'Hopefully the powers that be are working out a way to stop them . . . before it's too late. Let's keep moving. If we don't stop and the roads are fairly clear, we should get there later this afternoon.'

'This afternoon.' I almost choke on the words. I can't hide my excitement that we'll be so close to where I think Sylvia is.

As we go further, we start to see people. They run out at us sometimes and Len speeds up and swerves to avoid them. I know we can't help them, but I can't look at their faces; I don't want to think of the people that we are leaving behind.

Perhaps they are like us and are desperate to journey somewhere, to get to someone, but there's no room now on the motorcycle for anyone else.

We go past some houses, small clusters of them that sit together. A village that looks deserted. Some of the doors are left wide open and through the open doorways, I can see upended furniture and things scattered where they shouldn't be.

One cottage we go past has a heavy, overhanging thatched roof. It looks like something from a fairy tale in a picture book: its front door is shiny and red, its windows are made out of wonky diamonds of glass.

As the motorcycle reaches it, the front door flies open suddenly.

Greys throw themselves out desperately on to the road.

One after another, they pile out of the house.

I feel Len lean forward a little. The engine revs. We accelerate past the Greys and even though they try to follow us, they cannot catch us up.

I hear Len shout something back to me that I can't quite make out, but then he points to the sky. The sun has disappeared behind a cloud.

It makes me nervous now whenever we pass by any other buildings and whenever I can't feel the sun beating down.

The Greys are simply hiding.

They're waiting for the right moment to pounce.

HOW TO (ALMOST) LOSE YOUR BAG

I try to ignore it at first.

The sound, like grinding metal, as though there are huge, steel teeth grating against one another. It starts small, like something close to a ticking, but then it grows louder; it turns into a crushing, grinding sound. I can imagine them, those metal teeth: large dull hunks, rubbing against each other until they are only worn-away nubs, until they are almost, in fact, no more.

I can see Len's shoulders tense as he hears it and it grows sharper and more defined until it becomes a mechanical pounding that shakes the motorcycle with each vibration. I have to cling to Len tightly to stay upright.

He shouts something to me that I can't understand but then I hear the engine winding down and we begin to roll to a stop.

We're out in the middle of the countryside and I can't see any buildings around us. There's just the brown stretch of a ploughed field and the jagged outlines of some trees in the distance which, when I squint, look not unlike figures, their arms raised and outstretched as though they are waving to us, or warning us away.

But before we come to a complete stop, there's a flash of something in front of us. At first I only catch a glimpse of the patterned material – it's the soft type that pyjamas are made of, white covered with tiny pink dots which, when I look again, I can see are in fact small rosebuds. It's a type of nightie, or it used to be, hanging in pieces from a Grey that's run out from the parting in the field and almost collided straight into us.

The Grey shrieks with an awful voiceless whine. It lets its mouth hang wide open as it cries, raised up towards the sky, as though it is trying to catch the thin, fine raindrops that have started falling lightly around us.

Len kicks the motorcycle into gear again and we rush forward. We whip around the side of the Grey, despite the metal clunking which now reverberates like thunder through the bike. The Grey claws for my bag as we pass it, managing to grab hold of one of the straps. It almost pulls me from the bike but I cling on tightly to Len, binding my arms around him as closely as I can.

But the Grey grips on too and we end up dragging it behind us, shrieking and screaming and screeching all the way.

Len looks over his shoulder at what is happening.

'Take your bag off!' he shouts. 'Take it off! I've got you!'

I struggle to get out of the straps. I don't even think of what's inside it, I know that I have to let it go. I can only do it one arm at a time and it's when the rucksack slips a little away as my first arm is freed that the Grey makes a lunge towards me.

HOW TO USE A PICTURE FRAME (CREATIVELY)

I catch sight of the rectangular bulge of the frame that Angharad gave me jutting out from the side of my rucksack. I think of that photograph of her, smiling away with her dad and Julie. In another world, another time, one where she would never have thought that she would have to meet Steve and me.

The sharp corner of the picture frame is sticking out just by the head of the Grey and so with every bit of strength I have, I drive my bag and the pointed edge of the picture frame towards the creature. It lets out a shriek; of surprise, I think.

The Grey falls from the motorcycle and, in an instant, Len is pushing us forward, grinding the complaining engine on so we're propelled down the road, away.

Away from my rucksack filled with all my provisions, away from the photograph of Angharad with her mum and dad and away from the crumpled body of the Grey that is now starting to sit up.

I make myself turn my head and I watch it. I cannot turn away.

It stands up but from the way it's standing I can see it's injured from the fall. It doesn't try to follow us but, as though it's looking right back at me, it stares at us driving off down the road. I tell myself I'm imagining it, but the expression on its face looks to me something like sadness.

HOW TO GET TO SANDGATE

Len pulls the motorcycle into a lay-by after a few more hours of driving.

The metal rattle hasn't got any worse, but it hasn't got any better either. I've been waiting for the bike to give out completely, but luckily it is holding on. Just like me and Len.

I'm so stiff, I don't think that I can climb off the motorcycle; I feel like I'll be stuck in that same hunched position from now on.

Len stretches wide. His arms reach out sideways. He looks massive as he does it and seeing him standing tall, I think that I wasn't far off, thinking he was like a giant when I first saw him.

'That's better,' he says after stretching out for a few moments. 'That was a close shave back there, wasn't it? Well, Billy, this is where we say goodbye. I've got to try and get this old hunk of metal a little further still but you're not far now.' He touches the bike tenderly as though it's a horse or a dog, something that could feel his touch.

'Will the motorcycle be all right? Will it get you to your mum?'

‘It should just about get me there,’ Len says in a vague way that makes me not want to ask any more. ‘How’re you doing?’ Len peers down at me, shading his eyes so he can see me properly.

‘You’d better eat something,’ he says. ‘And have a drink. You’ve still got a little way to go yet.’ He rummages around in one of the bags and gives me a packet of biscuits and a bottle of juice in a plastic bag.

I feel my mouth fill with saliva just looking at them but I ask, ‘Are you sure you have enough?’

‘Sure,’ Len says. ‘Have them.’

‘Where are we exactly?’ I ask.

‘We’re about four miles outside of Sandgate,’ Len says.

‘Where is your mum again?’ I ask.

‘She’s in Folkestone,’ he says. Then he says it again, as though he is trying to convince himself: ‘She’s in Folkestone.’

‘You’d better go,’ I tell him. ‘Thank you so much for bringing me this far.’

‘It’s okay,’ Len says. ‘I just wish, I just wish I could take you all the way.’

‘No, it’s better that I go on foot,’ I tell him. ‘I can move really quietly if I do come across any Greys. It isn’t far now. But I don’t know if I would have made it if you hadn’t stopped.’

‘You would have made it,’ Len says. ‘You’re tough, you are. You wouldn’t have made it this far if you weren’t. And brave. By heck, when I saw you waving that torch in the middle of the road like you were, I thought: this kid’s got guts.’

'I don't know,' I say. 'I wasn't really thinking about what I was doing.'

'Well – look. I hope you find your mum quickly. And, Billy?'

'Yes?'

'I know you said things were . . . complicated with your dad, but I'd guess that he'll be worried about you. So, when you get to your mum, find a way to let him know you're safe, yeah? When the world goes mad like it is now, we see what's really important, and I bet, well, I bet, you're more important to your dad than you think.'

I blink, not knowing what to say to that.

Len shuffles awkwardly. 'Well, bye, Billy. And good luck.'

'You too. Goodbye, Len,' I say.

We're making all the noises like we are saying goodbye but Len doesn't climb on his motorcycle and I don't walk away.

Neither of us makes a move.

I don't know if it's because Len's worried about leaving me. Or if perhaps he doesn't want to be alone either. Maybe, I think, he's worried about his mother and finding out what's really going on with her.

Without thinking, I step forward and throw my arms around Len in a hug. I feel his huge arms enclose me.

I can't stop thinking that the Rule about not trusting anyone is once again out of the window. And that maybe I'm okay with that.

Without looking again at his face, I can walk away.

DAY 6

HOW TO MAKE A SOLAR STILL

I wake up sore and stiff, laced with dew drops.

It takes me a moment to realize that what woke me is the sound of heavy vehicles ploughing down a road.

There are deep shouts, now and again, that I can just make out through the rumble but they are shouts of action, not of despair.

I run towards the sound and through the trees I see a long line of huge army trucks roaring down the road. I hunker down so I cannot be seen but I can't stop myself from peeking out at the trucks. I haven't seen anyone since I said goodbye to Len yesterday. I don't want to risk the army thinking I'm lost and taking me back to Steve.

Once they disappear, there is no other traffic. The road becomes empty and still and I can only hear birdsong and the sound of leaves rustling in a gentle breeze.

I wander back to where I slept. I'd made a solar still the afternoon before by making a hole in the ground and lining it with green leaves. I placed the end of the biscuit packet so it made a sort of cup at the bottom of the hole, then stretched out and secured the plastic bag that Len gave me over the top of the hole. I weighed it down in its middle, just above the biscuit wrapper, so the condensation would run straight into it.

Fig. 14. – How to make a solar still

There's a couple of mouthfuls of water in the old biscuit packet. It will extend my supply a little, but partly I did it because it feels sort of like a miracle whenever I have made one – creating clean drinking water out of nothing. Plus running through the method distracts my mind from the bigger questions that are looming ahead of me. Will Sylvia be there?

What will she be like? Will I even make it? I reach down to the old wrapper to feel the small weight of water within it and tip it into my mouth. I eat one of the remaining biscuits, trying to eat it as slowly as possible to make it last a little longer.

I pick through a path in the woods, staying clear of the roads in case the army trucks come back, climb over stiles and walk on and on until my feet throb and my legs feel shaky beneath me. The sun shines down and I don't come across any Greys.

I try to ration out the few biscuits I have left and the last of the juice but I feel my hunger growing with every step that I take. I try to remember the last proper meal I had. We'd eaten at Julie's after Anwar and his dad had left. She and Steve had made pasta but they'd been talking over things and let it over-cook. It had turned a bit slimy in the pan but just the thought of it makes my mouth begin to salivate.

I find a bush of blackberries and I practically fall on to them. But they are not ripe, they're green and bullet-like and I know they will taste awful. But then I spot amongst the bushes some wild raspberry canes. The berries are almost overripe, darkly pink and swollen. My fingers tremble as I pluck them off the bush and shove them into my mouth and become stained with their juice. I'm sure that it's all over my face too, but I'm past caring.

Each one explodes in my mouth. Its tart sweetness rushes through me; I can almost feel the sugar reaching my brain.

It takes me a long time to leave those raspberries. I pick every berry I can see but each time I try to leave I tear back again to look for more fruit that I push clumsily into my open mouth.

I hear Sylvia's voice in my head once more: *Pace yourself. Don't give yourself a stomach ache.* I try to listen. I know I've eaten enough, but part of me is worried that I won't find more food on my way to the tower. Part of me, buried deep down inside, is also fearful that Sylvia might not even be there.

I had not let myself think this could happen.

I have only let myself imagine her there, in the Martello tower, waiting for me. To think of the alternative squeezes the breath out of me, it's a hammering in my chest, bearing down on me.

But now, now that I'm so close, that single thought, that little imagining that the tower is empty, swings through my mind like a pendulum.

If she is not there, I think, I will have to look for her. I think of the hospital that Steve and I saw her in. I would have to start there.

And if I couldn't find her there . . . I falter. And then I let myself think it: *If Sylvia is not in any of these places then maybe, like so many others, she has been infected.* She could be dead, or transformed into a Grey. But as quickly as I think that I bat the idea away. Sylvia's survival lessons had got me here, so she would be okay too. She would. She had to be.

I march on and on, one foot in front of the other.

I keep thinking that I can't possibly keep walking any more and each time that I do, I think: *Just one more step.* And after that, just one more.

After one more step, I tell myself, I can stop walking. But

after that one more step, I tell myself to take only one more.

Just like when I left Angharad at the farm, this is how I keep walking. Until eventually, there in the distance, is the outline of a grey building that I recognize as the tower.

It looks different to how I remember it. I worry at first that I've come to the wrong one. But then I think I spot the place where we parked the night that Sylvia brought me here.

'That's it,' I mumble to myself, although my mouth is parched, my throat sandpaper-dry. I sound strangled and hoarse as though I am a Grey myself.

I stumble on to the road now, the quickest route that will lead me directly towards it, although I almost tumble as my feet trip up on the loose stones on the tarmac and my legs speed up with a new energy I didn't know I had. I rush towards the Martello tower, breaking into a lolloping run.

I feel the raindrops fall on me before I realize it's raining. They patter on the road around me, like drumbeats.

I look up. The blue sky has been replaced with dark rain clouds.

I'm suddenly sharply aware of my footsteps pounding upon the tarmac in an offbeat and wild beat.

It takes me a moment to realize that they are not my footsteps I'm hearing.

HOW TO (ALMOST) GET CAUGHT

The Grey runs sinuously, moving with the grace of a cheetah. It's growing closer with every pace. Its legs look like they are moving so fast it might trip up over itself to reach me.

I feel the same way; I am running so fast that I am almost falling over myself to get away.

I try not to look back as I know this will slow me but at the same time, I can't stop myself from glancing back, just to know it's not on top of me.

Its face is crumpled and shrunken. There's something mesmerizing about it, definitely human but not at the same time. I can't help but try to imprint something living upon what is left behind.

I turn back as my shoes skid over the wet ground and the unbalance catches me: my heart is bursting and pounding. This fear still feels new, raw, even though I've faced it before on the journey to get here.

But I can't stop. I can't let the Grey touch me. So still I run. And then I trip, the black road dampened by raindrops coming up to meet me.

I plummet to the ground, spinning and breathless. Skidding over the uneven ground until I fall in a heap and with nothing left to protect me, I clasp my arms over my head, waiting for the claws of the Grey to hook around me.

'Get away!' I hear someone bellow. 'Get away from him! You'll infect him!'

And then I hear footsteps again, loud and insistent, but this time they are running away. When I look up, I see a car – it's not one of the army trucks but a large Land Rover that's covered in mud, and beyond it, I see the Grey running away into the distance as though there is something invisible that is chasing them and they have to get away from it.

Before I can even start to think about why the Grey is running, the car screeches to a halt at an angle ahead of me and the doors are thrown open.

HOW TO FIND YOUR FAMILY

Angharad is there first, flinging the door open and running towards me so fast that we collide into one another in a crash, crying, laughing and hugging all at once.

Steve darts from the driver's side of the car and before I know what is happening, he has me wrapped up in his arms.

'Oh, Billy, oh, Billy,' Steve is saying into my hair. He smells of sweat and a little of petrol.

'I've got you, I've got you,' Steve says. He thrusts me away from him and looks at me all over as though to check that I still have two legs, two arms and a head. 'Are you all right? Are you all right?'

But before I can answer him, he suddenly starts crying. Large, noisy tears that rack through his whole body.

'You are all right, aren't you?' he manages, through sobs.

I nod and then we are hugging each other again. So tightly that it hurts just a tiny bit, so tightly that I have to remind myself that this is Steve, not Sylvia.

'I thought I'd lost you,' he says when we stop hugging. 'I

couldn't bear it – I thought that I'd lost you again.' He looks at me like he can't believe that I am really there.

He won't let go of my shoulders. He is still clenching them tightly.

I peek a look up at him. Tears are still streaming down his face. It seems like they won't ever stop.

'Really?' I say quietly.

'What?'

'You really didn't want to lose me?'

'Billy – of course not! You are . . . you are my world. I can't imagine being without you.'

'Even though . . . even though I was the reason you left us, because I made Sylvia sick? Even though I was the one that changed her?'

'What are you talking about?'

'I heard you and Julie talking about it. You said that she changed after I was born. *I'm* the reason she was taken to hospital. *I'm* the reason I can't see her any more.'

Steve's face slowly changes; it goes from being wretched and confused to finally understanding. He remembers saying it, he can't hide the truth.

'Oh, Billy! I didn't know you were listening, and didn't really mean it like that. Your mum, well, she did change after you were born, yes. Some of those changes were a bit scary for me – the survival stuff took over, she couldn't seem to put it aside any more. But there were other changes too – changes that were so wonderful. I'd never seen your mum as happy as she was when she was with you. It was like someone had switched a light on inside of her, you know? None of it, none of that bad stuff, is your fault. It's my fault – for not being able to deal with it properly. Maybe a bit of your mum's fault too for driving me away, but I should have tried harder to stay around and help her. But you are not to blame for *anything*, I promise. Do you understand me? It's very important that you understand me.'

'But you don't like me doing my survival stuff? All I do . . . is upset you and make you mad,' I blurt out.

'Billy, that's not true! I mean, yes, at first I didn't like the idea of you carrying on with all the survival things, but I think that's because I got it all mixed together in my head.' He pauses. 'You *enjoying* learning all those skills is very different from your mum feeling that she *had* to do those things. I realize that now. And I was stupid for being cruel to you when we were travelling to the farm. Where would we have been without you? I was scared, that was all. I felt like I was letting you down, and now I see that I was, but just in a different way, and I'm so sorry for that.'

I stare down at the floor, not sure how to process everything he's saying. It's not my fault, he doesn't blame me . . .

'I'm the one who needs to deal with what happened between me and your mum,' Steve continues. 'But, Billy, you must know, I love everything about you. I know I'm not good at showing it or saying it, but I do. I never wanted to have all that time of not seeing you. I used to drive to London sometimes and sit outside your flat. Just so I might be able to catch a glimpse of you. I missed you so, so much.'

'You were the man in the car!' I exclaim. 'I saw you! On Christmas Day morning.'

Steve is nodding.

'Did you ever follow us into the woods?' I ask. 'When we made a fire.' I remember the figure by the dying fire on the day the storm started, on the last day of term. Has he really been watching me all this time? Wishing he could see me again?

'That was me,' Steve says, a little sheepishly. 'Your mum was always too good at spotting me. I know I'm not her – I'm not as exciting and I'm sure you've been really bored living with me. I just can't believe how talented you are, how brave and kind and strong – I just can't believe you're my son, that I'm your dad.'

'You don't bore me, Dad,' I say in a rush.

Steve looks up sharply when I call him that. He starts to smile and then quickly looks like he is going to start crying again.

He embraces me again in a tight hug, squeezing me so tightly that I don't know where I begin, where I end. When he lets me go, there is only a beat of a moment before Julie and Angharad are wrapping their arms around me, just as closely.

'Billy,' I hear Angharad say into my hair, as though she is sighing. When we release each other, her eyes are a swirl of tears.

'You broke your promise again . . .' I say.

'I'm sorry! I know you're going to be mad at me, but I had to,

Billy. Your dad, my mum, they were so worried and I couldn't stand the idea of you being all alone—'

But I cut her off. 'And I'm glad that you did.'

She smiles back at me.

'I can *keep* secrets, you know,' she says. 'In fact, I'm pretty good at it. But—'

'There are secrets you know you must keep,' Julie finishes for her. 'But there are others that you decide to break because you know it will help someone. The trick is knowing the difference. It's so good to see you again, Billy. So good.'

They hug me again.

'I just can't believe you're all here.' Even as I say the words, even as I see them in front of me, I can still barely believe it.

'Of course we are,' Angharad says back. 'We wouldn't leave you behind. We stick together now.'

'That's right,' Steve says. 'We're a family now.' He says the words slowly, looking around at us all for reassurance that what he's saying is right. Julie and Angharad nod through the tears that stain their cheeks in shiny, wet lines. I feel Angharad's fingers reach for mine and squeeze them very gently.

'And that means you don't have to do all the hard stuff on your own,' Julie says to me. 'Because we help each other – we'll always be there to help each other.'

I feel the words sink into me. They make me feel warm inside, like when the sun spreads its rays gently across your back, and slowly something inside me begins to unknot.

'And Sylvia, of course,' Julie adds. 'Your mum is important to you, Billy, so she's an important part of our family too.'

'I think she's hiding in there,' I say, pointing out the stubby, grey building in the distance.

'Let's go then,' says Steve. 'The news reports are saying that things have calmed down since we left the city. The army's been deployed now and things are getting better, but we still need to keep our wits about us.'

'Have they said anything about the Greys reacting to sunlight?' I ask. 'Len said . . . Len's a motorcyclist who drove me most of the way here, he thought that they have to avoid bright sunlight.'

Julie nods. 'Your friend was right. It's been on the government briefings that we saw at my dad's house. They've been saying that sunlight repels the Greys, especially when they are first infected. But they think they might get desensitized to it over time. So if it's sunny like now it doesn't necessarily mean that they won't be around. There's a lot they don't know yet.'

'And apparently they're behaving differently than they did when they first got infected,' Angharad tells me. 'Some of them seem like they are avoiding people now and some scientists even think that they can understand you when you speak to them. They've had reports that when people have told Greys to stop before they get too close, they can sometimes understand.'

'Is that why you yelled at that Grey?' I ask. 'Told it that it would infect me?'

'Yes. I wasn't sure it would work, but I had to try.'

'Well, I'm glad it did.' Julie reaches down to grasp Angharad's hand.

We all climb into the Land Rover. It's so high off the ground that I have to clamber up to get inside. Steve passes me a bottle of water that I drain immediately, then he gives me a chocolate bar that I tear into – it's melted a little at the edges but at that moment it's the most delicious thing I've ever eaten.

Steve turns the key in the car but the engine whines and then cuts out. He tries again and this time it whines for a shorter time and dies more quickly. The next time, it can barely make a chugging sound before there's silence.

'Right,' Steve says in the way that I know means he doesn't really know what to do.

'Let's walk to the tower,' I say. 'I really do think Sylvia will be there. She's good at fixing cars. She'll probably have some tools there.'

Steve hesitates for a moment, taking in the distance left between the car and the tower, but then he looks round at us all.

'Let's go,' he says.

As we approach the tower it looks deserted.

There are no signs of life at all. There's no face at the window, no vehicle parked close by, not even any rubbish on the ground.

There are just lots of rocks that are scattered around – large, grey boulders – amidst the trees and bushes. I don't remember them from before but then I remember again that it was night when I came here; I easily would have missed them in the darkness.

'So you've been here before?' Julie asks me.

'Once – just before the fire happened. Sylvia was stockpiling supplies and things and driving out here every night, while I was asleep, to get it ready.'

'Can you remember how to get in?' Steve asks.

'There's a door just round that side, at the back.' I point. As I reach out my hand, something catches my eye.

It's a flicker of a movement. It's so slight, like the spark that starts a flame, that it's only clear that it's something moving as the movement grows.

It's one of the rocks that are surrounding us.

One of the rocks is moving, and then another, and then another.

The movement catches, it passes from one to another, as though it is an infection.

They aren't rocks at all.

We are surrounded by Greys.

HOW TO (TRY NOT TO) GET INFECTED

'Get behind me,' Steve says. 'Stay behind me.'

The Grey that first moved has unfurled to standing.

'Stop!' Angharad shouts out. 'Stop! You'll infect us if you get too close.'

The Grey turns its head sharply as Angharad's words echo around us. I see its stony eyes flash with understanding and there's other emotions there too; the same sadness I saw in the Grey on the road, and there's fear as well. It looks afraid of us.

'Get back!' Julie cries out.

The Grey makes a movement backwards, slow and deliberate, but at the very same moment its arm extends out, its clawed hand reaches and stretches towards us.

It struggles against its extended arm but it's as though it is being pulled by a stronger force and in the next moment it has turned towards us and it's stepping forward.

It screams. That dead, hollow sound seems so empty of meaning, but from the look in its eyes I can tell it's trying to tell us something. It's not afraid *of* us; it's afraid *for* us.

'You are both going to run, okay? When I tell you to run, run. You understand?' Steve keeps his voice very low and calm.

'Don't look back,' Julie says. 'Run as fast as you can.'

My eyes flash to the grey, squat tower. There's no sign of life. I reach out for Steve's shirt and feel the soft fabric knot between my fingers. I want to keep hold of him. I can't lose him, because in this moment, I know that Sylvia is not here.

If she were in the tower, then she would be out here, helping us. If she were in there, she would do something, she would save us, she would save me.

'Get ready, Billy,' Steve says. 'You have to run and get as far from here as you can, okay?'

'I can't leave you,' I say. 'I don't want to leave you.'

'It's okay, it's okay. It's going to be okay. But you have to run, when I say. You have to run.'

His hand snakes behind his back and finds mine. He squeezes it, without looking round. His eyes are fixed on the Greys that are one by one waking and slowly uncurling to stand.

'Mum, we'll stay with you, we won't leave you,' I hear Angharad say fiercely. The first one that rose writhes against its arm that still reaches towards us, seeking us out. For a moment, it looks like it might be stronger and it pulls its clawed fingers back by just a few millimetres. But in the same moment, another Grey lunges forward, its hand outstretched.

'Run! Run!'

Steve is screaming the words; his eyes are bulging, white and wide with fear.

I can hear his screaming but my legs are frozen where I stand. My heart is in my mouth; I can feel its wild beating almost choking me.

'Bil-ly!'

It's Angharad and she's shouting my name so loudly it slices across the clearing. Her hand is in mine, and she's trying to pull at me, to pull me away. But still, I can't make myself move.

I feel as though I am not in my body any more, but that I have risen above everything that's happening and I am looking down on us from a great, great height.

And in those moments, I can see it all so clearly.

The Greys, all around us, their bodies making a wall that encircles us.

They could be mistaken for grotesque statues, cast out of stone or metal or any other leaden material.

Almost.

If only their arms didn't twist away from their bodies like branches growing from a tree.

If only the sound of whining shrieks and wrenching screams didn't ring from their crooked mouths.

If only they weren't rippling towards us.

There are so many more of them and they are everywhere.

More and more rise with every moment that passes.

There are too many.

It's suddenly so clear to me: this time, we will not escape them.

Julie screams out for them to leave us. Steve stands in front of us, his arms out wide, his body the only barrier between the Greys and Angharad and me. And the Greys forge towards us, getting a little closer with every step.

Never stop trying – you must never give up! I hear Sylvia's voice so clearly, it's as though she's right there next to me.

And in the next moment I am back in my body, back in my feet, and my hand's in my pocket.

I feel the reassuring lump of the old chocolate tin that Anwar dug out for me. My mind runs through everything that's inside it in case there's anything of any use. And then seemingly out of nowhere my brain grasps onto a plan. I have no idea if it will work. I have no idea, in fact, what will happen at all but I have the strongest feeling that it's the right thing to do.

I pull out the survival kit and wrench open the lid.

Its contents fall to the ground with a patter.

I step around Julie, Steve and Angharad so I'm the one that's closest to the Grey and direct the shiny lid of the tin – the heliograph – right into its eyes.

Its irises look like old mottled coins, but as the beam of sunlight hits them they suddenly flash amber. It's like an explosion; the burst of colour, the flecks of gold.

The Grey rears up. It looks huge, it looks giant as though it has grown taller and wider somehow. The amber in its eye does not die away.

It looks like it is about to crash down on us when all of a sudden, it turns sharply to its side and dashes away.

Away into the trees the Grey runs, as fast as it can move; it's a swirl of legs, a blur of speed.

I direct the heliograph to the next Grey approaching, pointing the light into its eyes as before but just as I am taking aim, another pounces forward, colliding into them. They fall towards me, knocking the heliograph right out of my hands. All I can do is watch as it tumbles onto the ground, out of my reach.

In the next moment, I sense, from the corner of my eye, a flashing light.

It's coming straight from the tower, a beam of light, and I know, with a certainty, that it's the light from another heliograph. It's Sylvia. She is here. She knows what to do.

She directs another ray of light right into one of the eyes of a Grey. It shrieks and runs off into the trees.

I dash forward, snatching up the heliograph and then leap backwards, flashing the beam of light again and again into the eyes of the Greys, and watch them wince and scatter. They cannot bear it when the light hits their eyes.

Steve is still shouting: 'Run! Billy! Angharad! Run!'

There are still Greys rising; they are just steps away from us, their backs turned towards the tower and so the light cannot be directed into their eyes. There are too many. I flash the heliograph, but I know I won't be able to reach them all.

I hear Angharad cry out as a Grey reaches towards me, its arm swiping and slicing the air.

Its arms reach out for me.

It is about to touch me.

*

I look into the face of the Grey and the many twisted and searching faces behind it, as they make their almost voiceless, whining howl. Shadows hang in their dull, dead eyes, a gloom that surrounds and engulfs me. I feel myself start to let go. It's too late. There were, in the end, too many.

But then Steve's there. His strong arms pull me up and away, just as the Grey's arms swipe the space where I was standing.

I hear a scramble of footsteps, coming from the tower. There's someone beside me.

Anwar. He's sticking his lip out, the way he does when he's concentrating hard, directing light from the heliograph I made him, right into the eyes of the Greys that are surrounding us. It's only been a few days since I saw him last, but he looks older somehow.

I have to save my friends. I have to find Sylvie. I feel a rush of energy and start once again to shoot the sunlight in one direction and then the other, towards the advancing Greys.

The irises of the Greys burst into colour as the flashing light reaches them and they run off, one by one, until finally, we are alone.

Finally, we are safe.

HOW TO UNDERSTAND

'You made it!' Anwar exclaims, turning towards me. 'We were wondering when you were going to turn up.'

Before I can reply, Steve wraps his arms around Anwar in a huge bear hug. 'Anwar!' he roars.

'Easy, Mr G, easy!' Anwar says, which makes us all laugh.

It feels like such a relief to be able to laugh again. Like bubbles rising, floating upwards, inside me.

'The heliograph,' I say. 'Good thing I taught you how to use one.' Anwar grins back at me.

I think back to Sylvia showing me how to use one all those months ago, on Christmas Day. The way she wanted to tell me something about them when we visited her in hospital. All this time she had known; all this time she had been right.

'When did you get here?' Angharad asks Anwar.

'A couple of days ago. Sylvia was pretty surprised to see us, I think.'

Suddenly I sense her as a flash of silver that one moment is behind me and in the next is silently beside me, and we are standing together as though we have never been apart.

I can barely turn to look at her but when I do, my breath catches in my throat and I cry out, for she is there. Sylvia is really there. She is solid beside me. I reach for her and her dry, warm hand catches mine in hers in a fierce clasp. It's a tight ball of fingers. Her hair is pulled back into a loose ponytail, which glows silver in the sunlight, and she's smiling at me, a small half-smile, one that seems to know something that I do not.

'Billy,' she says slowly, lingering over every sound.

It's the sound of a bell ringing; it's laughter, it's light.

'Billy, Billy, Billy!'

'Mum!' I don't mean to call her that but it's the word that comes out and it feels good, suddenly like the only name I could possibly use for her.

She wraps her arms around me, buries her head into my hair as though she is trying to breathe in every bit of me.

'You made it,' she mumbles into my head.

'Of course I did,' I say.

'And you've not come alone,' she says, looking towards Steve, Julie and Angharad. Behind her, I can see Anwar's family slowly emerge from the tower.

'No,' I say back. I worry for a moment how she is going to react. Will she be cross that I've broken the rules? But her gaze remains steady and warm. 'I've worked out it's better to stick together with the people close to you.'

She nods her head furiously and smiles but at the same time

she looks like she is about to cry.

'That sounds like a good rule,' she says. 'Come on, let's all get inside before any more Lumens come along.'

'Lumens?' I ask.

'That's what I call them,' Sylvia says as we all trail into the tower. 'Anwar says that you call them Greys. He's filled me in on what you've been through.'

She looks over at Steve and Julie. I realize I'm holding my breath.

'Hi, Steve,' she says simply.

'Sylvia, I—' Steve begins to say.

'It's okay,' she says. 'It's okay.'

Steve continues to bluster over what to say, but then he says just two words: 'I'm sorry.'

'It's okay, it really is,' Sylvia says. 'I know we all could have handled things a bit differently.' Then she fixes him with a hard, blazing look. 'Thank you – thank you for looking after our boy when I couldn't. You were right to do what you did.'

'I never didn't want to see him,' Steve says in a rush.

'I know that,' Sylvia says. 'That was my fault.'

I realize that something's lifted from my chest. Hearing them speak to each other, properly, has been something I didn't know I had been missing so much until this moment.

'And you must be Julie,' Sylvia says. 'Anwar told me about you and Angharad.'

'Hello,' Julie says a little anxiously.

'It's good to meet you,' Sylvia says with a small smile and I see Julie's face brighten in relief. 'Right, let's get you all inside, where it's safe.'

Sylvia and I had walked behind everyone and as the others went ahead, it seemed so weird and so normal at the same time that it was just the two of us, again: Sylvia and I.

After she'd closed the thick metal door with a clang and bolted it securely behind us, I'd asked her about the Greys or the Lumens, as she called them. I wanted to know if I was right in thinking that she knew about them before.

She told me that she was one of the first to see the virus in her old job. The diagrams I had seen of them in the tower on the night that she first brought me here were from that time. They had discovered a cell mutation in a patient – it was not someone that Sylvia had ever seen; she'd been working in the laboratory processing the samples. She'd submitted her report to her bosses and told them how dangerous she thought it was, seeing how the potential for infection would be massive if it spread, but no one had listened. No one wanted to hear. Sylvia thought that they were looking to see how they could make money from it and how they could control it. They wanted to keep it hidden until then.

She didn't know where the virus came from – there was some speculation that it might have developed in relation to severe changes in climate caused by pollution. What was concrete was what it would do if it attached to a host. It could be fatal or cause a physical transformation, turning people's skin grey, changing the vocal chords, altering how they move.

She'd tried to find out more about that first patient when she thought she'd discovered something else about the mutation. That, although the virus caused the extreme physical changes that rendered the patient seemingly inhuman, it seemed to react differently over time with exposure to UV light. But it was when she started to ask more and more questions that they sacked her.

I have so many questions and I want to talk to Anwar and Angharad about it all too. But then someone, I think maybe Anwar's mum, calls for Sylvia and she leaves me in the little room, the same one where she'd laid out the two sleeping bags all that time ago, that had smelled musty and damp.

As I look around now, I can see that it's not as bad as I remembered it to be. Part of me thinks about rejoining everyone else, but I also want to sit quietly to think. We've been through so much and so many things have turned out to be different than I thought. I can almost feel it all settling in my head like snowflakes swirling towards the ground. After a few moments, I start to feel as though I can, for the first time in a long time, begin to understand things around me a little more clearly: Sylvia, Steve, our family, the Greys.

Then Sylvia comes back through the door.

'Are you okay?' she asks. 'Food's almost ready.'

'I was just wondering,' I say. 'What does the light do? What was the research that you were doing before you stopped working?'

'It's just a theory I had based on some of the science I was working on around the virus, but I think the light makes them able to consciously resist infecting new hosts. I believe the virus retains more humanity than people think, but until the UV comes into play, it takes over and makes the infected drawn to new hosts so the virus can spread and spread.'

'Angharad said they had seen something on the news about them being able to understand what people are saying?'

'Yes – exactly. Those are probably the Lumens that have been exposed to more light. Directing the UV into their eyes seems to speed up the effect.'

'Did you know that before? When you gave me the heliograph?'

'I think so, although, Billy, you have to understand that even though our adventures all started because of my research, that the doctors and your dad weren't wrong. I wasn't well, and I'm still not completely well. It all took over too much and that wasn't fair on you.'

'Do other people know?' I ask. 'About the way they react to light?'

'A few days ago I spoke to some army officials who are taking back my research to their headquarters. We radioed them to come and see us out here. Now the cat's out of the bag, there's nothing my old bosses can do about me going public about what I know. They can't discredit me now. It should have been done a long time ago, but it's a start.'

As I turn over in my mind everything that she's telling me,

my thoughts are distracted by a rich smell of cooking coming from inside that makes my stomach turn and grumble.

Sylvia hears my tummy rumble and says, 'That's all Fatima. She's a great cook.'

I realize she must be talking about Anwar's mum; I'd only known her as Anwar's mum before.

Sylvia reaches towards my face and she studies it intensely, just like on the day that I saw her waiting outside school early, the day she lost her job.

'You've been very brave, Billy,' she says. 'I've missed you very, very much.' She looks almost embarrassed as she asks me: 'How have you been . . . really?'

'Oh, you know,' I say. It feels like too big a question to answer when I think of the fire and moving in with Steve and the twisted knot of feelings that I carried around. Then I remember meeting Anwar, the day he just came up to talk to me while I was standing all alone in the playground, and all the times that Angharad stuck up for me over and over again. And then I think of the fallen man, walking down the street in that odd, disjointed way that first seized my attention, and all that has happened since then. And I realize that I do have an answer: 'I'm okay,' I say. 'I'm all right.'

Sylvia beams down at me. 'You're more than all right,' she says.

'How are you?' I ask. 'How are you feeling?'

Sylvia is silent for a moment. She takes a breath, exhaling slowly, and then she starts to speak: 'Better than I was. Fear and worry can make you act in strange ways if you don't talk about things. My fears, though they were based on real things at first, just took over. And I'm so sorry that I sometimes put you in danger because I was concentrating too hard on keeping you safe. That I nearly lost you.'

'And now?'

'Now?' Sylvia asks. 'I know what I need to do if I feel like I'm losing myself like that. My time in hospital was hard, but it's what I needed to do to prove that I can look after you. I know I need to get better for myself and for you.

'And I think what you said was right – we do have to stick together with the people that are important to us.'

We walk up the stairs to the main room of the tower. Anwar's mum is handing out steaming bowls of food and his dad and Steve look like they are deep in conversation. Both have their sleeves rolled up and look like they are matching. Anwar's two little sisters are simultaneously singing and trying to climb on to Angharad's back, making the beads of her hair click together, while Anwar shouts at them to get off. He tries to lift up Taifa, who simply wraps her legs around his waist, hangs off his neck and prods him in the nose in a way that makes him laugh. I see Julie walk towards Sylvia, a warm smile spread across her face.

'Whatever happens next,' I say to myself, 'I just know we'll be prepared.'

DAY 7

- EPILOGUE -
HOW I SAVED THE WORLD IN A WEEK

'It's on!' Anwar calls out. 'Everyone get in here, squeeze in!'

We crowd around the small tablet.

It's a squash for us all to be able to see the screen.

I can barely hear the prime minister's voice over the scramble of Anwar's sisters complaining that they can't see and Steve trying to calm them down and make room and Anwar telling them to shut up because they're about to watch history in the making and Anwar's mum telling Anwar off for saying shut up.

For a moment there's quiet and then I hear part of the broadcast: *Here's the footage that has marked a significant turning point in the management of the infection . . .*

It cuts to a film and suddenly the room is filled with an explosion of whoops and shouts.

'There you are, Billy!' Anwar's dad says delightedly, squeezing my shoulders.

It's not just me. There's Steve, Julie and Angharad and the group of Greys, of course, all around us, edging ever closer. Then I'm pointing my heliograph towards them and they're running away. It's a film of what happened yesterday, caught on the CCTV which Sylvia had rigged up back when she was prepping the tower all that time ago when we were still living together. It's a little bit grainy and you can't see our faces really, but it clearly shows the Greys darting away as I direct the light into their eyes.

It was what Sylvia called 'the final piece of the puzzle' – conclusive evidence to prove what she'd been researching and theorizing, that the effect of UV on the Greys brought about a change in the virus, affecting how the Greys behaved and that it could, in fact, spark their recovery. That they weren't actually Greys, they were still the people they had been before. Everyone yesterday that had been exposed to the UV rays by the heliographs were now recovering; they'd been found by the army and taken to a secure medical facility. The film cut to a medical advisor talking about the patients. They were still in quarantine, but they believed they were no longer infectious. Their skin had lost its grey colour and some of them were talking, slowly, but talking nonetheless about what it had been like to be infected.

We are at present rolling out the UV exposure therapy to those infected and continue to see startling results, remarkable recoveries. World leaders are united in their gratitude to the young hero shown in the CCTV film whose actions have conclusively shown that this works. He and his family have asked not to be named but his bravery and quick thinking have essentially brought about an unexpectedly swift resolution to this crisis.

'It doesn't feel that swift,' I say.

'We only left Bristol a week ago,' Angharad points out.

'One week?' I reply. It feels like far, far longer.

Anwar grins. 'That's all it takes for you, Billy Weywood – one week to save the world.'

I smile back and I can feel Sylvia kiss the top of my head and Steve squeeze my hand in his.

Like most things, it doesn't feel like how it sounds – saving the world in a week – but what feels real is everyone around me.

My world, for the first time in a long time, feels secure.

TOP RULES FOR ~~SURVIVAL~~
LIVING

1.	*Always be prepared*	–	*~~have~~ KEEP ~~everything~~ EVERYONE IMPORTANT TO YOU ~~ready and~~ CLOSE TO ~~with~~ you ~~at all times~~*
2.	*Pay attention*	–	*keep ~~constant observations of your surroundings~~ COMMUNICATING WITH THE PEOPLE YOU LOVE*
3.	*Trust ~~no one~~ THE PEOPLE YOU CAN TRUST*	–	*you ~~may only be able~~ <u>DON'T</u> HAVE to rely ONLY on yourself*
4.	*YOU CAN Master your fears*	–	*through practice, planning, ~~and~~ taking action AND ASKING FOR HELP*
5.	*Never stop trying*	–	*you must never give up~~!~~ ON A PERSON*

AUTHOR'S NOTE

I read the following books to help me imagine Billy's survival guide from Sylvia: One, which I liked so much that I borrowed its title, was *How to Survive* by Brian Hildreth. Others which also proved extremely helpful were *Survival: The Ultimate Guide to Staying Alive in Extreme Conditions and Emergency Situations in the World* by Anthonio Akkermans, Peter G. Drake, Bill Mattos and Andy Middleton and *Survival Skills*: *How to Survive in the Wild* by Simon Ellar.

I also spent quite a lot of time on YouTube watching people making fires. One of the most useful and enjoyable videos I watched many times over was called *Advanced Tips For A Successful Bowdrill Fire* by Survival Lilly.

I hope you might enjoy researching some of the incredible skills that Billy mastered and perhaps you can try them out for yourself. But, as Billy learned, they're most fun when they're done together – just don't forget to ask permission!

Polly Ho-Yen